THE CONFESSION

Tellaro drew from his cassock Father Manzoni's letter to His Holiness and re-read it. Manzoni was shifting the grave responsibility for the discovery and its interpretation onto the shoulders of the Pope. Tellaro drew his gaze from the letter to the small lead casket. Like a time-bomb, it threatened to destroy two thousand years of blind faith.

He reached forward and drew back the lid of the casket again, looking down at the dirty brown roll which lay there so innocently. Yes, he was convinced. If this document were genuine then he, Giona Tellaro, would decide the future of the Church. His would be the power!

Also by Peter MacAlan and
published by Star:

The Judas Battalion
Airship

THE CONFESSION

Peter MacAlan

A STAR BOOK
published by
the Paperback Division of
W. H. Allen & Co. PLC

A Star Book
Published in 1986
by the Paperback Division of
W. H. Allen & Co. PLC
44 Hill Street, London W1X 8LB

First published in Great Britain by
W. H. Allen & Co. PLC in 1985

Copyright © Peter MacAlan, 1985

Printed and bound in Great Britain by
Anchor Brendon Ltd, Tiptree, Essex

ISBN 0 352 31786 8

ACKNOWLEDGEMENTS

While accepting full responsibility for any errors of fact made in this novel, I would like to express my gratitude for the invaluable advice given to me by Dr A.D. Bayness-Cope, principal scientific officer of the British Museum, and T.S. Pattie, of the Department of Manuscripts, British Library. While it is impossible to list all the background reading material which went into my research, I would like to single out Stuart J. Fleming's excellent study *Authenticity in Art; The Scientific Detection of Forgery* (Institute of Physics, London, 1975). It was the erudite scholarship of Dr Hyam Maccoby, the Biblical scholar, whose outline of the conflict between Paul of Tarsus and Peter the Apostle inspired the central theme of this book and I must pay tribute to his work *Revolution in Judea* (Ocean Books, London, 1973). I am also indebted to my archaeologist friend, David Seton, with whom I first discussed the basic premise of *The Confession* and who gave me encouragement to continue. Finally, I would like to dedicate this 'entertainment' to two good friends – Jim and Mary Cardiff.

Peter MacAlan

Confession of our faults is the next thing to innocence.

Publius Syrus
First century BC

Chapter One

The crack of the pistol shot caused Sergeant Hans Wiessen to halt abruptly as if every limb in his body had suddenly frozen.

It was not simply the unexpected noise of the explosion which caused him to gaze in shock towards the dark ornate oak doors from beyond which the sound had come; it was the fact that these doors sheltered the private papal apartment of the Vatican.

For twenty years Sergeant Hans Wiessen had served in the *Cohors Helvetica*, the Swiss Guard. His rows of papal medals – the *Cavaliere di San Silvestro*, the *Pro Ecclesia e Pontifice* Cross and others – were colourful testimony to the excellence of his service. That was why he was one of the privileged sentinels to the private apartment of the Pope on the top floor of the Apostolic Palace, stationed in the hall where the lift from the courtyard of San Damaso gave entrance to the sanctuary of the Bishop of Rome.

Beyond the dark ornate doors, Sergeant Wiessen knew that there lay a small library, an office for the Pope's private secretary, the Pope's own study, his bedroom, dining-room and chapel. Nearby was a room used by the Pope's valet-chauffeur and a cloistered room for a group of Polish sisters of the Maria Bambina Order who cooked, cleaned and laundered for His Holiness.

Wiessen was perplexed. He thought the apartment was empty. The Pope had departed yesterday to stay a week at his summer villa at Castel Gandolfo in the Alban Hills, twenty miles south-east of Rome.

1

Slowly Wiessen recovered the power of movement and reached for the large brass door-handle, turned it and pushed it open. He hesitated on the threshold for a moment, feeling a little in awe at the idea of entering the private living quarters of the successor of St Peter, a place where so few had licence to enter.

Then he sniffed, smelling the acrid stench of cordite in the air, and drew himself together, remembering his duty.

He strode into the library, the reception room where His Holiness received his closest advisors. The sun streamed in through the tall windows which opened overlooking St Peter's Square. The bright rays of the sun sparkled against the cream-coloured walls, against the white and black marble of the floor, on which richly woven carpets were strategically placed. There were a few comfortable antique chairs placed around the room while, looking absurdly out of place, a telephone stood on a small ornately carved table in the centre of the chamber. On three walls stood bookshelves and a few selected seventeenth-century paintings. On the fourth wall hung a rich tapestry – Christ giving the keys of heaven to St Peter. A work influenced by the painting by Raphael. It was this tapestry which caused Sergeant Wiessen to stare with widening eyes. Red paint had been daubed across it forming one word – '*Amentissimus*!'

Sergeant Wiessen supposed it to be Latin, though he was no scholar. He gazed in disbelief at the desecration, moving forward to examine it. His foot kicked at something. He glanced down to see an aerosol paint-can rolling away on the marble floor before him, coming to rest against the obstruction of a black bundle of material.

The body of a young man, clad in the dark robes of a Benedictine friar, sprawled on the floor. He lay on his back, one arm across his chest, the other outstretched behind him. The fingers still gripped a small automatic pistol. The left side of his face was a bloody pulp where the bullet had shattered it at close range.

Sergeant Wiessen dropped to one knee by the body, automatically feeling for a pulse in the right side of the neck

2

while, at the same time, knowing that it was a futile gesture.

The young man was clearly beyond aid.

Sergeant Wiessen genuflected and began to mutter a prayer for the dead.

'*Requiem aeternam dona ei, Domine*... Eternal rest to him, O Lord...'

Then he turned and reached for the telephone.

The prefect of the Civil Guard stood uneasily before the large antique desk. He glanced nervously at his side where the colonel-commander of the Swiss Guard remained in a stiff military posture, seemingly aloof from his surroundings. The room was drab, almost cold, with little else in it save the desk, a large bookcase and several metal filing-cabinets and a large but elderly looking safe. Seated on the other side of the desk, regarding both the prefect and the colonel-commander grimly, was the Cardinal-President of the Central Security Office of the Vatican City State – Cardinal Giona Tellaro.

Tellaro was a tall man. Even when seated his height was apparent, although he slouched in his chair, leaning well back, his hands clasped in a prayer-like attitude in front of his chin. He was young to be a prince of the Church, scarcely more than fifty years old. His dark curly hair had only a few streaks of silver amidst its blue-blackness. His eyes were dark too, so dark that they seemed to have no pupils. His skin was swarthy and his jowl showed faintly blue. He had a broad forehead, high cheek bones, an aquiline nose and his lips were thin and red. The prefect of the Civil Guard felt that Tellaro had a face which one could not help but dislike on sight, a face which would grace a Renaissance visualisation of Lucifer.

'Well?' The question was snapped out coldly. 'Do you have anything to add to this report of your sergeant, Hans Wiessen?'

His deep black eyes were staring at the colonel-commander.

'None, Eminence,' replied the man with equal coldness.

'Very well, I need detain you no longer.'

There was a silence while the colonel-commander, straight-backed, clad in the dark blue and black non-ceremonial uniform of the Swiss Guard, strode from the room.

The prefect of the Civil Guard, a small, fussy little man who had spent a life of service in the Vatican police force, glanced nervously into the fathomless black eyes which Cardinal Tellaro turned to him.

'Has the body been identified?'

The prefect, a Venetian by birth, strained to catch the swift, rolling Sicilian accent of the Cardinal.

'Yes, Eminence. The young man was Girolamon Solaro, a member of the Benedictine Order. But little else known which is pertinent to our enquiry. He graduated in palaeography and classics from the University of Rome about six years ago and then joined his Order. Two years later he was employed by the Secret Archives under the Palatine Administration. He worked as a *scrittore*. He was apparently happy in this work and the Cardinal Archivist informs me that Brother Girolamon was on a short list for possible promotion to archivist.'

Tellaro drummed his fingers on the desk top.

'And?'

'That is all, Eminence.'

'All?' The word was a sneer in Tellaro's cold tones. 'A young friar manages to break into His Holiness's private apartment with a gun, then shoots himself after desecrating a sacred and priceless tapestry and all without apparent reason. Surely there is more?'

The prefect of the Civil Guard shifted his weight, his unease causing him to flush slightly.

'There is no more that my department could ascertain, Eminence,' he replied nervously.

Tellaro sighed deeply. 'Your report is complete then?'

The prefect nodded.

'Very well. You may go.'

The prefect of the Civil Guard turned and hurried from

4

the room. In his thankfulness to be released from the Cardinal's company he did not care that his departure might be slightly undignified. Behind him Cardinal Tellaro watched his scuttling departure with a faint smile on his thin lips. Then he shrugged and turned his attention to the reports before him.

Only a hour before the Secretary of State had been on the telephone from Castel Gandolfo expressing His Holiness's personal concern about the tragedy and implying, in a not too subtle fashion, that a clear-cut reason for the young friar's suicide should be established before the news was officially announced in the *Osservatore Romano* or on the Vatican Radio.

Tellaro glanced at his wristwatch. It was 11.00 a.m. The *Osservatore Romano,* the Vatican's own daily newspaper, went to press at 3.00 p.m. and, presumably, the Secretary of State expected some announcement to be made before then. That did not leave him long to finalise the report.

He reached for the telephone and was answered immediately by his secretary, Sister Beatrice.

'Will you telephone the Cardinal Archivist at the Secret Archives and ask him if he is free to receive me within the next fifteen minutes?'

A moment later Sister Beatrice was back on the line. 'The Cardinal Archivist will meet you in the Cortile del Belvedere, Eminence, by the entrance to the Secret Archives.'

Cardinal Tellaro put the receiver down and turned to stare at the reports of Brother Girolamon's death. What was the word that he had daubed on the tapestry? *Amentissimus!* He dredged his church Latin. *Amentia* – senselessness, folly, insanity, meaninglessness. What was? Had Brother Girolamon's life become meaningless? If so, why? What had made him commit the mortal sin of taking his own life?

Cardinal Tellaro shrugged as he rose leisurely and placed the reports in a filing-cabinet. Making sure it was locked, he turned from his office and joined the people moving along the black-veined marble coolness of the corridor. The unhurried, purposeful movement of the functionaries of the

Governorato, the Government Palace, was a feature of all workers in the Vatican City. He moved among them anonymously, inclining his head now and then as he passed a colleague.

Outside, on the steps leading to the piazza in front of the building, he paused and glanced up at the bright blue Roman sky.

A uniformed chauffeur, a bull-necked, ugly-looking man, came hurrying forward but Tellaro smiled and shook his head.

'I shall not need you at the moment, Salvatore,' he said in Sicilian dialect. 'I am not going far.'

'At your command, Eminence,' growled the chauffeur and turned away.

Hands clasped easily before him, Cardinal Tellaro strolled across the piazza, away from the imposing white stone and brick edifice which rose pretentiously behind the Basilica of St Peter. The building had originally been intended as a seminary but was converted into the headquarters of the administration of the Vatican City State, housing a bewildering number of officers from which the numerous activities of the state were controlled. The building rose above a large basement area which served as a store for all kinds of goods, the exports and imports of the state, while other parts of the building were reserved as guest apartments for important visitors to the Vatican. Yet another suite consisted of the official residence of the Pro-President of the Commission for the State of Vatican City.

Tellaro strode across the piazza and through the green gardens by the imposing statue of St Peter, down towards the Palace of the Mint and passed the Fountain of the Sacrament to the Stradone dei Giardini. Here he entered an arch into the buildings which housed the Vatican Museums and Libraries, and which enclosed the Belvedere courtyard. Tellaro allowed a smile to flicker on his lips as he gazed around the now tiled courtyard. A few years ago it had been asphalted to make a car park but Pope Paul VI had been so annoyed that the historic courtyard, which had been used

6

for jousting in Benvenuto Cellini's day, had taken on such a mundane appearance that he had ordered it to be tiled.

The Cardinal Archivist of the Secret Archives and the Apostolic Library was waiting for him across the courtyard. He was a short fragile-looking man with white hair but with bright blue eyes that continually examined the people to whom he was speaking. He was answerable directly to the Pope for his office, and to no one else, for the Pope was the owner of the Secret Archives and had absolute authority over their management and use.

If there was a department in the Vatican which held a scent of romance for Cardinal Tellaro then it was the Secret Archives. He had often felt annoyance that he had not trained in scholastic discipline for he day-dreamed of the great historical secrets which the archives held. They were as old as the history of the papacy, although the reliable history of the Vatican documents did not begin until the fifth century AD. Nevertheless, the collection of manuscripts in the Secret Archives was beyond price. It was said that the archives lay like a vast graveyard where, from time to time, the dead rose up to confound the living. Much of the material was unclassified and unsorted, and great treasures often lay forgotten until some scholar stumbled across them by chance. Among the treasures which members of the public were tantalisingly allowed to see were the oldest-surviving Latin manuscript, a fourth-century copy of Cicero's *De Republica*, a fourth-century Greek Codex Bible and a fourth-century manuscript of the work of Virgil. Cardinal Tellaro had frequently wondered what other fabulous treasures lay buried, unknown and unseen, in the endless vaults of the archives.

He caught himself abruptly.

'I am grateful that you could spare the time to see me, Eminence,' he smiled dryly at the Cardinal Archivist.

'Not at all, Eminence,' replied the elderly man brightly. 'Each morning about this time I take a stroll in the Cortile del Belvedere for the fresh air. When one works amidst the dust of old manuscripts and books, a walk in the fresh air is

7

essential to the constitution.'

The Cardinal Archivist began to walk as he spoke and Tellaro fell in step beside him.

'I wish to talk about Brother Girolamon.'

'I thought as much.' The face of the Cardinal Archivist did not change expression. 'But I have already told the officers of the Civil Guard what I know of the affair.'

'Which is?'

'That the young man worked in the Secret Archives; that he did well at his job and was due for promotion. That is all.'

'You knew no more?'

The Cardinal Archivist raised a shoulder and let it fall.

'I have a prefect, a vice-prefect, five archivists and nineteen general staff in my office. I only know them in connection with the work they do.'

'Of course, Eminence,' smiled Tellaro pacifyingly. 'But you see my difficulty? There must be a reason why a Benedictine friar decides to kill himself in the private papal apartments. His Holiness is taking a special interest in the matter...'

Tellaro paused as the Cardinal Archivist glanced suspiciously at him.

'Naturally,' he replied a little stiffly, 'I wish to co-operate with your investigation.'

'Of course. Of course. Perhaps you could tell me who worked closely with Brother Girolamon?'

The Cardinal Archivist grimaced. 'Father Manzoni was his immediate superior. Father Manzoni is our curator of ancient Greek and Latin manuscripts.'

Tellaro nodded encouragingly. 'Then I wish to speak with Father Manzoni.'

The Cardinal Archivist frowned. 'That will not be possible.'

Tellaro stared hard at the man who returned his gaze impassively. 'Perhaps you will be so good as to explain why?'

'Father Manzoni had a heart attack two days ago while working in his office. His condition, so I understand, is not good.'

8

Chapter Two

Toni Ciperello was sweating freely. It was not simply due to the fact that the day was scorching hot and that Ciperello was middle-aged and overweight. The colder sweat of fear mingled freely with the perspiration caused by the fierce heat of the noon sun and the wreathes of his flabby flesh.

For the seventh time in as many minutes, Toni Ciperello glanced at his wristwatch. He came out of the dingy *pensione* on the waterfront Via Del Porto and glanced nervously across the dockland of Palermo. The streets of the Sicilian capital were deserted and silent. At this hour most Sicilians were taking a siesta or nodding over their coffee in the shade of some bar.

Ciperello paused, shaded his eyes, and looked around like a man expecting to see something he has no wish to. Then he moved swiftly across the dusty street and unlocked the door of the battered Alfa Romeo saloon. The heat inside the car was almost unbearable. He wound down the windows and cursed that he had been unable to find some shade in which to park it. He carried a small suitcase which he flung onto the back seat. The he climbed in, muttering and screwing his face up at the stifling atmosphere.

He was in no mood to delay. He started up, placed the vehicle in gear and sent it forward rapidly, turning up the Via Cavour and right into the Viale Della Liberta. The streets were deserted but his wide, strained eyes, kept flickering to his driving mirror and several times he turned off down side streets, winding in and out until he found himself on the Via Noce heading towards the small town of Carini. He halted by the old castle there, leaving his engine running, and sat gazing into his rearview mirror. Finally, he threw the car into gear again and went squealing away towards Montelepre, climbing up into the mountains which rose behind Palermo. The road he took was a small twisting route which made its way up via incredible hairpin bends to a small group of houses clinging precariously to the side of the great granite thrust. It was hardly a village – a solitary church, which stood in need of immediate restoration, and a collection of tumbledown buildings.

A sign, fading with years of neglect, bore the legend 'Welcome to Taretta'.

Ciperello drew up in the solitary street just by a Coca-Cola sign which also carried the word 'Bar'.

He left the car and pushed through the beaded curtain into the cool of the small room beyond. It contained a few small tables and an odd assortment of chairs. There was a bar in one corner on which stood a coffee machine and a colourful assortment of bottles. Behind it stood a large refrigerator which grumbled softly to itself. There were crates of assorted bottles stacked against the wall.

Ciperello stood in the middle of the room hesitantly.

The place seemed deserted.

Then there was a movement beyond the bar and from a hidden door, behind the refrigerator, came a stocky man in a dirty sweat-stained singlet and even dirtier trousers. He had greying rumpled hair, chewed on a self-rolled cigarette and carried a grimy newspaper.

His eyes flickered nervously as they fell upon Ciperello. 'So . . . you have come?'

Ciperello exhaled as if in a gesture of relief. 'Did you get it for me?' he asked, eagerness edging his voice.

The stocky man flung down his newspaper on the bar and scratched his nose. 'Sure. A promise is a promise. After all, you're family, aren't you?'

Ciperello forced a grin. 'That's right,' he replied un-enthusiastically. 'We're cousins, after all.'

'Well then . . . we look after family.'

'Then you have the air ticket to Boston?'

The man bent down behind the bar and came up with a large buff envelope and placed it on the counter. 'It's here, Toni. No problem. Plus the thousand dollars.'

Ciperello strode forward and seized the package anxiously. He emptied it on the bar and examined its contents. The barman chuckled.

'What's the matter, Toni? You don't trust family?'

'I can't afford to trust anyone,' he replied. 'Would you if you were in my position?'

The barman looked suddenly serious. 'I would not be in your position, God willing.'

Ciperello was stuffing the money into his pockets. 'I'd better get to the airport.'

'No hurry. Have a beer for the journey. It will be a long time before we see you again.'

He turned and reached into the old refrigerator for the cold bottles of Peroni beer.

There was a sudden squeal of brakes as a car halted outside.

Toni Ciperello glanced at the barman with the face of a hunted animal. The man simply threw himself down behind the bar as Ciperello turned towards the door.

A shadow moved there and even as Ciperello turned to flee through the door beyond the refrigerator, there came two soft 'phuts!' Blood appeared as if by some miracle across Ciperello's back and some unseen force sent him staggering forwards, colliding with the tables and chairs, crashing headlong into the debris.

A tall, dark-haired man moved through the beaded curtains and stood gazing scornfully down at Ciperello's body. He wore a dark-blue suit and a matching silk tie which contrasted with the brilliant white of his shirt. Dark glasses shaded his eyes but did not conceal the broad slope of his aquiline face, his thin cruel mouth and blue-black hair. He had the appearance of an undertaker.

The barman struggled to his knees, moaning softly at the bruises he had sustained in his attempt to find safety. He saw

11

the dark man's gun with its silencer swinging in his direction.

'For the love of God, *signore*!' he almost screamed. 'I am a friend of the friends!'

The gun stopped swinging.

The barman, trembling slightly, rose and dusted himself down. 'You got him then?' he laughed, a little too harshly, as he gestured to the body of Toni Ciperello.

The tall dark man made no reply but walked across to the inert form and bent down feeling for a pulse.

'Is he dead?' asked the barman.

The tall man's mouth quirked without humour. 'He is dead.'

The barman came bustling forward and knelt down, his hands rummaging through the pockets of the dead man. 'He nearly made off with the money and the ticket,' he said, feeling the eyes of the dark man staring at him through the sunglasses.

There was no reply.

The barman, having retrieved his money and ticket, suddenly felt uncomfortable. He made to say something but closed his mouth. It was not wise to interfere with the *gentile* of the Honoured Society, especially with this grim-faced man who was known simply as 'the Executioner'.

The tall man rose and stared disdainfully at the barman. 'You know what you must do?'

The barman swallowed nervously and nodded.

'That is good,' replied the dark man softly. Then he put his automatic in his pocket and strode out.

The barman heard a car start up, heard the roar of its engine race down the mountain road; waited until he heard its noise die away on the hot lazy air. Then he wiped the sweat from his brow and stared down at the sprawled body of Toni Ciperello.

In ten minutes he would telephone the police.

Having served his customer, he had been out in the back yard. That was when he had heard the shot. He hurried back into the bar to find his customer dead. Yes; he had heard the sound of a departing car. That was all. He knew nothing else.

The police would be dissatisfied. They would suspect. But they would do nothing. The Honoured Society had simply punished one who had transgressed its unwritten laws.

Cardinal Giona Tellaro's black Mercedes was hardly noticed as it weaved among the traffic of the Viale Aventino towards the Piazza Albania into Rome's richest suburb. The car was not out of place amidst the opulence of Aventino, the southernmost of the Seven Hills of Rome which, in imperial times, was the aristocratic quarter and still retained its aura of elegance and good living. Here were the villas of the city's wealthy and powerful, enclosed by walls in wide avenues lined with palms and cypresses, and interspersed with some of the city's most beautiful churches.

Impassively, Salvatore, the cardinal's Sicilian chauffeur, eased the vehicle along the Via di Alessio towards the elegant tree-filled Piazza dei Cavalieri di Malta, turning with the traffic into the Piazza di Sant' Anselmo, and coming to a halt before the imposing gates of the large Benedictine Seminary with its church of Sant' Anselmo rising in Lombard Romanesque flourishes against the bright blue of the sky.

Salvatore sounded his horn impatiently.

A small grille in the gate opened and then the gates themselves began to swing inward as the observer spotted the emblem of a cardinal on the waiting vehicle.

Salvatore eased the car into the cool of the courtyard beyond.

A Benedictine friar came forward, hurrying as quickly as propriety would allow.

'Good day, Eminence,' he bobbed nervously as Cardinal Tellaro climbed out of the vehicle.

'I am here to see Father Manzoni.'

It seemed that the Benedictine looked startled, his wide eyes meeting Tellaro's narrowed ones for a moment.

'Eminence, may I conduct you to the Father Prior?'

Tellaro sighed impatiently. 'Very well.'

The Benedictine turned and led the way through the

marble-flagged corridors of the seminary building to a wooden door on which he knocked cautiously. A voice bade him enter and he opened the door, hesitating as he realised that he did not know Tellaro's name.

'What name, Eminence?' he hissed quickly.

Tellaro grinned at the young monk's discomfiture. 'Tellaro of the General Secretariat of the *Governorato* for the State of Vatican City.'

The young monk's eyes widened further.

'What is it?' demanded a gruff voice from inside the room with not a little impatience.

The Benedictine stumbled over Tellaro's name and title.

Tellaro moved into the room to find a red-faced, elderly man struggling to rise from behind his desk, trying to disguise his expression of astonishment.

'Eminence, forgive me. I had no word of your coming.'

Tellaro nodded grimly as the Father Prior bent to kiss his ring.

'No word was sent, Father Prior,' he replied evenly.

The Father Prior spread his hands helplessly and waved dismissal to the young monk who had been his escort.

'What can I do for you, Eminence?'

'Father Manzoni, who works at the Secret Archives, lives in this seminary, does he not? I believe he has been ill. I would like to see Father Manzoni.'

A troubled expression crossed the Father Prior's face. 'That is not possible, Eminence.'

Tellaro raised an eyebrow. It was the second time that he had been told that it was not possible for him to see Father Manzoni. 'Not possible?'

'It is my sad duty to inform you that Father Manzoni suffered another heart seizure early this morning. He is dead, peace to his soul.'

Adriano Tellaro whistled softly to himself as he swung his Fiat sports car around the curving bends of the road which wound down from Taretta towards the main road to Palermo. He was well satisfied with his day's work.

He was a tall man, above six feet in height, with dark, swarthy Sicilian features. His complexion was almost sallow, with a permanent dark shadow on his cheeks and chin no matter how many times a day he shaved. He had thick black curly hair and dark eyes, so dark that they seemed to have no pupils. He preferred to wear sunglasses most of the time. He was a fastidious man, especially when it came to clothes. He preferred to dress in dark suits and so sombre was his appearance that many mistook him for an undertaker. In that they were not far wrong, for death was Adriano Tellaro's profession. Among the *gentile* of the Honoured Society, Adriano's sobriquet was 'the Executioner'.

Adriano spotted a telephone kiosk at the side of the road, slowed his vehicle and halted by it.

From memory he dialled a number.

A hollow voice answered.

'This is Adriano, *Signor*,' the young man said slowly.

'Yes?'

'It is done.'

'No problems?'

'No problems, *Signor*.'

'It is good. We shall be in touch.'

Adriano put down the receiver and smiled thinly. He turned and climbed back into the Fiat and sent it racing away towards the distant white and russet towers, domes and steeples of the red-roofed city of Palmero, through the groves of orange and lemon trees where once Norman kings hunted stags, deer and wild boar, and whose palaces still lay by artificial lakes and fountains in the immense parklands which surrounded the city. Adriano's mind was not on the beauties of his surroundings. He had seen them many times before. No; he was eager to return to his apartment in Palmero – to his apartment and to Cosima.

The Father Prior paused before a small door.

'This is Father Manzoni's room, Eminence,' he said to Tellaro. 'We will be taking him to the chapel within the hour

15

for the mass.'

Cardinal Tellaro nodded slowly. 'I will go in and pray a while,' he said. 'You may wait for me.'

The Father Prior opened his mouth to say something, then shrugged and inclined his head.

Tellaro stepped inside the room.

The immediate smell was one of camphor and tallow.

The body of Father Manzoni was laid out on the bed; two candles were burning on the bedside tables either side of the head of the bed. The curtains were drawn across the window, making the atmosphere close and the odours stronger.

Tellaro genuflected and approached the body.

Father Manzoni had been an old man with a shock of white hair and a deeply etched face. In death his features remained troubled; the pain lines had not eased with his passing. His frail hands clasped a silver crucifix on his chest.

Tellaro gazed down for a moment and then swung round to examine the room. The Benedictine priest had lived frugally. There was a desk piled with books and papers, a visible sign of Manzoni's calling as a scholar and archivist. Apart from the cluttered desk there was a curtained-off wardrobe space in which a few clothes hung from a line. There was also a small dressing-table with a few personal items on it.

Tellaro went to the desk and quickly flicked through the papers strewn across it. Most of them were in Greek with a few pages of translation and notes in Latin. The papers meant little. Tellaro's Latin was fundamental, adequate for ecclesiastical purposes, but he was no scholar.

It was then that Tellaro's searching eyes fell on a worn leather briefcase at the side of the desk. He bent and picked it up. It was not locked. Inside were a jumble of papers, some magazines which appeared to be connected with archivism and religion, and a mass of unrelated notes. He thumbed through them, examining the odd scraps of paper, the few envelopes...

Then his dark eyes grew suddenly round.

One of the envelopes was sealed and addressed. It was the

address that caused Cardinal Giona Tellaro's face to become a mask of astonishment. The envelope was addressed for the private attention of His Holiness, the Pope.

There was a gentle tap at the door.

Tellaro swiftly shoved the envelope into the folds of his cassock, closed the briefcase and replaced it. Then he swung to the bed and dropped to his knees in an attitude of prayer just as the door swung open and the Father Prior gave a discreet cough.

Tellaro genuflected and rose to his knees.

'A moment of prayer, Father Prior,' he smiled thinly. 'Alas, Father Manzoni will be sadly missed at the Vatican. Have you informed his colleagues at the Secret Archives?'

The Father Prior nodded. 'I believe the Cardinal Archivist will be attending the funeral services himself.'

Tellaro moved from the room. 'I shall trouble you no more, Father Prior. Thank you for your courtesies.'

The Father Prior hastened after him. 'It is always an honour to be of service, Eminence.'

Outside in the courtyard Tellaro climbed into the back seat of the Mercedes.

'Where to, Eminence?' demanded Salvatore, easing the car through the seminary gates.

'Drive to the Parco Savello and halt in some quiet spot.'

'At once, Eminence.'

Salvatore nursed the vehicle across the piazza and along the Via Sabina, passing the church of Sant' Alessio and down to Santa Sabina, one of the most beautiful of Rome's many churches, originally built in the fifth century AD on the site of the house of a sainted Roman matron. Beyond the church, at the top of a rise overlooking the Tiber Valley, one could see the panorama of the city of Rome. Here, at the spot, stood the walled garden of the Parco Savello.

Salvatore drew the car to a halt and Tellaro climbed out.

'Wait for me,' he said shortly.

The tall cardinal entered the walled garden, which was open to the public. There were a few elderly people seated among the fragrant orange trees, enjoying the view across

17

the river Tevere below, whose stately pushing waters were known to every schoolboy as the Tiber. From one corner of the garden, steps led down to the ancient river.

The people in the garden cast curious glances at Tellaro's tall figure dressed in his black cassock trimmed in scarlet, denoting his cardinal's rank. Tellaro ignored them and walked to an empty seat by the gate which led out into the Piazza Pietro d'Illiria with its splendid wall fountain. He sat down and took out the envelope, and gazed at it curiously, turning it over and over in his hands.

Why would Father Manzoni address a letter to His Holiness?

Tellaro had no feeling of guilt at having appropriated the letter, only an overwhelming curiosity. It was the same curiosity which he felt when Brother Girolamon had been discovered in the papal apartments having taken his own life. For fifteen years Giona Tellaro had been connected with Vatican security and he found that he no longer thought as a priest but more as a policeman. Some instinct in him caused him to feel that there was a connection of some sort between the death of Father Manzoni and his assistant Brother Girolamon; some meaning to the word '*Amentissimus*!' sprayed in red paint across a priceless tapestry in the papal apartments.

He gazed at the envelope with a frown, examining Father Manzoni's thin and scrawling calligraphy.

'For the eyes of His Holiness only' had been underlined several times.

The envelope was badly sealed, scarcely stuck at the edges.

Deliberately, Cardinal Tellaro inserted a forefinger and tore the envelope open.

Chapter Three

Adriano Tellaro drove through the hot dusty streets of Palermo, coasting down the Corso Vittorio Emanuele towards the waterfront where the road ended abruptly at the harbour. Before he reached that point, however, he turned at the Parco Marine and into the Via Alloro by the museum. It was at the back of the old museum building that he had his apartment, the top floor of an ancient block. He parked his Fiat sports car in the shade, locked it and made his way up the stairs. As he let himself in a voice called: 'Adriano?'

A girl in her early twenties appeared in a doorway across the small hall, a shapely blonde in a bikini, whose body was softly honey-coloured with a tan. Her corn-coloured hair and wide blue eyes gave her the appearance of being Swedish or German. She had well-shaped legs, dancer's legs, but perhaps a little too long for her otherwise perfectly proportioned body.

'Adriano, you are back early. I was going to spend the day at the beach.'

Her Italian was unmistakably Neapolitan — a rolling, slurring dialect distinguishable by a failure ever to pronounce word endings. Cosima Colombo was a child of Naples despite her blonde hair and fair features. It was not unusual. Naples being an international port, the people of the city were of very mixed origin.

Adriano smiled as he heeled the door shut behind him. 'Don't let me spoil your day.'

Cosima came quickly to him and kissed him. 'You never spoil anything for me, *mio tesoro*.'

19

He moved into the cool of the apartment, taking off his jacket and throwing it on a chair. 'Get me a cold beer.'

He flung himself on the couch, glancing up to make sure that the fans were working and the windows, which opened onto the balcony overlooking the waterfront, were wide open.

'It's hot,' he muttered as she handed him an opened bottle of Peroni. He never liked to drink beer from a glass, preferring to sip from the bottle or can.

Cosima nodded and grimaced. 'Is it always like this in Palermo?' she asked.

Adriano had met the girl a month before in a night-club in Naples, where she had been part of a cabaret act. Cosima had little talent except for her figure, which had been tucked away in a chorus line. Adriano had been with a few of the *gentile* of the Honoured Society celebrating a successful piece of 'business' and had asked the owner to send some girls over to keep them company. That was how he had met Cosima and when he had suggested that the girl might like to give up her job and come to spend time with him in Palermo, Cosima had been willing enough.

Cosima Colombo was a great believer in fate; she never planned for the future or made conscious decisions on how to fulfil her ambitions. Her ambitions were simply to acquire a comfortable standard of living, an escape from her working-class Neapolitan background. Colombo was not even her real name. She had simply taken it from the name of a main thoroughfare in the city. It sounded good when she applied for the job at the night-club. From school to night-club, entertainer to mistress of a member of the Honoured Society was an easy progression. Not that Adriano had told her about his profession; not that anyone had told her. She knew instinctively by the way others treated Adriano with a mixture of respect and fear. But it mattered little to her what Adriano did. It mattered that he was handsome, intelligent and kind to her. It mattered more that he had position, money and respect. It never occurred to her that she had any moral choice to make. And if Adriano discarded her

sometime in the future? *Non importante!* That was in the
future. It was today that mattered.

She noticed that Adriano's eyes were hungry as they fed
on the contours of her lithe body. She stood shivering a little
in pleasure. Adriano stood up abruptly, swallowing the
remains of his beer and wiping the back of his hand across
his mouth. He put the bottle down and turned towards her.
She came to him without hesitation, feeling his mouth cruel
and demanding on her own. His hands moved rapidly over
her body, fumbling with her bikini top.

Cardinal Giona Tellaro sat on the bench in the Parco Sevallo
and began to read the poor scrawl of the dying Father
Manzoni with a tightening mouth. His throat seemed to be
suddenly dry and aching, his chest felt curiously constricted.

> *'Holiness,'* he read:
> *'For many years it has been God's will that I have
> worked as an archivist in the Secret Archives,
> safeguarding the great records of our Christian Faith.*
>
> *'Brother Girolamon Solaro, whose tragic death I
> have learned of today, was my assistant in this work.*
>
> *'This letter is but an attempt to give a reason for his
> death and, similarly, to my illness from which I doubt
> to recover, but God's will be done. His mercy is
> infinite.*
>
> *'Holiness, does it not say in* Hebrews *that faith is the
> substance of things hoped for, the evidence of things
> not seen? For years I have laboured in the archives
> among the evidence of our Faith.*
>
> *'In the Secret Archives it is known that there is a
> section of documents which only the heir of St Peter
> himself may examine. It has been my job to safeguard
> and preserve such documents. Four weeks ago I was
> revising the catalogues of these documents when I
> chanced upon a reference to a manuscript of whose
> existence I had no previous knowledge. It was listed in
> a mediaeval cartulary as* Confessio Paulus Apostulus

and marked clearly that only the eyes of an incumbent of the throne of St Peter could look upon it. A gloss in the margin of the cartulary mentioned that the document was read on 20 August 1492 AD by His Holiness Alexander VI, after which it was resealed in a lead casket and replaced in the vaults of the Secret Archives. It has never been opened again.

'As archivist it was my duty to ascertain whether the manuscript known as Confessio Paulus Apostulus was still in safekeeping and whether it stood in need of restoration, perhaps having decayed over the centuries. It took many days before I finally discovered the sealed lead casket in the vaults and, in the presence of Brother Girolamon, I opened it to discover an ancient papyrus. My initial tests place the papyrus to the first century AD – the very century of the foundation of the Church. The papyrus was much decayed and stood in need of restoration and copying for future use.

'I commenced upon the task of first making a rough note of its contents.

'Holiness, when Faith becomes opposed to known learning and investigation, it is not worth the breath used in giving it expression. Have we been so wrong these twenty centuries? Is our Faith but a dream? A fragment of one man's egocentricity? If this document is genuine, then all our labours are meaningless.

'It was as I was digesting the significance of the document that my feeble body was unable to withstand the strain of the conflict which it aroused within me. My heart was unable to deal with it. Brother Girolamon had me taken back to Sant' Anselmo, where I live. While recovering from my heart seizure I learnt that Brother Girolamon, who was of my Order, had taken his life. Before doing so he had, so I am told, written a single word – Amentissimus! I can only presume that, in my absence, Brother Girolamon read my translation and compared it with the original. God be merciful to him; he was a young man and could not *bear the weight of its implications.*

'I beg you, Holiness, send for the papyrus, have it examined and evaluated by the leading scholars of the day; scholars whose word may be trusted. And when they have given their verdict, only you can decide, in the light of knowledge, what must be done according to God's will.*

'I remain, your brother in Christ. Father Manzoni, Ordinis Sancti Benedicti'

'I'm not asking for charity!'

'Get out of here, you damned lush!' The red-faced barman moved around the edge of his bar in a threatening manner.

The man sprawled on the stool shaking his head. Then he tried to rise with dignity but only succeeded in knocking over the stool and falling against the bar.

'. . .'s OK, 's OK,' he mumbled as the barman bent down and hauled him, not too gently, to his feet. 'I'm not asking for charity.'

The rest of the occupants of the bar looked on indifferently as the man was propelled towards the street door.

'You don't come back here no more, understand?'

'Sure, sure . . . anything you say.'

The barman reached the door, still with a firm grip on the drunk and gave the man a quick thrust which sent him sprawling on the sidewalk outside.

'No need . . . no need . . . for that,' the man muttered as he tried to pick himself up.

He stood swaying, blinking into a winking mass of neon lights which flashed along New York's Canal Street. A sea of humanity hurried this way and that along the street, pushing him along, hardly noticing him. Those who did see him carefully avoided him. The man's dirty, torn and rumpled raincoat, the filthy open-necked shirt, the trousers with jagged tears and the worn shoes with the soles and uppers nearly parting company, proclaimed him to be just another Bowery bum. They did not have to bother to gaze at his

23

sunken, unshaven face, the matted hair and wild eyes, glazed from cheap booze. His sort were common enough along Canal Street at this time. In another hour men like him would drift down to where the Bowery intersected Canal Street, finding doors and alleys and gutters along its route where they could fall into a semi-comatose alcohol-induced sleep. If they were lucky they would be able to snatch a few hours of peaceful oblivion before a prowling patrol car edged along and they would be prodded back into harsh reality with the tip of an officer's night-stick.

The swaying man took a few paces against the surging sea of the crowd, found the safety of a wall and leant against it.

His face was puckered as he tried to think.

Automatically he began to fumble in his pockets, first one pocket and then another, hoping against hope that he would find a coin, some forgotten coin which might help him purchase another drink. He tried to remember when he had had his last drink. Some time ago now, he thought. Too long ago. Life was interminable . . . measured between one drink and another.

His search was fruitless.

He tried to heave himself away from the wall, succeeded and pushed towards an anonymous blur of a figure.

He thrust out a hand. 'Spare a dime?'

His mind heard a distant whining voice call out, dimly recognising it as his own. 'Spare a dime?'

A rough hand pushed him away, sending him crashing back against the wall. 'Get out of my way, you bum!' a voice screamed.

He recovered his balance and pushed forward again. 'Spare a dime?'

People either avoided him or pushed him roughly aside.

The man stood engulfed in a sea of passing humanity, totally alone. He could have been any age, so unkempt was his appearance. Only a close observer could see that he was young, probably not much more than thirty. It was hard to say whether his hair was prematurely grey or whether the greyness was the product of the dirt and dust which adhered to it. The eyes seemed colourless and listless. They did not seem to have the ability to focus on any object but stared permanently into the middle distance.

He suddenly felt something pressed into his outstretched hand.

Someone nearby chuckled.

Automatically his hand closed over the object. It was soft and squelching. The man tried to focus, bringing his palm near to his face. Someone had pressed a blob of masticated chewing-gum into his hand. He tried to wipe it off on the sleeve of his dirty raincoat.

'Bum!' hissed a voice.

The man began to push his way through the torrent of faceless bodies towards the Bowery.

Chapter Four

The Carmelite brother watched the swarthy-faced cardinal with an anxious expression. On the instructions of the prefect of Archives he had escorted Cardinal Tellaro through the maze of corridors of the library buildings, with their tall recessed windows, across the huge reference room, which ran under the Sistine Hall and which was crammed with long desks and countless chairs, down frescoed aisles, until he halted before a door.

'This is the office of Father Manzoni, Eminence,' he said softly.

Cardinal Tellaro inclined his head. 'Is it unlocked?'

The Carmelite started, flushed and fumbled for a key, swinging the door open.

'Thank you,' said Tellaro gravely. 'I need not detain you.'

The Carmelite bobbed his head. 'If there is anything you require, Eminence, please use the telephone. The line connects directly with the library switchboard.'

The monk turned and made his way sedately back along the corridor.

Tellaro stood for a moment watching him go. He found his pulse was beating rather quickly, he was breathing too rapidly, feeling like a small boy about to make his first raid into a forbidden apple orchard.

He turned into the room and closed the door carefully behind him.

He stood surveying the office which Father Manzoni and Brother Girolamon had used. It was lit from a large, single window across which the shutters were partially drawn

26

giving a murky atmosphere to the room. A large bookcase ran across one wall. A work-bench ran the length of a further wall on which stood microscopes and scientific apparatus, chemical bottles and photographic equipment. Tellaro could not even begin to guess the purpose for which most of the equipment was used. In the centre of the room were two desks. On one desk stood an ancient typewriter but both desks were tidy of any other materials except two telephone extensions. Behind the desks were a series of filing-cabinets and cupboards.

Tellaro placed the briefcase which he had been carrying on the nearest desk and moved to the window to open it, letting the warm sunlight flood the room.

He turned and sat down at the desk without the typewriter, deducing that this was Father Manzoni's desk. Slowly, methodically, he opened the drawers one by one. Manzoni had obviously been a scrupulously tidy man. His drawers were neatly arranged, piles of paper were carefully stacked. Tellaro soon realised that there was nothing of consequence to be found in this desk and so repeated the process with the other, with similar results. However, Brother Girolamon's desk was the antithesis of Father Manzoni's tidiness. Papers were scattered everywhere, screwed into balls; there were even the remains of a sandwich curling into biscuit hardness. Tellaro shook his head and sighed.

He turned his attention to the filing-cabinets and cupboards.

As he expected, everything was locked. From his cassock pocket he drew out a bunch of keys which he had appropriated from Father Manzoni's briefcase and tried them until he found the right one.

It was in the bottom drawer of the filing-cabinet that he found it.

It was an innocuous-looking casket, some twelve inches by six inches by six, without any distinctive marks on the outside save some roughly scratched characters on the lid. There was evidence that the lid had once been sealed but had recently been prised open with a sharp instrument.

Cardinal Tellaro suddenly felt nervous. His hands trembled slightly as he removed the box from the filing-cabinet and placed it carefully on the top of Father Manzoni's desk. It was very heavy. The grey metal was obviously lead and it smelled curiously of the poisonous metal mixed with the odour of age.

He stared down at the casket and found that the scratches were decipherable to him. They were the letters 'CPA' and the numeral '2'.

Slowly Tellaro sat down and stretched out his hands towards the casket.

The lid was easy to remove although it fitted snugly, making the casket almost airtight. He supposed that the addition of the wax, or whatever had sealed the rim, had made the box completely airtight. He stared inside. There were several sheets of modern paper folded in haphazard fashion on top. He recognised the sprawling writing of Father Manzoni. He reached down and picked them out. As he did so he saw the small scroll lying in the bottom of the box. It was about six inches in width; a papyrus wound around a strip of once-polished wood. He gazed for a long time without touching it. He had not the knowledge to touch it. Instead he placed the lead lid carefully into position again and sat down to read the sheaf of notes which Father Manzoni had written.

'*Confessio Paulus Apostulus:* Secret Archive, Manuscript Register CPA 2.'

Tellaro stroked his nose nervously.

> '*This papyrus is registered for the eyes of the Pope only,*' Manzoni had written. '*It is a "lost" manuscript reference to which was only discovered by myself in a record to the Cartulary of the Monastry of St Severus, which stood on the Via Merulana, Rome. The cartulary is dated to the thirteenth century AD. A gloss records that this manuscript was last known to have been seen by His Holiness Alexander VI on 20 August 1492 AD, after which it was resealed in a lead casket and*

placed in the Secret Archives.

'On 2 April, this year, I discovered the sealed casket and, in the presence of Brother Girolamon, opened the seals. The manuscript was in poor condition and urgently needed restoring and copying to preserve its text. However, I was able to make an adequate translation of the work. In view of the contents of this, I made several tests to ascertain the age and credibility of the papyrus. It is my opinion that there is a high degree of probability that the papyrus is genuine. I have always used the term "probable" or "highly probable" according to the degree of certainty that I felt. It is the nature of an archivist to be cautious.'

Tellaro turned to the next page. It was headed: – 'A letter from Paul of Tarsus to Linus; a rough translation of the text into Italian'.

Tellaro grew tense as he began to read, his face going pale, his eyes widening. The trembling of his hands grew more acute until he was finally forced to place the sheets of paper on the desk top in order to be able to read them. He read right through the translation and then returned a second time and even a third time before he sat back and gave a long shuddering sigh.

'Take it easy.'

He swam up out of the blackness into blinding consciousness which caused him to groan and whimper like a baby. He struggled and turned his head away from the light.

'Take it easy, mister,' repeated the voice near at hand.

The words were pronounced so loudly, so clearly, that he started up with the feeling that they had been shouted directly against his ear-drums, causing them to vibrate in rebellion.

He was lying in a stuffy prison of a bed. He tried to struggle upwards, feeling that the sheet and blanket were some confining enemy intent on smothering him.

A cold impersonal hand was poking at his wrist.

He blinked and focused on a figure in a white coat. A

29

young healthy looking face surmounted by a blond crew-cut stared down at him good-naturedly.

'What the hell . . . ?' he began.

The face grinned.

There was a pinprick on his arm; something warm slid into his bloodstream.

'There you are, mister. It didn't hurt a bit, did it?'

He tried to wet his dry, cracking lips. 'Where am I?'

'In hospital.'

'What for?'

The fresh-faced young man in the white coat bent over his bed and he saw the syringe in his hand.

'Where am I?' he repeated again. 'What have you given me?'

He suddenly became aware of a cacaphony of sound around him: mutterings, screamings, sobbings – a bedlam of human misery.

'What's that?' he demanded.

'Your fellow patients, mister. I told you, you are in hospital.'

He frowned at the white-coated man in annoyance. 'Where?'

'Bellevue. The alcoholic ward.'

He stared up at the man in disbelief. Cautiously he turned his head. He was in a long high-ceilinged room with a concrete floor, bare of anything except beds, most of them low, more like pallets. The beds were filled. Next to him was an old man with wide staring eyes who kept smiling and chuckling and addressing the ceiling in a loud voice. Beyond him was a negro who was singing and babbling alternately. The figures stretched anonymously way down the long ward. He could see one or two of them were in straightjackets. He turned back to the amused stare of the nurse. His body began to sweat and he felt tremors in his limbs.

'Why was I brought here?' he managed to mumble.

The nurse grinned. 'You've gotta be kidding.'

'Why?' The word was almost a scream.

'Your blood was one hundred percent proof, man. You

30

fell down some subway stairs, nearly broke your goddam neck. You were brought here by ambulance.'

He tried to remember and couldn't.

The crew-cut nurse was taking out a black-covered notebook. 'Name?'

He dredged his memory. 'Kane.'

'C-A-I-N-E?'

'K-A-N-E.'

'First name?'

'David.'

'Okay, Dave,' smiled the nurse. 'Let's have the address.'

Kane shook his head.

The nurse cocked a laconic eyebrow.

'Hobo?'

'No! I ...'

The nurse gave a world-weary smile and made an entry in the book.

'Look, Dave, you had no ID on you and no money. We've probably had to incinerate the clothes you were wearing. I reckon they could have walked away by themselves. You sound educated, you're not old ... what's with the vagrancy? Drink get you into this mess, eh?'

Kane shrugged indifferently.

The nurse sighed. 'Next of kin?'

A bitter look crossed Kane's features. 'None!'

The nurse raised an eyebrow at the harshness in his tone and flicked shut the notebook. 'You realise that I'll have to pass the details to the local precinct?'

Kane merely said: 'My head hurts.'

'I guess it would,' grinned the nurse.

He turned down the ward leaving Kane lying gazing up at the paint-peeling ceiling. He felt the stiffness of the short white nightgown which barely reached to his knees. It was tied at the back of his neck. He debated whether to attempt to leave the bed and decided that he was in no condition to do so.

He heard a footfall next to his bed and opened his eyes. It was the blond male nurse. He held a glass with some clear liquid in it.

'What's that?'

'Paraldehyde. Drink it down... you'll feel better.'

Obediently he reached out and suddenly withdrew his arm. It shook and trembled as if it had a life of its own.

The nurse reached down and placed the glass against his lips. The liquid was foul-tasting, more bitter than anything he could conceive of. Nevertheless, after a few moments he miraculously began to feel better. His hands stopped their trembling. A new thought occurred to him.

'How long have I been here?'

'Two days. The doctor will be round to see you soon, Dave. Take it easy.'

The nurse drifted away.

The doctor!

Kane suddenly smiled.

Doctor David Kane! That was a hoot! But it was true. Oh, he was not a doctor of medicine, his doctorate was in palaeography, specialising in ancient Greek and Latin manuscripts. At thirty he had been one of New York University's up-and-coming young men. His papers on ancient inks and papyri had been widely quoted in the academic world. Now, at thirty-four, he was just a drunken Bowery bum without a future, without a past. One of the anonymous hulks which drift along the Manhattan thoroughfares in their own twilight world.

The doctor is coming to cure the doctor!

David Kane began to chuckle softly to himself. It was amusing. Highly amusing. Devastatingly amusing. The babble of his laughter merely blended into the cacaphony of the mad world about him.

Giona Tellaro was a career priest. By his brilliance at organisation he had risen swiftly from the curacy of a small Sicilian parish to the secretariat of the Bishop of Catania and from thence, by leaps and bounds, to the various organisational positions in the Roman Curia. He had been thirty-one when he entered the portals of the Vatican as

Father Tellaro, an assistant on the Council for the Public Affairs of the Church. Now, scarcely twenty years later, he was not only a prince of the Church but he had one of the most powerful jobs within the Vatican – head of the Central Security Office, which he had joined fifteen years before. His talent for the Church's security matters had been noticed by the secretary of the Council of State, the Marchese Don Giulio Torrella, and within five years Tellaro had been made undisputed head of the most intriguing security force in the world.

Along the way his priesthood and his faith had come to be less important than the poltical power he wielded.

To Giona Tellaro the priesthood had never been a vocation; it had been merely a way of escape from the poverty of the working-class eastern suburbs of his native Palermo; from a large squabbling family in which he had grown up; from the memories of a mother unable to cope and a father who had been gunned down one Sunday morning, just after mass, because he had talked unwisely about the Honoured Society. Giona Tellaro was exceptionally intelligent; even at the age of ten years he had seen that life could offer him few alternatives and he had deliberately chosen the easiest path of escape. He frequented his local parish church. He ingratiated himself with the local priest who, realising the intelligence of the child and misled by his apparent piety, had ensured an education through which Giona Tellaro was able to enter a seminary and take holy orders.

Faith?

Giona Tellaro was a good Christian, a good Catholic. Wasn't everyone? He accepted without question. Not for Giona Tellaro were there any conflicts of faith, any questioning of the teachings of the Church. Never did he have to go into a retreat and meditate on his religious convictions and the role of his Church in the modern world. While some priests had to overcome doubts and scruples, Giona Tellaro simply believed. He was like a soldier enlisted in an army carrying out his functions without questioning

33

how that army had come into being and for what purpose it existed. 'My country, right or wrong' was a maxim which could easily be transferred to Tellaro's attitude to his Church.

His life was devoted to what he was best at: organisation, manipulation, finding the best ways of getting a job accomplished. He had no moral scruples to prevent his garnering personal wealth along the way by using his position to bestow favours on those who would pay him for the privilege. He owned a villa in Rome, the Villa Tiburtina, and a villa in Sicily, a modest summer residence on the slopes of Mount Etna near the village of Zafferana. Needless to say, the deeds of these properties appeared in another name – that of a cousin who managed them for him. It was not that Tellaro was dishonest; he was a man who liked power and position and enjoyed the benefits that those things brought. He was human and thoughts on higher morality did not appeal to him. The mediaeval Vatican, with its vast properties, riches and the feudal military power of its prelates, appealed more to him than the poverty of early Christendom.

Sitting at Father Manzoni's desk, gazing at the spidery scrawl of the dead priest, Cardinal Giona Tellaro, prince of the Universal Church, was bewildered.

He knew the tenets of the faith, he knew the history of the Church. He knew more. If what he had just read were true then the entire fabric of the Church would be rent asunder. The very rock on which the Church was founded would be smashed to a thousand fragments. The papyrus constituted a more considerable threat to the Church than the heretic Luther ever did.

Both Father Manzoni and Brother Girolamon had believed that the papyrus was genuine. The young man, unable to cope with the knowledge, had taken his own life. Hence his last word '*Amentissimus!*' – Senseless! – splattered on the tapestry in the private papal library. Father Manzoni had been old and the terrible burden of his discovery had proved too much for his heart.

34

Tellaro drew from his cassock Father Manzoni's letter to His Holiness and re-read it. Manzoni was shifting the grave responsibility for the discovery and its interpretation onto the shoulders of the Pope. Tellaro drew his gaze from the letter to the small lead casket. Like a time-bomb, it threatened to destroy two thousand years of blind faith.

Tellaro bit his thin lips.

At least he was no emotional prelate. He had acted as chief policeman to the Vatican for ten years, dealing with various threats to the safety of the Church and its property and personnel. Here was simply another threat and one which had to be dealt with.

Firmly, he replaced Manzoni's letter in his pocket, refolded the translation and notes and stuffed them after the letter.

The Church had to be protected. But to have protection from a threat one must know fully the nature of the threat. Manzoni and his assistant believed the papyrus to be authentic but perhaps their examination had not been thorough? Perhaps they had been too emotional in their judgement? Tellaro scratched his chin thoughtfully as he gazed down at the dull grey exterior of the casket.

The first step would be to become fully assured as to its authenticity. Perhaps to get some non-Catholic, a non-Christian with the right knowledge, to examine it? Have more scientific checks conducted, a further translation, without the translator seeing Father Manzoni's text, in order to be absolutely certain.

What then?

Then – that would have to be decided. The decision would be his and his alone. If the document were genuine then perhaps it should simply be destroyed; lost in the vaults of the Secret Archives. After all, no Pope since Alexander VI had seen it and that had been five hundred years ago. Perhaps another five hundred might pass before... A thought suddenly caught at his mind. Alexander VI! Roderigo Lenzuoli-Borgia... one of the most profligate men who dared to ascend to the throne of St Peter. Tellaro had a good memory for facts and figures. Alexander VI had examined the papyrus on 20 August 1492 AD. That was exactly eleven days after he had become Pope. Was the cause of the subsequent events of his reign that very act of reading the papyrus? The deeds of the Borgias became a by-word for evil... was it because they *knew*?

Tellaro shuddered slightly.

He reached forward and drew back the lid of the casket again, looking down at the dirty brown roll which lay there so innocently. He stretched forth a tentative, inquiring finger to touch it, drawing swiftly back as if afraid of contamination or some electric shock.

Yes, he was convinced. If this document were genuine then he, Giona Tellaro, would decide the future of the Church. His would be the power!

The present Bishop of Rome, the Father of the Church, was a man of simple belief; straightforward, honest and a hopeless idealist in search of truth and justice. Put such a decision in his hands and the Church might well be destroyed, for truth is not always a weapon for good. Only the other week His Holiness had preached a sermon based on the Gospel of John, chapter eight, verse thirty-two: 'The truth shall make you free.' Well, if this were truth, then it would mean anarchy. Dimly Tellaro recalled another quotation but he could not place it. 'Whatever satisfies the soul is truth.'

The decision was his but the first step was to ensure the authenticity of the papyrus.

He picked up his briefcase and opened it. Then he placed the casket inside. No one would question the head of the Central Security Office as to what he carried in his case as he left the Secret Archives.

Cosima Colombo sat back in her chair painting her toe-nails and watching Adriano emerge from the shower. There was a soft proprietorial smile on her full red lips. Her eyes wandered over his tall broad-shouldered frame, the flat belly, the dark cropped hair and the cruel though handsome face which bore the lines of harsh experience around the thin mouth. The chiselled features, the strong hands excited her, and she stirred a little uneasily on her chair.

'A drink?' she asked, putting down her nail varnish.

Adriano grunted.

She walked carefully to the small bar at one side of the room as Adriano wrapped a towel around his middle, lit a cigarette and sat on the edge of the bed. He watched her enacting the ritual of slicing the lemon peel and measuring the drinks.

'Mix mine dry,' he said, turning to stare through the window across the Foro Italico to the bright blue sea beyond.

'I'm sick of Palermo,' he suddenly said. 'I think we ought to have a holiday.'

Cosima smiled brightly. 'You have no more work for a while?'

Adriano exhaled the smoke of his cigarette with a deep sigh. 'I was thinking of Sorrento,' he said without answering her. 'I want to lie in the sun and swim and eat and drink...'

She came towards him carrying two cocktail glasses. She placed them on the bedside table and nestled onto his lap.

'I'd love to go to Sorrento,' she said.

The telephone shrilled and she pouted with annoyance.

Adriano lifted the receiver. '*Pronto?*'

The voice on the other end of the wire was cold. 'Adriano, this is your cousin in Rome.'

Adriano's jaw dropped. He had only one cousin in Rome, a cousin Giona.

'Adriano,' the voice went on. 'I have some work which I think you are best qualified to do. I would like you to come to Rome to see me. Can you be at the Villa Tiburtina in the Via Angelo Emo tomorrow afternoon? Say, at four o'clock?'

'Yes,' replied Adriano.

'Excellent. You will find the job is well paid.'

Adriano gazed at the buzzing receiver for a moment and then replaced it. He had not seen his cousin Giona in ten years although he had acted as a middle man for him in connection with buying the villa near Zafferana. He wondered what had prompted his cousin to telephone him.

Cosima was watching him uncertainly. 'Something is wrong?'

He smiled and shook his head. 'Just a small change of plan, Cosima. Tomorrow morning we fly to Rome for a few days at least. You may do some shopping there.'

Cosima clapped her hands and laughed. 'Shopping in Rome! Oh, how I've wanted to go shopping in the Via Frattina and the Via Condotti! Adriano, you are wonderful.'

Adriano glanced at his watch. 'I'll make the reservations. Get changed. We'll go out for a meal this evening.'

He turned and reached for the telephone.

Chapter Five

David Kane glared defiantly at the small, balding doctor named Klugerman. He was seated in a consulting-room with only a desk between him and the good-natured psychiatrist who was thumbing through his notes.

'Well,' the doctor was saying, 'I guess it's up to you now. We've done our best. We've pumped you out, dried you out... but...'

He shrugged.

Kane said nothing.

'You haven't been the most co-operative patient,' Klugerman ventured.

'I didn't ask for your help,' snapped Kane.

'True,' granted the psychiatrist. 'We could have easily let you kill yourself.'

'It was my choice.'

Klugerman's good-natured mask suddenly broke. 'Don't come that crap with me. You're far too intelligent. Your only trouble is that you are too damned self-indulgent.'

Kane laughed harshly in response. 'Aren't you forgetting your role, doc? You're supposed to be murmuring sympathetic sweet nothings into my shell-like ear, asking me to lie down on your couch and taking my mind back to my mother's womb. Thereupon you will declare that my problem lies in my latent oedipal complex, my hatred of the old man and my predilection to alcohol as an escape route.'

Klugerman's eyes glinted dangerously. 'Is that your diagnosis?' he asked softly. 'Did you want to screw your old woman?'

Kane swore.

'Then why bring it up?' responded Klugerman. 'If you want to hear that crap, I'm not your man. The facts are pretty plain. You are drinking to blot out the death of your wife, Janine.'

The statement was so direct, so unexpected, that Kane had no time to prepare for it. He reeled in his chair as if from some physical blow. He tried to recover his poise, staring at Klugerman, his mouth working but no sound would come.

'We're not all morons here, Kane, as much as you would like to think we are. You can't just vanish into anonymity.'

'So?' Kane's voice had a dangerous edge.

'David Kane, Ph.D. and half a dozen other degrees. Expert in early Greek and Latin manuscripts. Palaeographer. Former lecturer at New York University. Drunk. Vagrant. Why?'

'Suppose you tell me?' invited Kane, his voice growing more even.

'Three years ago you married a girl called Janine. The day after the wedding she was attacked, raped and murdered.'

Klugerman said the words clearly, deliberately, giving each word its own weight and watching Kane's knuckles whiten as he gripped the arm rests of his chair.

'All right, David,' Klugerman suddenly bent forward sympathetically. 'We can sympathise with you. It was a terrible thing. A senseless thing. A great shock. The men who did it were caught, tried and sentenced. You never recovered from the shock. You took to the bottle as an escape route. We all want escape routes in life. That's understandable. But the one you chose, David, is a one-way ticket to oblivion; a ticket to hell. That's no escape.'

Klugerman flicked through his notes.

'At first everyone was sympathetic to you. The University bent over backwards to help you. After all, you were a leading man in your field. You had great promise. You were given chance after chance. The registrar managed to fix up a course of therapy for you; you were given counselling. Then you went right back to emptying every bottle in sight. The result was that the University had to dismiss you. So there you are, in New York, with no job, no prospects and all the makings of an alcoholic. You sold everything for the bottle – your car, the apartment, furniture – everything. Now you're a Bowery bum, just another one of the countless drunks in this city.'

He stared hard at Kane, his eyes flashing.

'That's why I am so damned angry, Kane,' his voice grated harshly again. 'You have talent, intelligence. You could have been at the top of your field. You've thrown it all away. You don't need me to tell you why, or to tell you what you must do to save yourself. You know it all.'

'So?'

'So nothing! The doctor on the alcoholic ward suggested that I have a chat with you. He thought I might be able to help. I know better. I've read your notes.' He tapped the file before him. 'I know that you are just another useless, stupid, sonofabitch who will walk right out of here, hit the nearest bar and be back on the Bowery by tonight. You are useless, expendable junk of humanity and the sooner you poison yourself with booze the easier it will be on the rest of us.'

Kane sat staring at the man for several long moments before he let his mouth form into a bitter grin.

'You know,' he said, 'for a shrink, you are damned good. And shall I tell you something in return? Your prognosis is one hundred per cent correct.'

Klugerman bit his lip. He was hoping that his un-sympathetic approach might have hit a spot. Sympathy had been tried with David Kane too many times without success. The man was just impervious to all suggestions.

'Why don't you accept that your wife is dead, Kane?' he said quietly. 'She's dead and you are alive and there is nothing else for it but to go on living.'

Kane's lower lip trembled. 'The hell with it!' he snarled.

'Sure,' Klugerman plucked at his lower lip. 'The hell with it. You have just sentenced yourself to death. But you are a damned coward, Kane. You haven't got the guts you were born with. Shall I tell you for why? Because any person with guts would go out, buy a gun and end it all there and then. Bang! No more problems. No more guilt feelings. And guilt is the central issue here. You blame yourself for Janine's death. You feel guilty. It is your feelings that you can't live with. And that's self-indulgent. It's nothing to do with what you felt for Janine. It's what you feel about yourself. Rather than end the problem cleanly, you prefer the coward's way – slow poison by means of the bottle. Jesus, you make me sick!'

David Kane stood up, swaying slightly. 'Is that all?' he asked evenly. 'Any more great theories, sage advice, platitudes about the value of human life and dignity?'

'No. Go kill yourself.' Klugerman turned back to his notes and began writing.

Kane hesitated, feeling that he ought to go out on his own terms and not be dismissed like some recalcitrant, erring schoolboy. He made to say something, shrugged and left.

Behind him, Klugerman glanced up and swore softly.

What a waste of a human being! If only he had been able to get through the shell which Kane had succeeded in establishing. He had been so sure that a direct shock might have broken through. He lifted the telephone and dialled the alcoholic ward. The ward doctor, Bono, answered.

'Kane's on his way down. Nothing for it but to discharge him.'

'He won't respond?'

Klugerman pinched the bridge of his nose and sighed. 'The man's already dead,' he said heavily.

Doctor Bono put down the telephone just as Kane was being escorted into the ward by a male staff nurse. 'Klugerman tells me that we can discharge you.' Bono nodded as Kane came up to him.

Kane gazed at the doctor without replying.

'Where will you go?'

'What's the chance of my getting welfare in this condition?' he smiled sourly.

The hospital had supplied Kane with some second-hand newly laundered clothes; a pair of slacks, white shirt, threadbare jacket, socks and a pair of canvas sneakers. His appearance was passable. Doctor Bono thrust a card into Kane's hand.

'Try this place, Kane. Father Keegan at the Cathedral of St John the Divine up at Amsterdam and Cathedral Parkway. He'll give you a place to sleep until you get something organised.'

Kane obediently put the card into his pocket.

Doctor Bono was bent over a desk writing out a form.

'This is your discharge paper. Keep it in lieu of an ID.'

Bono paused and then pressed something else in Kane's hand and made an embarrassed gesture. 'Take it. You don't deserve this luck, Kane.' He turned and strode away down the ward.

Kane stared bemused at the twenty-dollar bill and shrugged. He turned and was let out of the ward by the grinning blond-haired male nurse. 'See you soon, buster,' the man smirked.

Kane paused. 'You reckon that I'm coming back?'

'Oh sure,' nodded the nurse. 'They all do. Either in a coma or in a pine box. You'll be back. Just like all the rest. They all come back.'

The door of the alcoholic ward slammed shut behind him.

Outside he stood gazing at the twenty-dollar bill and then he drew the card with Father Keegan's name from his pocket. Taking it between thumb and forefinger, he tore it into strips and let the pieces fall to the floor. Then he turned and followed the stairs down to the entrance hall, emerging from the grim portals of Bellevue onto First Avenue.

The study of the villa was dark and cool and protected from the stifling heat by partially closed shutters. It was an expensively furnished room with period furniture, a desk, chairs, a small table and various ornaments, the sale of which, Adriano Tellaro calculated, would allow a man to live in comfort for the rest of his life. One wall was lined with books while the others were covered by a variety of original paintings none of which seemed more recent than the seventeenth century. Not that Adriano was an expert but one couldn't help but acquire a working knowledge of art when one aspired to the more indolent life of the Italian leisured classes.

A hollow cough caused him to raise his eyes from the marble floor and gaze at the man seated across the desk from him.

'It might be difficult, Eminence,' he said.

Cardinal Giona Tellaro gave a thin smile. 'There is no need for formalities in private, Adriano,' he said softly. 'I realise that the commission is not easy if one tackles it without a firm starting-point.'

Adriano raised an eyebrow. 'You have an idea, Em... Giona?'

Tellaro nodded and reached for a small magazine which lay on his desk and thrust it towards Adriano without speaking.

Adriano took it with a frown.

'*Studia Archivum ...*' He pronounced the title carefully and looked up at his cousin. 'I was not able to learn Latin in my school.' There was a tone of rebuke in his voice for Giona knew the hardship of life in eastern Palermo.

'It is a magazine for archivists,' explained Tellaro. 'It is read by the sort of person who would qualify for the job that I have in mind. It is a sort of professional journal. This issue contains a small paragraph which might be the starting point for your search. The issue is dated six months ago.' He reached for the magazine and flicked it open. 'I will translate for you: "New York University's Department of Palaeography has announced, with regret, the dismissal of Dr David Kane, senior lecturer in the department. Dr Kane, who has edited the new standard text of *Anecdotes of Valerius Maximus* as well as a work on the critical dating of the works of Ammianus Marcellinus, has been reported to be suffering an illness." That's all.'

Cardinal Tellaro put the magazine down and smiled. 'This David Kane has all the right qualifications for the job I have in mind.'

44

'But the illness?' pressed Adriano.

'You must discover the facts. All I know is that it is very rare, if not an impossible event, for a University to dismiss a faculty member of Kane's reputation simply on grounds of ill health. I find that this dismissal has an interesting connotation, Adriano. I suspect... but suspicion is not enough.'

'What exactly must I do?'

'Go to New York and make enquiries. You already have connections there – the friends of the friends, eh?'

Adriano shifted uncomfortably.

Cardinal Tellaro smiled thinly. 'I have already indicated the terms and conditions of my proposed employment. Find this man, Kane. If he qualifies, I leave it to you to persuade him to come to Rome.'

'And if he does not qualify or if he refuses?'

'You must continue your search.'

Adriano nodded. The terms of his cousin's commission were generous – very generous. He nodded and rose to his feet.

'Let me know if there are difficulties,' Tellaro added.

Adriano hesitated, wondering whether he should kiss his cousin's ring, but he thought better of it in the circumstances, bowed his head and left the study.

Chapter Six

Kane tossed and turned in his own sweat, twisting from side to side and occasionally whimpering like a child. He was dreaming. Dreaming or remembering?

They had been married on the Saturday from Kane's apartment in 63rd Street, between Columbus and Amsterdam, a mere five minutes' walk down to Central Park. They had decided to stay at the apartment until Monday and then fly down to Florida for a holiday – they called it a 'holiday' because they found it hard to agree with the old concept of a 'honeymoon'. After the riotous Saturday night party which followed the wedding, they had spent most of Sunday in bed. It was evening before Janine sat up and groaned.

'I'm hungry. What's there to eat?'

Janine was a well-proportioned, attractive redhead who looked the farthest thing from the stereotype librarian, which profession she followed at Columbia University.

Kane gazed up with a lazy grin.

'I think we have a Mother Hubbard situation,' he replied with mock gravity.

Janine pouted. Kane watched her slim figure as she slid from the bed and walked to the kitchen. After a moment she reappeared and leant against the door jamb.

'As you say, the cupboard is bare. Do you want to go out or eat in?'

Kane chuckled.

'I'd prefer to eat in bed.'

Janine grinned.

'OK, lover. Is there a take-away place open near here?'

'There's a Chinese place around the corner on Columbus. I use it quite a lot. It's called Lee Fong's Kitchen.'

'Right,' Janine began pulling on her clothes. 'I'll go and get it. You start tidying up, Mister Kane. We want to catch that plane from Kennedy bright and early and I don't want to leave the apartment looking like a cyclone hit it.'

Kane nodded sheepishly.

After she left he began to tidy up in a half-hearted fashion. It was an hour later when he began to feel irritable. The Chinese restaurant was five minutes away at most and they were never busy at this time. He frowned and tried to peer down from his apartment window. The street outside was fairly deserted. It was a typical late Sunday. He waited another fifteen minutes and then telephoned the restaurant.

'Hello, Mister Lee. This is Dave Kane.'

He was a regular patron of the restaurant.

'Ah, Mister Kane. You wish to order?'

'No. I just wondered if my wife has been in. A tall, attractive redhead.'

'I see no redhead come in, Mister Kane. Anything wrong?'

Kane frowned.

'I don't know,' he said brusquely as he rang off.

It could be that Janine had changed her mind and gone to another restaurant. It could be that she had missed Lee Fong's place and gone elsewhere. But... he turned and threw on some clothes, let himself out of the apartment and walked slowly towards Lee Fong's Kitchen, carefully examining the other shops and eating houses *en route*. There was no sign of Janine. He reached Lee Fong's and looked in.

Lee Fong smiled as he entered. 'You miss your wife, Mister Kane? She no come in here.'

Kane began to panic now.

He turned and hurried home, hoping – somehow – that he had missed her and that she would have already arrived back at the apartment. The place was cold and cheerless. It was two hours since Janine had left. He telephoned the police.

The sergeant to whom his call was referred was

sympathetic but not really interested.

'Did you have a row?'

'For Chrissake, no! We were only married yesterday.'

'Mister, I've known a wife to walk out on her husband as they came out of the church door. You're certain there was no row?'

'I've told you the facts. She went out to get some food.'

'All right, mister. Tell you what . . . if she hasn't shown up by tomorrow, call in to see me at the precinct and bring the latest photograph. You have checked all the local hospitals?'

For the next hour and a half, Kane rang every hospital on Manhattan.

It was midnight when the sad-faced police sergeant and patrolman appeared at the apartment. They had Janine's bag with them.

'The body of a young woman has just been found in Central Park. The bag was nearby.'

In a dream, Kane allowed them to take him to the police morgue.

She lay in one of the long drawers as if she were simply asleep. She looked peaceful apart from the ugly bruise to her eye, the gashed lip and three dark wounds around her heart.

Kane could not remember much of what happened then. The world seemed to explode. He was screaming, hitting, yelling . . .

He sat bolt upright in the bed and peered around the small hotel bedroom with its brown paint peeling off the walls and layers of dust. It was dark and musty. What else could one expect of a Lower East Side doss house? He stretched out of the creaking bed and gripped the quart bottle of rye. It was almost empty. Kane sucked at it eagerly.

There was a crash against his door and it swung open as a stocky negro entered. The man wore a dirty string vest, pants several sizes too large which were held to his protruding belly by a thick leather belt. A filthy trilby hat was perched on the back of his head and he chewed in rhythmic motions at the butt of a cigar.

'You say your name was Kane, hey?' he demanded.

'Couple of guys downstairs to see you.'

Kane blinked.

'And you've been here two weeks without paying the rent, man. I don't run no charity doss. I need a fifty bill and now.'

Kane rose from the bed. He was still dressed and began to rummage through his pockets. He knew that he had no money. The last dollar had gone on the quart of rye.

'I don't seem to have it...' he began to mumble.

The negro swore loudly and colourfully. 'If you can't pay, you shift your arse elsewhere. Like now!'

He began to push Kane through the door. Two men were climbing the stairs. They were short and dark and smartly dressed.

'Is that Kane?' demanded one.

Kane felt sick and dizzy. He tried to focus on them.

'So what?' Kane's voice was thick.

The negro shouldered by him. 'If you guys are friends of this bum then you can pay the rent he owes me.'

One of the men turned towards him. His eyes were like a snake's, the expression was cold. 'No, we ain't friends of this guy. We want him just the same.'

The negro spat disgustedly on the floor.

'Cops! I might have known.'

The two men had gripped Kane's arms and were propelling him down the stairs of the drab tenement and out into the street.

'Seems we arrived just in time, Kane.'

From some place far away Kane said: 'You never arrive in time. If you'd arrived in time she wouldn't be dead!'

'How's that?' demanded one of the men glancing at him in puzzlement.

His companion shrugged. '*Ubriacone!*' he said by way of explanation. '*É pazzo!*'

Kane tried to jerk himself away.

'I can speak Italian, you know. I lived in Rome once...'

The grip simply tightened.

'Then, *beone*,' sneered one of the men, 'you get into this car now, eh? Otherwise I might have to break your fingers, *capisce?'*

Kane found himself pushed into the back of a dark limousine between them. In front sat the driver, his eyes masked by dark glasses.

'This isn't a police car,' objected Kane.

The shorter of the two men smiled. 'Did we say that we were cops?'

The car drew quietly away from the sidewalk, its powerful engine purring through the streets, weaving in and out of traffic until Kane felt the world spinning before him.

'Who are you? Where are you taking me?' he said thickly.

Some still-functioning part of his mind recognised that the car was moving downtown but he couldn't keep pace with its constant weaving.

'You'll see.'

'Who are you?'

'You'll find out later.'

Kane blinked. He felt he should protest but he didn't really care.

'Got a drink?' he demanded hopefully.

The taller of the two men swore in gutter Italian.

Kane sighed and closed his eyes. The last thing he was conscious of was crossing Houston Street and turning down Delancy towards the Williamsburg Bridge. Then he was being pushed from the car and hauled into some building. He was in a small elevator being held upright by his escorts. He felt increasingly dizzy with the rapid ascent. Then he was aware that he was in someone's apartment. It was bright and sunny and smelled of fresh flowers. The carpet was so thick that it was like cotton wool under his feet.

He blinked but his vision kept clouding up.

One of his escorts was speaking rapidly in an Italian that Kane could hardly follow. He dimly realised that it was a Sicilian dialect. The man spoke with respect and called someone Don Valluchio. Kane sought to focus on the man but did not succeed.

Another man was speaking. 'You have done well, Giancarlo. But he is in no condition to be received by me nor by my good friend. You will take him and sober him up. Return him in the morning.'

'Very well, Don Valluchio.'

Kane found himself being hauled back into the small elevator and then he passed out.

Chapter Seven

Kane seemed to be swimming, swimming through waters of velvet blackness in which disembodied heads would suddenly appear with crystal clarity and fade again. Heads of people he knew or had known. Accusing heads, sympathetic heads, angry heads, sad heads. Janine's head!

He cried out!

He was laying on a bed with someone holding his arm. He was aware of a sharp prick. He tried to protest but he fell back into the black waters.

He was swimming after the shadowy figure of Janine. Janine, clad in a delicious two-piece bathing suit. She kept turning towards him and smiling; waving her hand for him to follow her. It was like an old Esther Williams fantasy of the 1950s. He raised a hand to call her back but she was swimming away, out of reach.

A dark shadow crossed the black waters.

Something struck his face sharply.

He was in bed again. The room around him came into clear focus with an abruptness which made him blink. By his side stood a short man with a vaguely familiar face. He was grinning viciously.

Kane frowned and raised a hand to his stinging cheek.

'Good morning, *beone*. Are you sober today?'

'Who the hell are you?' growled Kane, gently probing the numbed flesh of his face.

'Give me your arm.'

'Why?'

The small man sighed. 'Make it easy on yourself, *beone*.

Give me your arm.'

Kane did so and felt the jab of a needle. 'What's that?'

'Full of questions, aren't you? It's just something to set you up. Don Valluchio wants to see you in an hour and you wouldn't be able to make the door without a shot.'

Kane watched in curious detachment, feeling the soreness of his arm. He tried to recall the events of the previous day. This was not the hotel room in the Lower East Side. It had a strangely impersonal and antiseptic quality about it. Then he remembered the car ride, the elevator and passing out. He wondered what it was all about. Who cared anyway? It was a free bed. Whatever the man had injected him with was beginning to clear his mind. The door opened and another man came in carrying some clothes.

'Get dressed, *beone*,' he said. 'We don't want Don Valluchio to be kept waiting.'

Kane felt normal enough to feel anger. 'Don't call me a drunk,' he snapped. 'I can speak Italian.'

The man grimaced indifferently. 'Sure you can. You told us that yesterday, *beone*.'

Kane bit his lip and swung out of bed. There was a bathroom leading off the room and he luxuriated in perfumed soap and hot water. He shaved, put on cologne, which he found on a shelf, and combed his hair. Suddenly he felt good. Maybe there was something in the shot he had been given? He stood a moment and grinned at himself in the bathroom mirror. Yeah, he was passable. In the bedroom, the man sat picking his teeth, waiting while Kane dressed in new underwear, socks, a fresh crisp shirt, casual trousers, a sports jacket and smart shoes, all of which seemed perfect fits.

'Who's signing the cheque for this?' asked Kane.

The man said nothing. He stood up and jerked his head towards the door. Kane followed him through the rooms of what was obviously a private apartment and into a hallway. They entered a small elevator and within seconds they had emerged in a luxurious penthouse suite whose great glass windows overlooked the East River with the East River Park

53

just below them and a spectacular view of the Williamsburg Bridge alongside.

A middle-aged man with iron-grey hair and aristocratic features, dressed in a very expensive suit, came forward with a faint smile.

'Ah, good morning, Doctor Kane. I am pleased to see that you are looking better this morning.'

Kane frowned. 'Excuse me?'

'But you would not remember our little meeting yesterday? No matter. I am Charlie Valluchio.'

The man waited a moment as if expecting some reaction in Kane. The name meant nothing.

'This,' he suddenly turned to a small, insignificant man, seated in a corner of the room, 'is my *consigliere*. And this is my friend and compatriot, Don Adriano Tellaro, who has come from Italy to speak with you. Regretfully, Don Adriano speaks no English.'

Kane shrugged. 'I speak some Italian.'

'Excellent. We will speak in Italian,' said Valluchio dropping into a standard Roman accent.

Kane glanced to Don Adriano, a tall man with dark hair and an almost cadaver-like face. He gave no sign of greeting so Kane turned back to Don Valluchio, who was dismissing Kane's escort.

'I would offer you a drink, Doctor Kane,' Valluchio smiled apologetically. 'But perhaps it is not wise in the circumstances. A coffee maybe?'

Kane grimaced and watched while Valluchio poured a small *espresso* and gestured for him to be seated.

'What is this all about?' demanded Kane.

Valluchio smiled. 'Patience, doctor, patience. Let me first establish your *bona fides*. You used to be senior lecturer in the Palaeographical Department of New York University?'

'So what?'

Valluchio bent forward and took a folder from the coffee table and opened it with a frown. Kane saw that it contained several photostats of documents and a glossy photograph of himself.

'You have changed very much in recent years, Doctor,' Valluchio said pointedly.

'Perhaps your folder will tell you why?' Kane replied coldly.

'It does. Sympathy is an empty word these days, Doctor. Yet I sympathise. It is an evil world in which we live.'

'Let's get down to business,' snapped Kane. 'I presume that there is some business in this?'

Kane let his eyes move from Valluchio to the tall, almost sinister figure, seated opposite him. Adriano stirred under his gaze.

'We wish to employ your services, *doctore*,' he said softly.

Kane held his gaze. 'Does the file tell you that I was thrown out of my job for drinking? That I am considered a drunk? A vagrant? A hopeless case?'

'Naturally. We know all about you.'

'You know I have not worked for three years?'

'Nevertheless, doctor,' interrupted Valluchio, 'you were a leading name in your field and author of several distinguished papers.'

Kane laughed harsly. 'Any fool can publish a paper. You'd best take your job to someone who is not a society reject.'

'Sometimes, *doctore*, society rejects the wrong people,' Adriano said, his voice still soft.

'Why me?'

'Because you are most fitted for the job.'

'Which is?'

Adriano smiled and leant back in his chair.

'You will appreciate that I am merely a middle man in this enterprise? Good. My principal has in his possession a very old manuscript, a papyrus – so I believe it is called. It is a papyrus written in Greek. He needs someone to authenticate it and translate it.'

'Then he should go to a museum or library. They have all the facilities at their disposal. Any authentication needs to be a multi-disciplinary job, not the task of one man.'

Adriano frowned. 'I do not follow.'

'Technically . . .'

Adriano interrupted him with a wave of his hand.

'I will not be able to understand any technicalities. It is simple. There are certain valid reasons why my principal wishes to avoid sending his papyrus to a museum or library; publicity for one thing. The reasons are really no concern of anyone's. I am informed that you were a leading man in this field. My principal wishes to employ you to give your opinion on the manuscript. The job involves going to Rome, spending time there until you have arrived at your conclusions and made the translation. My principal offers to meet all your expenses, give you the hospitality of his villa in Rome and pay you a fee of . . . twenty-five thousand dollars. American.'

Kane's jaw dropped. 'That's ridiculous!'

Adriano exchanged a glance with Valluchio. 'Too little?'

'Too much,' replied Kane. 'There must be a catch.'

'Catch?'

Kane stumbled in Italian for the right phrase.

'My principal is not trying to cheat anyone,' Adriano assured him. 'He is simply a private collector who dislikes publicity, and publicity would inevitably ensue from a public examination of the papyrus. Total secrecy is, of course, a principal condition of the job.'

Kane stared directly into Adriano's dark eyes. 'Is the papyrus stolen?'

Valluchio laughed to ease the sudden tension. 'I would have thought, in the circumstances, that twenty-five thousand dollars would ease any pricks of conscience if that were the case.'

Kane chuckled. 'It might.'

He reached forward to take up his coffee cup, trying to steady the shaking of his hands. Valluchio and Adriano watched him drain it in silence.

Kane was thinking: what if the manuscript were stolen? So what? But his professional training reminded him that authenticity of an old document required back-up from an expert team and a wealth of equipment. Yet here was some idiot who was prepared to pay him a large sum for a few weeks' work. He was a vagrant. A drunk. He had nothing, and now someone was offering him money to spend time in Rome. He smiled grimly to himself. Better to drink himself into oblivion in Rome with cheap booze and plenty of money than to crawl the gutters of New York begging for dimes. He was aware of the anxious faces of Adriano and Valluchio.

'Well, Doctor Kane?'

'You said that it is an old Greek text written on papyrus?'

'That is so.'

'How old?'

'That is for you to discover but, I am told, very old.'

'The fee will be paid me for expressing my opinion?'

'The fee will cover you making a copy, a translation and doing any restoration work necessary to preserve it, in addition to giving your opinion.'

'That and no more?'

'That and no more,' agreed Adriano gravely.

'There is one problem...'

They looked anxious.

'... I have lost my passport and most of my personal documents.'

Valluchio nodded and smiled to the silent *consigliere*. 'Leave that to us. We will be able to put you on a flight for Rome within two weeks.'

Adriano frowned. 'Will it take as long as that?'

Valluchio raised an expression shoulder. 'It is best, Don Adriano, that he travel on genuine papers.'

'But I must return to Rome within two days.'

'Then leave the arrangements to us. I will guarantee that Doctor Kane is placed aboard a plane for Rome at the end of two weeks and will let you have word of his coming.'

'There is another thing...' interrupted Kane.

They looked at him in concern.

'If you want this work to be done properly, I shall need some specialist equipment.'

Adriano relaxed with a smile.

'My principal understands that and will fit out a small

laboratory according to any specifications you make. Perhaps you will let me have a list of such equipment before I leave for Rome? I can then ensure that it will be awaiting you on your arrival.'

'Your principal obviously has a lot of money to throw around,' commented Kane.

Adriano did not answer.

Valluchio clapped his hands and grinned. 'Excellent! Excellent. Everything is in order. We will ensure Doctor Kane is fitted out with travel documents, expenses and a new wardrobe, and allow him...' He broke off slightly embarrassed.

Kane parted his lips in a mirthless smile. 'Allow him to dry out, eh?'

Valluchio shrugged. 'You must be well to do this work, doctor,' he said simply.

Kane silently agreed. He was thinking of how much booze he could buy with twenty-five thousand dollars.

Chapter Eight

Through the double-glazed windows of the main Air
Terminal Building of Fiumicino, a group of men and women
gazed anxiously as the giant black shadow of a Boeing 747
jumbo eased out of the blue sky and set itself down on the
tarmac of Rome's main airport with a squealing of wheel
brakes and a roar of engines suddenly thrown into reverse.
Even as the noise of the landing aircraft was reverberating
across the airport a prim voice began to make an
announcement over the tannoy system.

'*Signore e signori*, Flight PA 305 from New York-Kennedy
Airport has now landed. Will those wishing to meet
passengers from this flight please proceed to the reception
area.'

There was a surge among the group of men and women
who had been staring through the window. They carried a
variety of notebooks and cameras which proclaimed their
collective profession. The reporters swarmed down the stairs
of the building to the waiting area outside the doors which
led into the customs section. Moving more sedately in their
wake strode an attractive-looking girl with Titian-red hair
and a stocky middle-aged man with a lugubrious face whose
jaws chewed rhythmically around a wad of gum.

At the age of twenty-six Juliana Gambretti's name had
been by-lined in almost every glossy magazine in Europe and
America. Her vital brand of photo-journalism was eagerly
devoured by editors in search of 'new angles'. She worked
exclusively for the Rome-based Italo-American News
Agency which syndicated her work throughout the world.

Her face had an Etruscan beauty, with a slightly high forehead; a young Katharine Hepburn, with a delicate Roman nose, deep, brooding green eyes and a mouth which seemed to have a permanent mischievous smile set on natural red lips. She carried her figure well and had often been mistaken for an actress or a model.

Beside her, Charlie Burgano, the agency's bureau chief in Rome, was apologising for the hundredth time that morning.

'I'm sorry, Julie, honest to God! I know airport crowds aren't your beat. But – hell! – this kid thinks he rates next to God with the press. An eighteen-year-old pop singer and he expects people to run after him. Goddam punk!'

'It can't be helped, Charlie,' Julie sighed as she stared unenthusiastically at the milling of her fellow journalists. 'If he deigns to be interviewed only while passing through an airport terminal, then that's where he gets interviewed... especially if *Oggi* are so desperate to get the story.'

Oggi, the leading Italian glossy, were making it worth while for Italo-American to put themselves out for a short session with the latest American pop sensation who went by the name of 'The Scream' but who had started life as Arnie Schwartz of Hackensack, New Jersey.

The doors to the customs areas began to open and a trickle of people began to push out, passing the waiting reporters.

'Looks like our friend is waiting to make a big entrance,' muttered Charlie Burgano, thrusting another piece of gum morosely into his mouth.

Julie smiled sourly. 'Let's hope he didn't make the plane and I can go back to my apartment and curl up with a good book.'

Charlie Burgano glanced reproachfully at her.

The doors opened again and a man stood unsteadily taking his bearings. He wore a belted raincoat but no hat and carried a canvas grip and a suitcase. Julie didn't know what made her give him a second look. Perhaps it was because he had clearly been taking full advantage of the in-flight hospitality. He was well built with sandy, untidy hair, with a face which had been rugged but which was now becoming fleshy and lined. His eyes were light blue, opaque with a mistiness which owed not a little to alcohol. She put his age about mid-thirties. He was not good-looking, not even pleasantly featured, she decided, though he might have been once. There was something degenerate about the face and yet . . . it was the haunted and melancholy expression which seemed to lie behind his features that captured her imagination.

Someone else pushed through the doors and bumped into him.

He staggered and then walked a little erratically through the throng of reporters. As he drew near to where Julie and Charlie Burgano were standing someone shoved him and nearly sent him flying.

'Goddamit!' he swore loudly and heads turned momentarily. 'Why don't you people learn some manners, pushing and shoving. That's all you do in this goddam country!'

Even from this distance Julie sniffed the stale odour of alcohol.

The man swung round, stared at her for a moment, and then turned and staggered off across the concourse towards the taxi rank.

Burgano's lips drooped. 'Guys like him give American tourists a bad name.'

Julie half nodded. 'He'd just had a skin full, Charlie,' she said.

There was a sudden chatter of people and the reporters surged forward, flash bulbs exploding and the cacophony of shouting rose in volume. 'The Scream' emerged with a small entourage and stood posing for the photographers.

Julie grinned broadly. 'The Scream' was not her idea of a new sex symbol. He stood five foot nothing, was thin almost to the point of emaciation, wore long hair streaked with a variety of colours and was hideously daubed with make-up. Julie wondered how he was able to get beyond the Italian passport control with his clown-like appearance. A black leather waistcoat left the singer's pitifully thin chest bare, save for a gold medallion, while tight black leather trousers encased his spindly legs.

A group of screaming young girls flung themselves forward to be hauled back by grim-faced policemen and the singer's bodyguards, two self-conscious muscle-men.

Charlie Burgano was pushing forward.

'Mister er... um Scream,' shouted Burgano above the noise of the other voices. 'We're from Italo-American News Agency. You agreed to do a short interview with us.'

'Yeah?' The strange nasal whine coupled with the New Jersey accent made Julie fight for control of her features. She had a wild desire to burst out laughing.

'That's right,' pressed Burgano. 'This is Julie Gambretti who will do the interview.'

The heavily mascaraed eyes turned to Julie and flickered in appreciation.

'Yeah? Do you do the interpreting for her, pops? I could fancy this one. Are Eyeties good lays, eh?'

Julie flushed but kept control. 'You'll have to grow up some, sonny, before you play grown-up games,' she snapped. 'And have a few baths first.'

The Scream dropped his jaw. Julie couldn't make out the expression behind the mask of make-up.

'You're an American?'

'Italian-American,' corrected Julie.

'Don't get me wrong, sister,' purred The Scream, apparently unabashed. 'I like you. You've got a great figure.'

'Well, suppose we stop talking about my figure, Mister Schwartz, and get on with the interview?'

'OK, OK,' mumbled The Scream. 'Come with me to my hotel and we'll do the interview in the car on the way.'

'Hey,' muttered Charlie Burgano, 'your press agent said you wanted to do it here at the terminal. Its twenty-six kilometres to Rome, you know. We came here especially...'

Julie laid a hand on his arm. 'It's all right, Charlie. You take my car and meet me at... what hotel are you staying in?'

A nervous ferret-faced man who was presumably The Scream's press secretary, moved forward. 'The Hotel

Hassler-Villa Medici near the Piazzi di Spagna.'

Julie handed Burgano her car keys. 'Meet me in the lounge bar there, OK?'

Burgano moved off while Julie accompanied the singer to the rented limousine awaiting him and his entourage.

By the time they had covered the journey from Fiumicino along the *autostrada* and crept through the heavy Roman traffic to the hotel, Julie felt that she needed a shower. It was not the heat of the Italian day nor the dust of the city which made her feel dirty. It was the continuous innuendo and smut of the nasty little boy who called himself the Scream. She was thankful when the limousine drew up outside the hotel and she was able to extract herself.

She went straight into the bar, wondering whether Charlie Burgano had arrived with her car. There were not many people around and no sign of Charlie. She went up to the bar and ordered a Campari and soda and turned to find herself a quiet seat.

A figure cannoned into her, sending her drink over the floor.

Julie Gambretti stared at the haunted, melancholy face which had excited her interest at the airport.

'*Mi scusi*,' mumbled the man, the slur of alcohol cutting the contriteness from his voice.

'That's OK,' replied Julie in English, automatically distant.

The man's eyes widened. 'You're an American. Sorry, let me buy you another drink.

Julie glanced at the insignificant amount of liquid still left in her glass and decided to accept the refill.

The man ordered a replacement for Julie and a rye for himself.

Julie didn't know what made her say it but on a sudden impulse she said: 'Don't you think you've had enough?'

The man swung round to her and for a moment anger creased his face. Then he relaxed and grinned. Oddly, it seemed a boyish, honest smile.

'No,' he said disarmingly. 'I never have enough.'

He slumped on the nearest bar stool and gazed at the amber liquid in his glass as if it were something special, something almost sacred. He glanced up and caught her stare.

'No need to feel sorry for me.'

'Was it that obvious?' Julie smiled contritely.

'Sorry. I didn't mean to snap,' he changed his tone again. 'My name is Kane. David Kane.'

'From New York? I was at the airport.'

Kane nodded.

'I'm Juliana Gambretti. Julie Gambretti.'

Kane frowned as he digested the name. 'You are American, aren't you?'

'I was born in Providence, Rhode Island. Italian parents. After I did my journalism course and spent some time on a hick-town newspaper, I decided to come to Rome for a year and do some feature work. That was three years ago. I've been here ever since.'

'Oh? You're a journalist?'

'That's right.'

'Then you were at the airport to meet that nauseating kid with all the make-up. A stewardess told me he was some kind of pop star.'

Julie grinned broadly. 'For my sins, I was. Nauseating is certainly the word for him. But what about you, are you here on business or just touring?'

'Just drinking,' replied Kane as he waved to the barman for a refill.

A shadow crossed Julie's face. 'You probably don't want advice, Mr Kane, but I really would ease up on the booze. It's a long flight from New York and you ought to get a shower and sleep.'

Kane stared at her for a moment. 'You're right,' he suddenly sounded sulky. 'I don't want advice.'

Julie shrugged. Charlie Burgano entered and she slid off the bar stool.

'Have a good trip anyway,' she said, moving away.

She felt hot in the face, like a damned silly social worker

who had been rejected by her good cause of the day. It was her own fault for trying to help a stranger. She wondered why she felt so sorry for the man. She kept seeing that odd melancholy expression in his face. She tried to pretend it was some journalistic instinct which made her sense a tragic story behind the man's obvious drunkenness.

Charlie Burgano was watching her curiously.

'Did you get it?' he said.

'What?' Julie startled out of her thoughts.

'For Chrissake! The interview with the Scream!'

'For what it's worth.'

'Then let's have a drink.'

Charlie Burgano started towards the bar but Julie held him back.

'Not here, Charlie. Let's go up to the Auriga, there's a better atmosphere there.'

Burgano shrugged.

David Kane watched the girl stride away with the middle-aged man and his lips twisted with a gesture of cynicism.

'So little miss goody-two-shoes has a sugar daddy, eh?'

He realised that he had spoken out loud.

'*Senore*?' frowned the barman.

Kane glanced at him. 'Sugar-daddy,' he suddenly said loudly. '*Protettore*, eh?'

The barman made an eloquent gesture. '*Come faccio a sapere*?' he said indifferently, and moved away to polish his glasses.

Americans! Drink and women! That's all they thought about. And if this one drank much more then he wouldn't even be able to find his way back to his room, let alone anything else.

Chapter Nine

The taxi deposited David Kane in a broad tree-lined avenue. The early-morning sun reflected on the intense white of the buildings which nestled comfortably behind the curious mixtures of olive and orange trees whose perfumes rose overpoweringly into the atmosphere. Even the high white-washed walls surrounding the rich-looking villas were edged with red roof tiles, echoing the tiling of the villas beyond.

'Villa Tiburtina, *signore*,' announced the cab driver.

Kane paid him off and walked to the tall iron gates. They were locked. He glanced round and found a bell chain at the side of the gates and pulled it experimentally. A strange metallic voice snapped out of nowhere: *'Chi é?'*

Kane located the intercom after a second's pause.

'David Kane.'

'Momento.'

The gates started to swing back and Kane, carrying his suitcase and canvas grip, walked through and up the short driveway towards the palatial villa beyond. It was a large three-storey building surrounded by neat lawns and well-tended shrubs and trees. The high wall protected it from the city outside as if it were in the heart of the countryside, miles from the nearest habitation.

Kane moved slowly up the tiled sweep of stairs which led to a terrace where a stocky man was waiting for him. He was bald-headed, with harsh, ugly features, and dressed in a chauffeur's uniform.

'Buon giorno,' Kane nodded.

The man regarded him suspiciously. 'I would like to see

your passport.'

Kane wondered whether he had heard correctly. 'Excuse me?'

'Your passport.'

Kane handed over the document with an indifferent gesture and stood while the chauffeur made an intent examination. The passport was thrust back at him.

'Don't I get it stamped or something?' grinned Kane.

'Leave your cases here and come with me,' was the uncompromising reply.

Kane dropped his bags and followed the man into the villa across the marble-flagged hall. He noted that the furnishings of the interior of the villa, though simple, were in keeping with the obvious opulence of the place. Oil paintings hung on the walls, two jardinières stood sentinel to an interior door and brimmed with plants he could not identify.

The chauffeur led the way up the staircase to the second floor of the building and turned across the landing to halt before two large oak-panelled doors. He tapped on them deferentially.

A voice called from inside and the man thrust his head through.

'Doctor David Kane has arrived ... *signor*.'

Kane frowned at the hesitation as if the man were unused to addressing the person he was talking to by that title.

'Show him in, Salvatore.'

Kane could detect in both men's voices the burr of a southern accent.

The chauffeur, Salvatore, gestured Kane to enter.

Beyond was a tall room, obviously a study, lined from floor to ceiling with books, and with old paintings decorating the walls where an absence of books allowed. Shutters were partially drawn across the several tall windows which opened on to a balcony. Even so, the room was light enough, the shutters unable to expel completely the harsh glare of the sun. The marble tiles of the room were strewn with exquisite rugs. The desk, chairs and table were clearly antique. Whoever owned the villa was not wanting in wealth.

Behind the massive carved oak desk in the corner of the room a tall and impressive figure rose to greet him.

There was something which caused Kane to feel uneasy in the penetrating stare of the dark eyes which seemed to have no pupils. The man's face was swarthy, the blue shadow of his facial hair gave it an almost sunken appearance. The open-neck shirt and casual trousers and jacket were worn with an air of self-consciousness which registered briefly in Kane's mind. The man kept fingering his shirt collar, his jacket sleeve, in a ceaseless rotation. His features were somehow familiar and Kane took a moment to recognise Adriano Tellaro in them.

'Please be seated, *doctore*,' the man said, making no effort to shake his hand. 'Do you speak Italian?'

Kane nodded. 'If you've seen my *curriculum vitae* you will know that I spent two years on graduate research at the Universitá Gregoriana Pontificia here in Rome.'

The man simply said: 'We will speak Italian then. My name is Tellaro.'

Kane congratulated himself on recognising the likeness. 'A brother?'

'Adriano is my cousin.' The man hesitated. 'My name is Giona Tellaro.'

Kane took the seat to which Tellaro gestured.

There was something in the man's manner which made Kane realise that Giona Tellaro was used to being obeyed; was used to command. He wondered whether the man was a military officer. That would fit the nervous way he fingered his clothes; a military officer wearing unaccustomed civilian clothes? Perhaps.

'We were worried about you, *doctore*.'

Kane raised an eyebrow.

'Yes, we were worried. Salvatore went to meet the aeroplane at Fiumicino yesterday. We expected you to come straight to the villa.'

'I didn't see your man, Salvatore. I went straight to an hotel to sleep off the jet lag.'

'No matter,' smiled Tellaro, easing his weight in his chair. 'My cousin has explained the nature of the task?'

'He has told me that you have a Greek papyrus which you want authenticated. I have explained that it is quite a task.'

'What I want is a scientific examination to establish the authenticity of the document. You are capable of doing that, aren't you?'

Kane did not rise to the insulting tone.

'By scientific examination, which people use rather loosely, I take it you mean a systematic examination by means of instruments? Science is not pursued with instruments, Signor Tellaro, but with brains. The instruments, whatever their type, are simply fancy spectacles which allow us to see smaller things and distinguish things more effectively. What information they give us is sorted out between our ears.'

Tellaro smiled thinly. 'Whichever way it is done, can you do it?'

'Perhaps.'

'Perhaps?'

'The generally accepted way of examining such objects is summed up by the phrase—"You look at it until it tells its own story, and not anybody else's, and then it cannot lie." All right. I can look at it but there are no hard and fast rules as to what it will tell me. The evidence which I might obtain by examination must relate clearly to the context. Even with what might be thought hard and fast facts, there may well be a range of values into which the object might not fit.'

Tellaro sighed impatiently.

'I am no academic. What you say means little to me. I want to know in layman's terms.'

'Very well. Let me try to make it simple. I can only reasonably date the materials used but I cannot absolutely date the action which physically placed the ink of the papyrus. Let's put it another way...'

He reached across the desk and took a piece of paper, took a pen and wrote the date on it, signing his name underneath.

'This paper bears a date. Under examination it will be

69

found that the paper and the ink are the correct materials for the period around which that date was written. But if you had not been a witness to my writing that date you could not, nor could anyone else, tell *scientifically* the exact day or time which I wrote that date.'

'I think I follow you.'

'Good. Given certain instruments I can check within a specified period at what age the materials were created. To check the authenticity of the contents of a document I could give you a considered opinion by an examination of the orthography and style of the Greek written, provided that it falls within the period that I have studied.'

'That is what I want.'

'But if you want a reasonable certainty with identifying and dating the type of papyrus you are speaking about you would want an entire team of experts. The usual course is to hand the document to a proper library or museum where a palaeographer, archaeologist, art expert, and historian could work on it from their various disciplines. You would get an expert in decay processes as well. Authenticity examination is a multi-disciplinary art, with no one person being able to master it all.'

Tellaro made an impatient gesture but Kane continued.

'No two examiners will proceed on absolutely identical lines, in the same sequence of operations or putting the same stress on data. Though each will produce an answer, each would receive comments from their colleagues which might direct them into new channels of research.'

'This is all very well, *Doctore* Kane. I am not an academic, as I have already said. All I want from you is an examination...'

'A considered opinion?'

Tellaro nodded. 'I felt it my duty to let you know the extent of one man's capabilities. Scientists are not conjurors. The only reliable method of dating an archival document is the proof of continued, unbroken, archival custody and, to be quite frank, my experience suggests that such proof is only rarely found, if ever. Archaeological integrity, dis-

70

coveries made during an excavation, where complete
freedom from disturbance can be proved, when the
document is found in a sealed unviolated tomb, for example,
is as good a proof as you can get. Do you know the history of
this document?'

Tellaro pursed his thin lips. 'I cannot reveal its history at
this stage. There is evidence, however, that it was kept in a
single archive since at least the eighth century.'

Kane's eyes widened. 'There are few archives which date
back continuously that far.'

Tellaro stood up abruptly. 'I have installed a small
laboratory for your use in one of the upper rooms, *doctore*,'
he said hurriedly, as if avoiding further discussion. 'The
room is equipped from the list of items you gave my cousin in
New York. Will you follow me?'

He turned and led the way out of the study, across the
marble-tiled landing and up a small staircase to what Kane
judged to be the top floor of the villa.

'This room is your bedroom,' said Tellaro moving through
a door into a small corridor and opening another door to his
right.

The room was well furnished with its own bathroom
leading off it. His suitcases had already been deposited on
the bed. There was a telephone by the side of the bed. Tellaro
followed his glance and smiled.

'The telephone is for internal use only, *doctore*. You will
appreciate that the prime condition of our contract is utmost
secrecy. If the papyrus turns out to be as valuable as I suspect
it is, then I do not wish anyone to know of your presence here
in the villa until I have reached a decision as to its future.
News travels fast, both in the academic world and the world
of collectors, is it not so?'

Kane couldn't argue with the man's logic.

Tellaro turned and led the way further down the corridor.

'Here is the laboratory which I have set up for you. With
the aid of your list of requirements, that is. If there is
anything further you want by way of equipment then you
have only to ask.'

71

Kane gazed about the room in surprise. There was a long work-bench, a desk with another telephone, a typewriter, paper and other writing materials. At one end of the work-bench were two low-powered microscopes. As Kane had specified, they were of the binocular variety, one with a zoom lens. He moved across and checked. They had a range of 3x to 40x. There was an assortment of chemical trays and bottles, photographic equipment and a photocopying machine.

'Across the corridor you will find a small darkroom for the photographic work. I trust everything is in order?'

Kane nodded slowly. 'You are certainly going to a lot of expense for just one document, *Signor* Tellaro.'

'Call it eccentricity on my part, *doctore*,' he said, stroking the bridge of his nose. 'I require absolute secrecy.'

'Well, you're certainly paying me enough to ensure that,' Kane grimaced as he squatted on a corner of the desk. 'When do you want me to start work?'

Tellaro suddenly frowned and stared hard at Kane. 'Tell me one thing, *doctore*, before we proceed. Are you religious at all?'

Kane looked at him in surprise. 'Religious? In what sense are you using the word?'

'Are you a Christian?'

Kane plucked at his lower lip and considered. 'Is it a requirement to this job?'

Tellaro shook his head impatiently.

'I'm an atheist,' Kane admitted. 'When I was a teenager I started reading Bertrand Russell and Charles Bradlaugh. I found that I'm just a natural sceptic. Does that blot my copybook?'

Strangely, Tellaro looked relieved. 'It doesn't matter. You were asking when you should start? If you are recovered from your journey I would suggest as soon as you like. After lunch, perhaps?'

'Sounds all right with me.'

'Excellent. Let us go down to lunch then and, as we go, I will tell you the "house rules" as I think the American expression is.'

'House rules?' repeated Kane.

'Yes. When I am not here, which, unfortunately, will be frequently, my cousin, Adriano, or Salvatore, will be on hand to get you anything you require. You have only to ask. You may also come across my cousin's... er... lady, Cosima. You will confine yourself to the rooms that I have shown you. Your bedroom and laboratory. I will arrange for food to be served in your rooms. You may walk in the grounds of the villa by permission only. Please do not try to leave the villa without permission. Do not request to make outside telephone calls nor write letters without permission.'

Kane stared at him with wide eyes. 'Jesus! It sounds as if I am in some kind of prison.'

Tellaro shrugged deprecatingly. 'I am sorry that it sounds so. Over the years I have taken an interest in matters of security, *doctore*. When it comes to objects of great value, which evil-minded people covet and take an interest in, I have learned not to underestimate security. Call this an eccentricity on my part, if you wish. I'm afraid I have to make it a condition of our contract.'

Kane shrugged his shoulders nonchalantly. 'You're paying me,' he said.

'That is good. I am glad that we are in agreement.'

Eccentricity was hardly the word for it, mused Kane as he regarded the tall man in curiosity. He wondered what really lay behind the enormous expenditure on one small ancient document.

Chapter Ten

Luncheon had been a leisurely affair. Salvatore, with his ugly, pugnacious features, served Giona Tellaro and Kane in the large ornate dining-room on the lower floor. Apparently Tellaro's cousin, Adriano, and the girl, Cosima, were out. Tellaro himself guided Kane through the inconsequential luncheon conversation as Salvatore brought in pasta, followed by fish and a salad and white Frascati wine. Finally, Salvatore brought in strong black coffee, the *caffè ristretto* favoured by Sicilians. It was Tellaro who suggested that Kane might like a siesta before starting work but Kane found himself curiously excited by the prospect of looking at the mysterious papyrus.

While Kane checked over the materials in the small laboratory, Tellaro went to fetch the small lead casket from the safe in his study.

'At the end of each day's work,' Tellaro told him, 'you will replace the papyrus in the casket and return it to my safe.'

Kane nodded absently as he stared down at the innocuous-looking casket which Tellaro, almost reverentially, placed on the work-bench before him. The casket was plain enough, measuring some twelve inches by six inches by six inches. There were some characters scratched on its dull grey surface – 'CPA 2'. He saw that there was some evidence that the box had been sealed and recently prised open with a sharp instrument. There was a strong odour, not just the oppressive smell of the poisonous metal but the must of age. He was interested to see that Tellaro's large bony hands shook nervously as they placed the casket down.

'Do you want to know anything?' asked Tellaro, gazing anxiously at him.

Kane shook his head. 'Not at the moment. Tell me nothing. Let me make a cursory examination without any preconceptions.'

Tellaro watched as Kane opened the casket, noting that it was still an essentially airtight vessel. Inside was a small scroll. He stood looking down at it for a long time, his eyes taking in the condition of the papyrus, which was wound round a rather well-preserved piece of carved wood – mahogany, he thought.

'The papyrus has been unrolled fairly recently,' he commented.

Tellaro grunted in assent.

'It is already breaking up,' went on Kane. He turned and from the bench took a pair of tweezers, reached into the casket and extracted a small particle of broken papyrus on which some ink, the loop of a letter, could be seen. He moved across to the microscope and inserted it, examining it for a few moments.

'Are there any polythene bags here?'

Tellaro moved to a drawer. 'Here is a supply, *doctore*.'

Kane held out his hand and Tellaro passed one to him. He dropped the piece of papyrus inside.

'This will do excellently. It will save a lot of trouble, having a piece broken off from the original.'

Tellaro did not understand.

'After I have stretched out the entire papyrus,' explained Kane, 'and photographed it, then this particle can be used for experiment.'

'Experiment?'

Kane smiled. 'I presume it will not be difficult for you to get access to radio carbon dating equipment?'

Tellaro stared at him for a moment and then shrugged. 'I know of a laboratory which is equipped with it,' he said hesitantly.

'I thought you might. All you have to do is hand them this sample and ask them to carry out tests on both papyrus and

75

ink. The particle is big enough for the test but small enough not to compromise the original by identifying it in any way.'

'But what will it prove? Will it date the papyrus?'

Kane shook his head with pursed lips.

'It's not as simple as that. What the test will do, within defined limits of error and the variations in the calibration curve, is provide the year in which an annual plant grew. Papyrus is made of paper reed, a tall plant, Cyperus Papyrus, of the sedge family, which was once common in Egypt. Its pith was cut in thin strips and pressed together for writing material. Being of plant origin we can therefore date it by the Carbon 14 method. It should be possible to give a date on the papyrus to within a plus or minus factor of fifty years. But that doesn't date it beyond all question. The same goes for the ink used. We have to work on a negative factor. The results of the tests would show that the papyrus and ink were contemporary materials. But that is all.'

'I see,' Tellaro frowned trying to follow the technicalities.

'The ink should be carbon-based in a papyrus of this age, or should I say, apparent age? They would use soot or lamp black.'

He bent over the papyrus again.

'Most institutions are usually reluctant to allow samples to be taken for chemical analysis, submitting pieces of manuscript to destructive tests is frowned upon by archivists. However, do I have your permission to conduct such tests on the fragments which have broken off?'

Tellaro hesitated. 'To what extent are these tests destructive?'

'I would require to remove several small samples. Naturally, everything would be clearly filmed beforehand but the pieces which are already broken off could be used for ultra-violet, infra-red and X-ray examinations, and an electron microscope examination, if you have access to one?'

Tellaro shrugged. 'You are the expert.'

'In that case, my first task will be to unroll the papyrus completely and fit all the broken particles together in order that I can take a series of photographs.'

'All right, *doctore*. I will leave it in your hands. I am not staying in the villa but my cousin Adriano will be here. I shall call every morning to observe and discuss your progress. Remember, the papyrus must be replaced in my safe each day when you have finished.'

Kane was already bent over the casket, and Tellaro, with a half-shrug, turned and left the room.

It was a soft knocking at the door which caused Kane to glance up and realise that the light was fading. It was early evening. He stared about him in amazement. He had become so absorbed in his task, unrolling the papyrus and fitting it carefully on a glass plate, that he had been totally unaware of the passing of time.

'One moment,' he called anxiously, worried that any sudden draught from the door might scatter the several small particles of the papyrus which he had spent hours fitting into a jigsaw pattern against the main body of the manuscript. He reached forward and carefully laid another glass plate on top, sandwiching the papyrus. He then found some small vice-screws and secured each corner of the two plates.

There was a second, more impatient knock at the door.

'Come in!'

The door opened and a young girl entered bearing a tray. She had blonde hair and blue eyes. '*Buona serra, doctore,*' she said brightly.

Kane's eyes widened in surprise. '*Italiana?*'

She looked so Nordic that he thought she must be Swedish or German, perhaps even American.

'*Si, Italiana. Da Napoli.*'

Kane shook his head with a smile. From Naples? Well, he supposed the fair-haired stock had filtered throughout Italy by now. He was always surprised when he encountered the red hair and blue eyes of Venetians, but for hundreds of years the area had been the territory of Cisalpine Gaul. As far south as Ancona, wave after wave of Celtic settlers had arrived and settled to be eventually conquered and absorbed in the *Pax Romana*.

'I have brought your dinner, *doctore*.'

The girl's rolling southern accent certainly identified her as Neapolitan even if her looks cast doubt on the matter.

'Thanks. Who are you?'

'My name is Cosima.'

He frowned. 'Do you work here?'

The girl pouted as if disgusted by the idea. 'I am a... friend of Adriano.'

Kane was not slow in catching the accent given to the word 'friend'. Then he recalled Tellaro's quaint phrase 'my cousin's lady, Cosima'.

The girl was examining the work-bench with curiosity.

'What are you doing, *doctore*?'

Kane grinned. 'Didn't they tell you?'

'Adriano tells me little about his work,' she shrugged. 'I know that you are engaged on some research for Adriano's cousin. That is all.'

Kane gazed thoughtfully at the girl. 'What does Adriano and his cousin do?'

A nervous expression crossed the girl's face.

'Cosima!'

Adriano Tellaro stood framed in the door.

The girl jumped in agitation.

'*Mi scusi, doctore,*' she mumbled as she hurried from the room.

Adriano Tellaro nodded towards Kane. 'It is a pleasure to see you have arrived safely, *doctore*,' he said coldly. 'Is there anything you want?'

'I seem to have everything at the moment,' Kane replied.

'Have you finished with the papyrus yet? I must ensure that it is returned to my cousin's safe.'

'Give me another hour with it.'

Adriano nodded slowly. 'Call me when you are ready,' he said, as he left the room.

Thoughtfully, Kane turned to the tray which Cosima had brought up. There was something about Adriano Tellaro which reminded him of a undertaker.

Chapter Eleven

Four days later Kane realised with a startled abruptness that, apart from the odd glass of wine with his meals, he had not touched alcohol since his arrival at the Villa Tiburtina. He felt a ridiculous glow of self-satisfaction. He could beat alcoholism if he wanted to, which proved he was no alcoholic. He had been so absorbed with the papyrus that he had not really had any time to think about anything else. Now he had finished his chemical testing, all that remained was for Giona Tellaro to get the results of the radio carbon tests and then he could commence the translation.

Life in the Villa Tiburtina was an odd sort of existence. He saw Giona Tellaro once a day, usually in the morning before lunch. The meals were mainly brought to him either by the pugnacious-looking Salvatore or the young girl, Cosima. Of Adriano he saw very little, and that was usually when he came to return the papyrus to the safe in his cousin's study. Well, he could endure the odd existence. He was being paid well enough.

He was beginning to check through his notes when Giona Tellaro entered the laboratory. He carried a paper which he thrust into Kane's hands without preamble.

'The result of the radio carbon tests, *doctore*.'

Kane took the paper and started at its embossed heading. 'The Vatican Library,' he said softly.

Tellaro frowned. 'Is there something wrong?'

'No,' smiled Kane. 'The Vatican Library is a good enough authority.' Kane had known of only two institutes in Rome which had the equipment to carry out the tests and he had been wondering which one Tellaro had access to. He scanned the report.

'Better than I expected,' he said, while Tellaro gazed at him anxiously. 'Radio carbon dating gives, within defined limits of error, the year in which the plant from which the papyrus is made actually grew. The report here suggests a date, with a plus or minus factor of fifty years, which would put both papyrus and the ink used on it to the first century AD.'

Tellaro flushed slightly with excitement. 'Perhaps to the middle of that century?' he pressed.

'It is a distinct probability,' Kane said absently, as he read the report again.

'Isn't it definite?'

Kane glanced at Tellaro and smiled thinly. 'The only terms one should use in such matters is "probable" or "highly probable".'

'But your own tests? Don't they confirm the date?'

'They only point to a high degree of probability that the papyrus and the ink belong to the same period, which is the first century AD. That is all.'

'And the text was therefore written at that time?'

'That remains to be seen. Because you have papyrus and ink which date from the same period, it does not follow that it was in that same period that the ink was placed on the papyrus. The provenance would have to be convincing.'

'What do you mean?' frowned Tellaro.

'Where does the papyrus come from? How long has it been in the same hands?'

Tellaro bit his lip. 'Is it essential that you know this?'

Kane nodded. 'I have already said that the only real method of dating a manuscript is by proof of unbroken archival custody.'

Tellaro sat on the edge of the desk. It seemed that he was making up his mind. Then he said: 'So far as can be ascertained, the papyrus was in the same archive for well over a thousand years.'

Kane stared at him impassively. 'Go on,' he prompted.

'Until recently it was part of the Vatican Secret Archives.'

Kane's eyes narrowed. His first thought that the manuscript had been stolen was probably correct. The Secret Archives did not make a habit of giving away its treasures.

'I am told that there is a reference to the manuscript in an eighth-century cartulary. Then it was listed as being in the Vatican Library when that library was first established in 1475 AD. It was marked as an item that was only to be seen by an incumbent Bishop of Rome. It would appear that only one Pope, Alexander VI, saw the papyrus, a few days after he became Pope. That was in 1492 AD.'

Kane frowned. 'Alexander VI? Wasn't he . . .'

'Roderigo Lenzuoli-Borgia.'

Tellaro paused as if waiting for further comment. Then he continued: 'In 1612 Pope Paul V appointed an archivist and a new register of manuscripts was drawn up. The papyrus was mentioned in that register. It was also listed again in the mid-nineteenth century in an inventory. When Leo XIII opened the archives to scholars in 1881 this papyrus, along with many others, was held back in the Secret Archives. However, it does seem that no one has ever examined it since the Borgia Pope.'

Kane exhaled slowly. 'I see. So we can say, with authority, that the papyrus can be placed in one spot as far back as the eighth century AD?'

'Yes. But what does that prove?'

'It is what it disproves that matters. How did it pass from the possession of the Secret Archives into your custody?'

Tellaro shifted uncomfortably. 'That must remain my secret,' he snapped. 'Your job is simply to evaluate, for which you are being well paid.'

'Don't be so touchy. I simply want to be sure that this papyrus is the same document as the one mentioned as being in the Secret Archives.'

'You can rest assured that it is, *doctore*.'

'At the moment I will accept your word. I would like the exact references you quoted and the whereabouts of the documents which refer to the papyrus.'

'I have already made such a list. It is in my study.'

'Fine. The next step is to start the translation and find out whether the actual writing, its orthography, style and contents conform with the date of the materials used.'

'How long will that take?'

Kane shrugged. 'It depends.'

He turned back to his work and was not even aware when Tellaro reluctantly left the laboratory.

Towards evening the girl, Cosima, came with a tray bearing the evening meal. Kane set aside his work and examined the girl with a smile as she set it down on his desk.

'Cosima,' he suddenly said, 'what do you know of Adriano's cousin?'

Cosima glanced up, startled. 'Know, *doctore*?'

Kane made an impatient gesture with his hand. 'What does he do?'

The girl looked uncomfortable. 'Surely, you, who work for him, must know that?' she countered.

Kane met her suspicious gaze and bit his lip. 'How long have you known him?'

'I do not know him. He rarely speaks with me.'

Kane sighed. 'Is he ... connected?'

Kane deliberately chose the Italian euphemism purposely and was rewarded by a flush which coloured the girl's cheeks.

'You should not ask questions, *doctore*.'

She turned and hurried from the room.

Kane was pretty sure that Giona Tellaro and his cousin, Adriano, were illicit art dealers. He knew that it went on and that dealing in rare documents was just as profitable as dealing in paintings. Collectors would pay a king's ransom for such historic treasures. There had recently been the case of a Texas millionaire who had paid an enormous fortune for an eighth-century Bible. He could see no other reason why the Tellaros were so secretive about their papyrus and why they were paying him so much for an authentication.

They were working outside the law, that seemed obvious. He frowned suddenly. He would have to be extremely careful.

He worked late into the night on the text and was so fascinated that he roused a disgruntled Adriano early the next morning to retrieve it from the safe so that he could continue. Lunch was brought up by Cosima, who purposely avoided any conversation, and it was only then that Kane realised that Giona Tellaro had not paid his usual morning visit to check progress.

After lunch he felt suddenly exhausted. The few hours' sleep and the heavy lunch suddenly told on him. He rose and returned to his bedroom, stretching himself on the cool luxury of the bed. It was not long before he passed into a deep dreamless sleep of an afternoon siesta.

When he stirred and opened his eyes he found that he had slept for an hour. He yawned and stretched. Then he realised that he wanted a drink. To his surprise he found that he fancied nothing alcoholic; just a cold, fresh fruit juice. He reached for the telephone but there was no answer. Well, the hell with ringing down for Cosima or Adriano to bring him a drink.

He rose and made his way downstairs and through the deserted marble-paved corridors to the back of the large villa. More by good fortune than anything else he found the kitchen and hunted for a drink. In a large ice-box he found some cartons of soft drinks and he took a glass and poured himself some orange, savouring its ice-cold sweetness.

The sound of a car drawing up outside made him move towards the window in curiosity.

A large black Mercedes had driven into the courtyard at the back of the villa. The man, Salvatore, clad in chauffeur's livery, his face impassive, climbed out and opened the back door.

Kane's eyes started as he saw a tall man with the scarlet and black robes and skull-cap of a cardinal climbed out. The man peered anxiously up towards the top-floor windows of the villa before hurrying forward into the house.

It was Giona Tellaro.

Chapter Twelve

In the quiet sanctuary of his bedroom, the first thought that came to Kane's mind was whether Giona Tellaro was a confidence trickster or whether he was robbing manuscripts using the guise of a cardinal. Then he recalled that Tellaro always looked uncomfortable in ordinary clothes and he had always had a quiet air of authority, as if used to obedience. Kane had initially suspected that Tellaro was a military officer. But perhaps he was a genuine cardinal, a prince of the Catholic Church? If he was, then many things would fall into place: the origin of the papyrus itself, the man's easy access to the Vatican Library... Thousands of thoughts began to whirl in his mind. Perhaps Tellaro and his cousin were involved in the removal of Vatican documents and their sale to private collectors?

The door opened abruptly and Giona Tellaro and his cousin Adriano entered.

'Good-day, *doctore*,' greeted Tellaro, now clothed in his open-neck shirt and casual trousers. 'I expected to find you in the laboratory.'

'I've taken to indulging in a siesta before the afternoon's work.'

Kane saw Adriano's eyes flicker towards the rumpled bed and he was thankful he had not straightened the bedclothes.

'How goes the work?' went on Tellaro. 'Will your translation be finished soon?'

'Fairly soon.'

'How soon?' demanded Adriano, cutting in. 'How soon before you can give us an opinion?'

His voice was eager and Kane saw Tellaro frowning at him.

'It's hard to say,' he replied. 'Not long.'

Tellaro nodded slowly. 'Then we won't detain you, *doctore*.'

In the laboratory Kane gazed thoughtfully at the enlarged photographs of the papyrus from which he was making his copy and translation of the text.

If Giona Tellaro was a cardinal and Adriano was a *mafioso*, for Cosima had unwittingly betrayed as much, then it followed that the cousins were working some crooked stolen art deal in which Tellaro smuggled items of value out of the Vatican to place on the black market. But why pay him such a fantastic sum to authenticate this papyrus? Tellaro knew its history well enough. Why not simply put it into an immediate auction?

He sighed and struggled to bring his mind back to his task. After several false starts he eased into the work of translation and became so involved that he did not even hear Cosima bring in the evening meal. The tray of food lay untouched and grew cold. Finally Kane wiped the sweat from his eyes and sat back.

He had a terrible headache, he felt like a drink and yet... and yet... he turned back to the pages of his translation with a shaking head.

The style, the orthography and syntax, were certainly within keeping of what he knew of first-century AD Greek. The earliest continuous texts of the New Testament writings dated from the third century AD and these were incomplete. He had seen these texts, the famous Chester Beatty and Bodmer Papyri, but their style was not as archaic as this. He rose and went to his reference notes. The earliest fragment of a New Testament text, a fragment of John's Gospel, assigned to about 120 AD, was a fairly close approximation of style. A few phrases resembled the earliest texts. It was agreed that Mark's Gospel must have been written about 70 AD and that the author was a poor educated non-Jew who wrote a very rough Greek. Yet the Greek of the text which Kane was examining was a very polished prose, written with a confidence which denoted that it was the mother-tongue of its author or that the author was a very competent linguist.

Kane was not a Biblical scholar but he had examined early Greek Biblical texts and found that he could make comparisons in phraseology to the *Septuagint*, the Greek translation of the Old Testament, which had been translated two hundred years before the birth of Jesus Christ. Similarly, there seemed an echo of Luke's Gospel, written about 85 AD with its cultured style and sensitivity to cadences in the language.

As a palaeographer Kane felt no doubt that the writing could be authentically dated to the first century AD and, bearing in mind the result of the tests on the papyrus and the ink, he was left with no other conclusion than that it was a genuine first-century document. Having come to that decision he found himself go cold with the implications of the text he had translated. He reached for his translation and began to read slowly and deliberately.

> *1 Paul, an apostle of Jesus Christ by the will of God, unto his brother Linus: grace be to you and peace from God our Father, and from the Lord Christ Jesus.*
>
> *2 Once I had cause to rebuke our brethren of the churches of Galatia for they removed from me who called them into grace and turned for comfort to the sect of Nazarenes who preached that only the circumcised may dwell in the peace of Christ Jesus.*
>
> *3 Well do you know the conflicts that curse our dealings with those of narrow minds. Did I not dwell with Simon Bar-Jona, who calls himself the Rock, for fifteen days in Jerusalem arguing that there is neither Jew nor Greek, there is neither bond nor free, there is neither male nor female, for you are all one in Christ Jesus. And if you be Christ's, then are you Abraham's seed, and his according to promise.*
>
> *4 Fourteen years passed since my meeting with Simon Bar-Jona and our quarrel. Then I went up to*

Jerusalem with Barnabus and Titus and argued once more that my mission was to preach Christ's word to those who were outside the laws of Judah. Then did James, the Lord's brother, and Peter and John, the pillars of the movement, attack me, claiming that they had better authority having heard the words from the living Christ on earth. I certify again that my truth is not of man, for I neither received it of man, neither was I taught it, but I knew it by the revelation of the spirit of Christ Jesus.

5 Thus did we argue; and finally they said to me – go, then, and preach to the Gentiles if you will but unless they become as we, circumcised in the faith of the Lord God of Israel, while they call upon the Christ, he will not hear. And so they gave Barnabus and I the right hand of friendship and we departed.

6. And when Peter came to Antioch he refused even to eat with those of my conversion who were not circumcised and converted to the faith of the Jews. Even Barnabus was swayed by him and I was compelled to argue with Peter before the assembly for counselling my converts to Christ to live like Jews. We parted on bitter terms. As one who knew and walked with Christ Jesus, Peter carries great force with the impressionable.

7 On my final visit to Jerusalem, James and Peter denied me, saying that I was perverting Christ's message, for he had come to preach to the Jews only and unless a man be a Jew, or become a Jew, he could have no faith in the Messiah. When I tried to enter the Temple, they drove me out with great tumult and I was brought before the Sanhedrin for blaspheming against the laws of Judah. Finally, I was driven into exile.

8 Still James and Peter sought to persecute me, sending out Nazarenes to preach in those places where I had preached, destroying the fabric of my work, demanding circumcision in the faith of the Jews before the acceptance of Christ Jesus.

9 O my brother, Linus, is there need for me to recount the vexations which beset me in this exile in Rome? Yet here I have converted many to the word and our community has grown strong in spite of the ill will of James and Peter.

10 Sufficient to my story is that in the year of the consulship of Caeius Laecanius Passus and Marcus Licinius Crassus, Peter appeared in Rome on a mission from James to the Jews of the city. He called me deceiver, an inventor of things not taught by his Christ. Imagine the consternation of the congregations at hearing this man, Simon Bar-Jona, who is accepted as the chief disciple of Christ Jesus, who it is said gave him the name of Peter the Rock as a token of faith in him as he who would build the church, so attack my preachings?

11 Everywhere are my followers in retreat before the onslaught of the Nazarenes and now here, in Rome, they were seeking to destroy my authority which was given me in a vision of Christ Jesus himself. Vainly did I preach that those who walked with Christ on earth, meaning Peter, had become old and had forgotten or betrayed the memory of him! How can one overcome the argument: Did you meet the Christ? Did you know him on this earth? How then is your argument more in truth than the argument of a man who, from the first, was the foremost of his disciples, who lived with him, suffered with him and knew all his life and sayings?

12 Thus did Peter mock me with his authority.

13 The preachings of Peter became a scandal from which I could not hope to recover my authority and leadership of our community.

14 Therefore I went up to a certain place outside the city and suffered two thieves, men who had formerly followed the eagles, to waylay Peter when he came to address a certain meeting of Jews. They left him hanging by his feet from a tree and talk went abroad that he had been martyred to the Word.

15 Thus did he end his life for the good of the
community which is more important than the
individual; for what is the suffering of one soul
compared with the joy of those who shall come after?
Now does our community grow strong and vigorous
and we may yet hope for the confusion of James and
his Nazarenes who envy us in Jerusalem.

16 Since the great conflagration there are whispers
against our community here and the emperor, it is said,
grows eager to encourage the fears of the populace
against us. I am encouraged to leave the city for
Antium and will deliver this epistle to the hand of our
brother Pudens who will send for you when this
current unrest against our community is resolved.

17 All that are with me salute thee. Greet them that
love us in the faith. Grace be with you all. Amen.

Chapter Thirteen

Kane was not religious. As a palaeographer he was prepared to accept that the papyrus was genuinely dated to the first century AD. Yet he was no Biblical scholar. So far as the materials were concerned, the use of Greek, its orthography and style, he could express his opinion as to the time the document was written, but it would take a Biblical scholar to really analyse the text, to judge any inconsistencies of known facts. The names, too, would have to be checked although he was sure he had rendered them correctly. The Hebrew name Jacob was usually rendered as James via a succession of Greek and Latin spellings, while the Greek name Cephas, meaning 'the Rock' was more popularly known by Christians as the Latin Petrus or Peter.

It was only as he pondered on the translation that Kane began to make sense of the significance of Tellaro's question as to whether he was religious. Had he been other than an agnostic, had he had unquestioning faith in the teachings of the Church, then the revelations of the text would be so unacceptable as to be a blasphemy. If the text was truly the work of Paul of Tarsus, then the ramifications were so enormous that the decaying papyrus would shake the very foundations of the Christian religion. If Paul the Apostle's confession were true, then the Roman Church had been founded on a myth and the egocentricity of a single man. The discovery was dynamite to the academic world.

He stood up abruptly.

Sooner or later he would have to give his opinion to Giona Tellaro and he was suddenly sure that the man already knew what was contained in the papyrus. It was about time that Tellaro explained a few things. He turned from the laboratory and began to make his way down to Tellaro's study.

Sister Beatrice was worried. She had worked in the offices of the *Governatorato*, the government offices of the Vatican City State, for fifteen years. For ten of those years she had worked as a secretary in the Central Security Office. Of those ten years four had been spent working as secretary to Cardinal Giona Tellaro, the head of the office, and not once had she had cause for complaint either about her working conditions or the attitude of her superior. At the age of fifty, Sister Beatrice had served a lifetime in the order of the Sisters of Notre Dame de Bon Secours de Troyes, although she had worked so long in the Vatican that a return to the normal routine of life in a convent was a prospect which she tried to avoid contemplating. Sister Beatrice was all too human. She liked her work, liked the power which fell to her, enjoyed the secrets to which she was privy and which she had sworn never to reveal.

Yet during the last few weeks she had begun to notice an odd change in the manner of her superior, Cardinal Tellaro. He was never the easiest person to get along with. A sallow-faced, austere man who was somehow always distant and grave, he was totally unlike the deputy head of the Central Security Office, Monsignor Ryan, a rubicund, ruddy-faced Irish priest who was always smiling and joking with everyone; whose twinkling grey eyes never missed an opportunity for mischievous humour. No, Cardinal Tellaro was not the sort of person one could share a joke or a confidence with. Nevertheless they had developed a good working relationship over the years but now... Now His Eminence never seemed to be in his office, was always short-tempered and nervous, almost secretive.

Sister Beatrice sighed deeply as she pondered the problem.

Glancing at the clock on the wall, she discovered it was late. She had missed the evening Angelus and she made a mental note to say an extra decade of the rosary as penance. Cardinal Tellaro had hardly been in his office all day. She wondered where he spent his time. It was so unusual for him to be away.

She stood up, made sure the drawers of her desk were locked, turned out the desk lamp and went out into the corridor, pausing to lock up the office as usual. As she started down the corridor she saw that the door of Monsignor Ryan's office was ajar. She hesitated, suddenly braced her shoulders and tapped on it.

Monsignor Ryan's tenor voice bade her enter.

The round-faced, silver-haired Irish priest glanced up in surprise.

'What can I do for you, Sister Beatrice?'

Sister Beatrice paused on the threshold, then turned and closed the door behind her. She looked ill at ease.

'Monsignor,' she began, hestitated and then started again. 'Monsignor, I am worried.'

Monsignor Ryan sat back in his chair and raised his eyebrows in silent interrogation.

'I am worried about His Eminence,' the nun plunged on. 'It is none of my business, I know, but I am wondering whether Cardinal Tellaro is overworking himself.'

Monsignor Ryan pursed his lips in an expression of concern.

'Explain, sister,' he invited.

Sister Beatrice, slowly at first but with gathering confidence, explained the reasons for her disquiet.

When she finished Monsignor Ryan stood up and came round the desk, taking Sister Beatrice under the arm and leading her gently to the door.

'Trouble yourself no further, sister,' he said reassuringly. 'We all tend to overwork at times. His Eminence, as you know, has a tough and very responsible job. We are not machines, thanks be to God. We all get tired and irritable. I would not let it bother you.'

'I worry for the health of His Eminence only,' replied Sister Beatrice primly, not wanting it to appear that she was complaining of the way Cardinal Tellaro was treating her.

Monsignor Ryan smiled benevolently.

'Of course, sister. I understand. Don't worry. All will be well.'

He shut the door behind her and returned to his desk shaking his head. Monsignore Ryan was a natural public relations man and it disturbed him that the behaviour of Cardinal Tellaro was a matter for concern to his secretary. As a matter of fact he, too, had noticed that Cardinal Tellaro seemed oddly preoccupied of late. It was not politic to approach Tellaro directly about it. Perhaps he ought to check through the projects with which the Central Security Office were dealing? One of them might be causing His Eminence unusual difficulties. An office such as the Central Security Office could not afford tension between its key personnel.

Kane paused outside Tellaro's study door and was about to knock when he heard voices from within: the sharp tones of Adriano Tellaro and the brisk commanding accents of Giona Tellaro. Some instinct made him hesitate. His previous feelings of misgiving came back to him abruptly. If the Tellaros were simply crooks then he was in no position to make demands. Yet if Giona Tellaro was really a cardinal then what was his motivation in paying such a large sum of money to have a private authentication of the papyrus – a document which could so damage his church?

Kane craned his neck towards the door, pressing his ear against it. The door was of thick oak. He could only hear an indistinct mumble.

He turned and saw that the French windows at the end of the corridor stood open, leading out onto a small balcony which ran the length of the villa on the first floor. He walked swiftly out onto this balcony and moved along to the study windows. Kane uttered a prayer of thanks that it was a hot evening. He halted by the open windows and stood with his back against the wall, listening.

'... nothing simpler,' Adriano was saying. 'But are you

sure it will work?'

'It must. The stakes are too high, as the expression goes.'

'You say that Kane is expendable?'

Kane's body began to tingle.

'As soon as he has finished his work, which will be within the next day or so, you will take him for a drive and he will vanish. Understand?'

'I understand, Eminence.'

'No one must ever know that he has been here.'

'No one will. If he is found, who would question the death of a drunkard? That is why we chose him, an insignificant and expendable young man. An alcoholic. Just another fragment of unimportant human flotsam.'

Outside, Kane's heart began to pound wildly and a cold sweat stood out on his forehead. He ran his tongue over his dry, cracking lips.

For the first time he began to get some idea of the situation in which he found himself, of the enormity of the ramifications of the ancient papyrus. If the document were made public it could topple the Catholic Church, deal a crippling blow to the Christian faith, by demonstrating that one of its most cherished beliefs and the corner stone of Christianity was simply a myth.

Giona Tellaro was a cardinal yet he was calmly ordering Kane's murder! For what purpose? To keep him silent about the papyrus? Yes, he supposed that much was obvious. But why? Because Tellaro was a religious fanatic determined to suppress this astonishing document? Perhaps. In that case was Tellaro acting on his own or for a higher authority? Was it possible? The Church had a great deal to lose if the revelation was made.

Kane's mind was in a whirl.

And where did Adriano Tellaro fit in, a man with Mafia connections? Was it simply that he was Giona Tellaro's cousin? Or was the Church not averse to using such people when it suited its purpose? Into his mind came half-buried memories of the Vatican's alleged Mafia connections, the unresolved case of Robert Calvi, director of the Banco

Ambrosiana, found hanging under a London bridge in 1982, and the scandal surrounding Michele Sindona, who was not only banker to the Mafia but had connections with Vatican finances.

Kane raised a hand and pressed it against his throbbing temple.

Whatever the reasons, the important thing was that Giona and Adriano Tellaro were plotting to kill him. He must get away.

He moved quickly back to the corridor and, holding his breath, he returned to his laboratory without incident. There he flung himself at his desk, drumming his fingers nervously on the table. He had only been there a minute when the door opened and in walked the saturnine Giona Tellaro.

'Good afternoon, *doctore*. How goes the work?'

Kane gazed up at the man's bland, unemotional face. He struggled to control his own expression.

'The tests are taking longer than I expected but I will be able to give you a report, say, within the next few days.'

Tellaro frowned. 'So long?'

Kane shrugged. 'These things take time,' he replied defensively.

'But your opinion so far?' Tellaro pressed him.

'I am not in the habit of making guesses,' snapped Kane. 'It would be wise to wait for my report.'

Tellaro's eyes widened a fraction in surprise at Kane's tone and Kane cursed himself for not keeping his cool. He must not arouse the other's suspicion.

'Very well,' Tellaro suddenly smiled thinly. 'Why not? I have waited a long time already. Is there anything more you want?'

Kane nearly demanded a day off to look round Rome but he bit his tongue. Tellaro was an intelligent and cunning man. He would see through such a request immediately; he would realise that Kane had learned something.

'I might need another look at the original papyrus,' he said.

95

He had been working from photographs during the last few days while the original reposed in Tellaro's safe.

'When you are ready, let my cousin know and he will bring it to you.'

Kane nodded unenthusiastically.

The idea of escaping from the villa with the original papyrus had entered his mind only to be dismissed a moment later as unworthy of consideration.

'There is nothing else?'

'No thanks,' replied Kane, turning back to his work.

A moment later he heard the door click as Tellaro left. He sat back and sighed deeply. He had to escape from the Villa Tiburtina – that much was evident. He had to find somewhere to hide while he thought about the situation. Yet if he tried to tell anyone, who would believe him? If he could not take the original papyrus with him, his story would seem simply a grotesque fairy tale. He gazed at the desk before him. The answer was staring him in the face. The photographs! He could take the photographs showing each step of the unrolling and of the text of the papyrus itself together with his translation and notes. That, at least, would be something. But then what? He couldn't think. Not in this place. He had to escape; had to find somewhere to hide. Then he would be able to think.

Chapter Fourteen

Kane lay on his bed fully clothed, listening to the hours strike on a distant clock somewhere deep within the endless corridors of the Villa Tiburtina. His body was taut as he lay waiting for the evening to tick away and pass into the quiet of the early morning. It was not until he heard the distant clock strike three that he slowly rose and drew out the small canvas hold-all from his wardrobe. In the bag he had bundled what clothes he could, his passport and remaining money, which was not much, and a folder with the photographs and notes. He had no definite plan in mind beyond escape from the villa.

He tiptoed to the door and stood listening. A chill silence hung over the villa.

Carefully, he opened the door and stepped into the corridor. The moon shone with the silver brightness of the early Roman summer and he was able to move through the unlit corridor with ease. At the end of the passage was the door separating his rooms from the staircase to the lower floors of the villa. He reached forward to open it.

It was locked.

Kane stared at it in amazement. He was only now becoming aware of the extent to which he was a prisoner in the villa. During the day the door was always open but that was when there were other people about to monitor his movements. He suddenly realised just how lucky he had been to be able to make it unseen into the kitchen to witness Giona Tellaro's arrival.

But what now?

Of the rooms on this third, upper floor, most gave exit through the windows onto small balconies, but there was no way from the balconies of these rooms to the lower floors or to the grounds of the villa.

He closed his eyes for a moment, trying to envisage the exterior of the building, cursing himself for not having paid close attention to it when he had arrived. He did recall seeing a fire escape, an iron ladder which ran down to the first floor and which probably had an extension to the grounds. He tried to work out what his position in relationship to it must be. No, it was no damned good! It must be on the far side of the building. To get to it he would have to scramble over the roof and there was no way up to the roof. No way up and no way down! Damn!

He began to walk slowly back to his bedroom, shoulders hunched in defeat. Then he halted and smiled before hurrying on to the small room opposite the laboratory which had been equipped as a dark room.

He entered, closed the door and locked it, clicked on the light and turned. Yes! He had not been mistaken. Just above him, in this small box-like room, the size of a large cupboard, was a sloping roof, and in it was a skylight painted over with black paint. If he could succeed in opening it, it would be large enough to squeeze through onto the roof. He clambered onto a stool and found that he could reach the skylight with ease. There were no visible signs of a catch. He swore softly. The catch had been removed and the skylight was fastened in place by means of screws and brackets. He examined them carefully.

If he could unscrew a couple of them, then he would probably be able to force the thing open. He climbed back down to the floor and glanced around for some substitute screwdriver. There was a small knife on the bench, an odd-job tool which really had no practical use in a darkroom. It was clumsy and fairly ineffective but, with dogged perseverance, he managed to start the screws turning and, after half an hour, he had prised them out. It took a long time of careful pushing and straining to ease the skylight open without making any noise.

From where he stood on the stool, his head was still eighteen inches below the opening so that he could not tell exactly where on the roof he had gained access to. Nevertheless, he decided to chance it, took his canvas bag and pushed it through the opening. Then he drew himself up slowly through the aperture. His muscles and limbs sent fires through his body as they protested at the years of disuse and ill-treatment he had given them. Sweat covered his brow, but he raised himself by sheer will-power. Then he was sprawling in relief on the cool tiles of the villa's roof. He lay there several minutes trying to regain his breath.

He was appalled to see how light it had grown. It would soon be dawn. Grasping his bag, he made his way carefully to the apex of the roof and peered around until he saw the dark iron arms of the fire escape. He reached it without mishap and started downwards.

At the first floor, some ten feet above ground level, the iron stairway ended. There was a sliding ladder which, once released, would extend the fire escape to the ground, but he could not find the means of releasing the ladder and gave up the attempt. He dropped his bag and hung on to the last rung. Then he let himself drop.

He was momentarily winded and stayed for a moment in a crouch before recovering his bag and picking himself up. He was bathed in sweat but, at the same time, trembling with cold. Or was it fear?

He glanced nervously about him.

It was no use attempting to get through the main gates of the villa. They were worked by an electronic device and probably wired to the alarm system. The only alternative was to go over the wall, which had obviously been designed to keep people out rather than keep them in, and which was at least eight feet high.

He smiled broadly. Now he knew that luck was with him. Across the lawn which stretched down to a wall was a series of olive trees – one grew close to the wall. He would be over it in no time.

He was halfway across the lawn when the shadow detached itself from the corner of the house and a ferocious barking filled the air.

Kane glanced at the shadow, his blood running cold as he saw the huge Alsation bounding swiftly towards him, snarling and yelping, its canines showing white in the half-light.

Kane ran, feeling the beast's jaws snapping at his heels. He sprinted for the olive tree and flung himself upwards, grasping the branches with one hand while the other seemed glued to his precious canvas grip.

The Alsatian leaped up and tore something from the leg of his pants. Then Kane was scrambling out of reach. He threw his bag over the wall just as a light flashed on in the villa. He heard a harsh voice calling, mingling with the furious yelping of the dog below him.

Kane did not pause. He reached out to grasp the top of the wall, suddenly feeling the row of jagged glass cemented into the top of it. He refused to heed the pain of the tearing flesh of his hands. He had to get away. He pulled himself up, lay for a moment on his stomach on the top of the wall, oblivious to the pricking of the cuts, and half rolled, half hauled himself over, dropping to the roadway on the other side.

Pandemonium was ensuing behind him.

He grabbed his bag and set off at a gasping run along the broad avenue. He was sobbing with his exertion as he staggered to the end of the deserted street. He had just reached the junction when he heard the sound of a car start up in the silence of the city.

Fear now lent him a new impetus. He saw the dark outline of a park across the road and ran for it, diving into the shrubbery and flinging himself flat. The headlights of a vehicle flashed across the road and a car tore swiftly down the avenue. He waited until it had sped by before getting to his feet and setting off at a right angle across the welcoming darkness of the park. From the light of dawn he judged that he was moving southwards. The only thought in his mind was to put as much distance as he could between himself and the villa.

He found his shoes becoming sodden with the heavy dew, but he pressed on until he came to a roadway. He slowed to a normal walking pace, hardly noticing where his dragging footsteps were taking him. He recognised the Porta San Pancrazio, the old gate of the city, which had been built by Urban VIII in the seventeenth century because it was here that the Via Aurelia started, the Great Coast Road which linked Rome to Etruria in ancient times. Still moving directly away from the Villa Tiburtina he continued southwards towards the Viale Glorrisom, crossing the Viale Trastevere.

It was just after six o'clock when he reached the Piazza Porta Portese on the banks of the Tevere, the Tiber as it was known in ancient times. There were many people about now for the Romans start their day early, preferring the hours before the sweltering summer sunshine, breaking their day with a siesta and working again only in the cool of the late afternoon and evening.

Just off the piazza Kane found a small workman's café, a *cantina*, and went in. There were only a few people inside having a morning coffee and hot rolls. The dumpy man behind the bar stared curiously at him as he entered.

'The *signore* has had an accident?'

Kane suddenly became aware of his dishevelled appearance, his torn trousers, sodden shoes and the blood stains from the cuts on his hands and stomach.

'Yes,' he said. 'Do you have a washroom?'.

The dumpy man nodded and gestured to the back of the *cantina*.

'Thanks. I'll have coffee and rolls,' Kane said over his shoulder.

'*Subito, signore*,' the man replied.

Kane cleaned himself up as best he could, but he realised that he would have to get the cuts properly dressed before he could effect a change of clothing for the cuts were still bleeding. He decided to continue wearing what he had on in

101

order not to spoil the only change of clothes he had. He returned to the *cantina*, found a table and sat down. The dumpy man promptly brought him the coffee and hot rolls. He ate ravenously while the man returned to his bar, watching Kane out of the corner of his eye.

Over coffee Kane tried to organise his scattered thoughts. He had little money, certainly not enough to leave Rome or go into any hotel. He could go to the American Embassy, of course. He could report himself as a distressed subject wanting to get home but... what then? He wouldn't put it past Tellaro to report his disappearance to the authorities claiming that he had stolen something from the villa. He should steer clear of officials. He needed a place to stay, to think, a contact... It had been years since he had lived in Rome and he knew no one in the city now. No one...

A vision of an attractive-looking girl with Titian-red hair, with brooding green eyes and a mischievous smile, swum into his mind. The girl in the Hotel Hassler Villa-Midici. The journalist. What was her name? Juliana. Julie. Julie Gambretti!

He did know someone in Rome!

He looked up and caught the eye of the dumpy man who was polishing glasses.

'Do you have a telephone directory?'

The man put down the glass and cloth, and reached behind his counter for a dog-eared directory, which he pushed across the bar. Kane flicked through its pages. Gambretti! Gambretti, Juliana! He uttered a prayer of thanks that there was only one Juliana Gambretti in the telephone book. Juliana Gambretti, Via Melania, Aventino. He memorised the address.

'Thanks,' he smiled and paid for his coffee and rolls, took his bag and moved out into the piazza. The streets were becoming crowded now and he noticed several people were glancing at his rough appearance. He ignored them and moved down towards the river, trying to dredge from his memory the geography of the city. It was not until he approached the bridge across the river that he realised that it was the Ponte Aventino, which led directly into the district of Aventino itself. He gave a chuckle as he crossed the Piazza dell' Emporio with its imposing Priory of the Knights of Malta and began to climb the hill into Rome's richest suburb.

It did not take him very long before he turned the Via di San Anselmo into the Via San Melania and came to the small apartment block at the address given in the telephone directory.

He hesitated outside and wondered what to say to the girl. Well, it was no use standing there wondering. He moved forward and pressed resolutely on the bell. It was one of those intercom bells and it was not until he was making his third stab at it, wondering if it were broken or if Julie Gambretti was away, that a sleepy voice said: *'Pronto?'*

'It's me,' he said, feeling ridiculous as soon as the words left his mouth.

'Me?' There was a noise like a smothered yawn. 'Who's that?'

'David Kane. We met briefly in the bar of the Hotel Hassler-Villa Medici.'

'David Kane?' The voice was bewildered, still half asleep. Then there was an intake of breath. 'Oh! You!' The voice came in English now. 'Do you realise what time it is?'

'Miss Gambretti, I must see you. It's urgent.'

There was a hesitation.

'Very well. I'm on the third floor.'

There was a buzzing sound and the door clicked open.

He pushed in and paused. There was a small lift across the hall. Somewhere down a corridor he could hear a woman's voice singing and the clank of a pail and broom. A *portinaio* was obviously already at her day's chores. Kane walked rapidly to the lift, crashed the gate shut and pressed the third-floor button.

As he stepped out of the lift, a door was opening across the hallway and Julie Gambretti appeared in the doorway, still yawning and blinking. She wore a silk robe around her well-shaped figure, and though her hair was tousled and her face

103

lacked make-up, she still contrived to look attractive. Julie Gambretti was obviously one of those women who did not need to resort to make-up to enhance their appearance.

She stared hard at his dishevelled figure.

'My, you must have been on an all-time bender.'

Kane ignored the sarcasm in her voice.

'I'm sorry... can I come in and talk to you? You see, there's no one else I know in Rome and...' He let his voice trail off lamely.

She raised a cynical eyebrow. 'Well, since you've got this far,' she jerked her head towards the door. 'But let's get one thing straight for starters... I'm not an easy touch so don't bother asking me for money.'

Kane flushed.

'You've every right to be angry,' he said meekly. 'I guess I was pretty much of a boor when we met. I don't blame you.'

Julie sniffed as she closed the door behind him.

'Come into the kitchen. I'm going to have some coffee. Do you want some? There's nothing stronger.'

'Coffee's fine.'

She moved across the living-room of the brightly lit apartment to a kitchenette separated from the living area by a simple bar.

'So what brings on this unexpected visit, Mr Kane?' she asked as she collected cups and saucers and filled the percolator. 'And exactly how did you get into that appalling condition? Get into a fight or just fall into something while you were drunk?'

Kane sat down in a chair and dumped his bag by his side.

'I guess I'm not really a candidate for the best-dressed man of the year,' he admitted. 'But it's a long story.'

Julie shrugged. 'Well, since you've made the journey to tell me, and since you've woken me about three hours before I should have woken, I've got the time to listen. But my reaction will depend on the punch line.'

Kane nodded. 'That's fair enough.'

Julie yawned. 'Go ahead,' she invited.

An hour later her tiredness had left her and she was sitting tensed and wide-eyed, staring incredulously at Kane.

Chapter Fifteen

Kane found himself starting with the death of Janine. He had not meant to but it was a logical place to start. The fact that he could speak of Janine to this girl surprised him, yet he found it strangely refreshing, as if he were expiating the years of guilt, as if a heavy weight were falling from his shoulders. He spoke of his drinking, of his suspension from his college and final sacking. He spoke of his time on the Bowery and in Bellevue. Then came the appearance of Adriano Tellaro, his trip to Rome, the Villa Tiburtina and the papyrus. He left no detail out until he had arrived at Julie Gambretti's apartment.

The girl was gazing at him in amazement. She had not interrupted him once, had not asked a single question, but sat in silence until he brought his story to a close.

Then she breathed a long sigh of released tension.

'Are you on the level?' she asked. 'Or is this some crazy drink-inspired fantasy?'

'It's difficult to believe, I know...' began Kane.

'It's impossible to believe!' snapped the girl irritably.

Kane said nothing but opened his bag and took out the folder. He handed the set of photographs to the girl. She glanced through them and sniffed.

'They don't mean anything to me. They might be anything. I have only your word that this – what do you call it? papyrus – is what you say it is.'

Kane bit his lip and exhaled sharply.

'I shouldn't have come here. I'm sorry,' he said, standing

up. 'It was just that I don't know anyone in Rome...'

He took the photographs and started to put them back in the folder.

'I'm sorry to take up your time, Miss Gambretti,' he said stiffly.

Julie stared at him. Suddenly he seemed like a small lost child. Some instinct made her reach forward and lay a hand on his arm. 'No, wait...'

He stared at her curiously.

'I may be a sucker,' she smiled awkwardly, 'but your story is just too crazy not to be true.'

She saw the ray of hope enter his eyes.

'The least I can do is try to check out what you have told me.'

'How would you do that?' he frowned.

She thought for a moment.

'Well, I'm a photo-journalist with several contacts. I can make some enquiries about your friends the Tellaros and the Villa Tiburtina, and see how they check out with your story.'

'But make sure they don't get to know of your investigation,' he advised. 'There is no telling what they would do if they realised that you were taking an interest in them.'

She stood up, suddenly all efficiency.

'While I make some telephone calls I suggest that you take a shower and get out of those bloodstained clothes. Do you have a change? Good. There is some antiseptic and bandages in the bathroom cupboard above the washbasin.'

She indicated the bathroom and grabbed the telephone. Her first call was to her bureau chief at the Italo-American News Agency.

'Charlie?' she dropped her voice to a whisper. 'Charlie, I want you to check out a few things for me and get back to me as soon as you can.'

Charlie Burgano protested.

'Jesus, sweetheart, I've just got into the office. Don't I have time to sort the mail?'

'No, listen to me, Charlie. I want a rapid check on the

106

career of a Dr David Kane who was sacked from New York University a few years ago. I want everything that is known about him.'

'Yeah? Dr... how are you spelling that last name?'

'K-A-N-E, OK?'

'Yeah. What was he a doctor of?'

'Something to do with ancient manuscripts.'

'Palaeography?'

'Something like that,' she shrugged. 'Can you do it?'

'Wonders I can do at once but miracles take longer, sweetheart. I'll get back to you when I can.'

'There's something else, Charlie. I want to know if there if a person named Cardinal Giona Tellaro. Also, I want to know who owns the Villa Tiburtina in the Via Angelo Emo.'

There was a pause while Charlie Burgano scribbled on a note pad.

'Are you on to a story, Julie?'

'Maybe.'

'I'll get back to you.'

'Charlie!'

'What now?'

'Top security.'

'Yeah.'

She put down the telephone receiver and, on an impulse, flicked through the pages of the telephone directory, glancing down the list of Tellaros. There was no one of that name listed at the Villa Tiburtina.

In the bathroom she could hear the shower running.

Suddenly the telephone buzzed.

'Sweetheart?'

'Charlie?'

'As I said, wonders I can work at once. Cardinal Tellaro, Cardinal Giona Tellaro is one of the big wigs at the Vatican.'

Julie grabbed her pad and pencil. 'Who is he?'

'He is an official of the *Governatorato*, the administration of the Vatican City State. In fact he is the head of the Central Security Office and has been so for the last five years or more. His is one of eight departments which come under the

General Secretariat of the *Governatorato* and that means he is in charge of all the security which surrounds the state and the person of the Pope.'

'How did you find out so quickly?' she asked amazed.

'No secret. He's listed in the handbook on the Roman Curia and its chief officials. Do you want more information about Tellaro? I've a friend on *L'Osservatore Romano*.'

Julie hesitated. 'No, leave it for the moment. What about the Villa Tiburtina?'

'It's a private villa which was bought five years ago by someone called T. Jonah.'

'Jonah? That doesn't sound Italian. Who is he?'

'No idea, but I'll work on it.'

'Thanks, Charlie. Let me know as soon as you can about Kane.'

She replaced the telephone again as the bathroom door opened and Kane emerged. His shirt was unbuttoned and he held his hands awkwardly.

'Sorry to bother you,' he held up his hands. "Fraid I just can't get the bandages on these. I've cut the palms rather badly.'

Julie moved across and looked down, wrinkling up her nose.

'You've still got some grit in the cuts,' she said, drawing him back into the bathroom and spending the next fifteen minutes with cotton wool and antiseptic. Finally, she bandaged the hands and did his shirt up for him.

He began to thank her but she grinned.

'At least you look better than when you arrived.'

Her smile was infectious.

'Did you find out anything?' he asked, trying to overcome a sudden wave of embarrassment.

She nodded as they returned to the living-room.

'It seems that your Cardinal is head of security at the Vatican.'

Kane's jaw dropped. He made an effort to recover himself.

'Is it possible to get a photograph of him to check whether he is the same man I met at the Villa Tiburtina?'

Julie frowned.

'I see your point,' she said slowly. 'You reckon someone could be impersonating him? But why?'

'Why anything in this goddamn crazy business?' replied Kane. 'I just can't see someone in such a powerful position engaged in shady activities over questionable documents.'

'It does sound crazy,' she nodded. 'Anyway, at least we know the name of the owner of the Villa Tiburtina, which suggests that Tellaro is not connected with it.'

Kane looked eager.

'Who is he?'

'The owner? Someone called T. Jonah. He bought the villa five years ago. The name isn't even Italian.'

She frowned when she saw the expression on Kane's face.

'What is it?'

'T. Jonah! Don't you see. Giona Tellaro. What's Giona in English? Jonah! Tellaro, Giona. T. Jonah!'

The girl stared in amazement. 'But he's a cardinal, head of Vatican security!'

'Which means that this could be a deliberate attempt to stifle knowledge of this document by the Vatican itself.'

'Then why wasn't it done within the Vatican? They have the capability and equipment to authenticate documents in the Vatican Library without bringing in an outsider.'

Kane shrugged. 'I don't know. I haven't any answers, yet, only questions.'

'Anyway,' she sniffed, 'while I'm not exactly a regular church-goer, I can't believe that this epistle of Paul, or confession, whatever you call it, can be anything other than a forgery.'

'That was exactly what Tellaro brought me to Rome to discover. I told him that authentication was a multi-discipline procedure. I've done all the tests I can think of. If it is a forgery it is impossible to detect because it was done in the first century AD.'

For the first time Julie began to realise the implications. Previously, she had been too concerned with Kane's adventures.

She bit her lip.

'You realise that if what you say is true then it would upset the entire basis of the Christian faith, especially the Catholic Church, which bases its authority on the assumption that Peter was told by Christ that he would found the church, that Peter came to Rome and was martyred here, and that St Peter's Basilica was built on the site of his tomb? And didn't they even discover such a tomb below the present basilica in the 1940s?'

'Julie, I admit that I'm no Biblical scholar. I can't judge the contents, all I can say is that the materials and the orthography of the Greek date the papyrus to the first century AD. You would need a Biblical scholar to make any further observations.' He scratched his head thoughtfully. 'The only one I know is a man named Myles, who worked at UCLA in California.'

'Have you heard of Jacob Rosenburg?'

He frowned at the abruptness of her question and shook his head.

'He's a dear old man, a professor from the Hebrew University of Jerusalem. He was in the newspapers about a year ago after having making some major Biblical find in... what was the name of the place?... some monastery in the Sinai. Bir Hasana, I think. It was some ancient text. He's been lecturing at the University of Rome for the last two months and I have interviewed him a couple of times, as well as having met him socially. He's an American by birth but now a Israeli citizen.'

Kane was excited. 'You think you might be able to get him interested in examining this text?'

Julie pursed her lips. 'He might. I don't know.'

'Can you call him and get him to come here? I daren't risk going to him just in case...'

The telephone buzzed.

It was Charlie Burgano.

'Pin back your lovely ears, sweetheart,' he said. 'This is the saga of Dr Kane. Ready?'

'Yes.' Julie's voice was low and tense.

110

She listened carefully.

'Thanks, Charlie. You've been a great help.'

She replaced the receiver and stared across at Kane until he felt uncomfortable.

'Something wrong?' he asked, unnerved by her silence.

She smiled abruptly, warmly. 'It seems that you have been telling me the truth about yourself, Dr David Kane.'

He raised an eyebrow in amusement.

'You've been checking me out?'

She nodded. 'Wouldn't you have done so in my position?'

He rubbed the bridge of his nose ruefully. 'Yeah ... yeah, I guess so.'

She picked up the telephone and dialled a number.

'*Si; posso parlare con il Professore Rosenburg? Si, Jacob Rosenburg.*'

Chapter Sixteen

Jacob Rosenburg was a small, thick-set man with a cherubic face. He was about sixty years old, balding yet with silver-white strands of hair fluffed untidily about his ears. He reminded Kane of a younger Ben Gurion. His bright, twinkling eyes shone with an infectious mirth. He sat in total silence, his expression of grave amusement not altering as Kane recounted his story, refusing the drink which Julie offered him with a curious negative motion of his head. When Kane finished, he did not move for several moments.

It was Julie who coughed nervously and asked: 'What do you think, professor?'

Rosenburg raised his head. 'Think? It's a fascinating story, so far as it goes. But I presume you have more than a story to tell me?'

Kane produced his folder. 'These are the photographs of the papyrus.'

Rosenburg flicked through them.

'And the original papyrus?'

'Locked in Tellaro's safe at the Villa Tiburtina.'

Rosenburg sniffed.

'This is my translation of the text,' went on Kane, pushing his notes forward.

Rosenburg waved them away. 'I would like to see the original Greek first, please.'

'Can you read it from the photographs of the papyrus or from the copy which I prepared?'

'Make it easy on an old man,' smiled Rosenburg. 'I'll read your copy before I tackle the original.'

Kane handed him the sheets. The professor took them, reached into his pocket and extracted a pair of small, gold-rimmed spectacles, and began to read. Although his face did not alter its superficial expression of amusement, Julie noticed a slight pallor overcoming his rosy features and a tightening at the corner of his mouth.

'So?' he said, sitting back. He gazed from Kane to Julie and back to the papers again.

'Well?' Again it was Julie who broke the silence.

'Your copy is excellent, Dr Kane. The form of Greek, its orthography and syntax are right out of the first century AD.'

'And the sense of the epistle?'

'If – note I say "if", my friend, because I would have to witness the tests on the original papyrus and see them performed in clinical conditions – if the papyrus and its ink can be dated to the first century, then the discovery of this document is more momentous than the discovery of the Dead Sea Scrolls. We would have in our hands the earliest surviving Christian document, but a document which takes away one of the foundation stones of the Christian Church.'

Kane moved uneasily. 'I can vouch for the authenticity of the papyrus based on my tests. I can even place the Greek to the first century. What I can not do, which is why we sought your help, is vouch for the authenticity of the contents of the text.'

Rosenburg scratched his chin. 'I think I'll have that drink now, my dear,' he said to Julie. 'A large whisky, if you have it.'

Julie went to pour the drink as Rosenburg turned back to Kane.

'I'll take a look at the photographs of the papyrus now.'

Kane handed them across.

The professor gazed at them intently, comparing them now and again with Kane's copy of the Greek.

'I cannot fault your translation, young man. You are obviously very competent.'

Julie handed the professor his whisky and glanced at Kane. Kane shook his head. Julie poured a drink for herself and sat down. They waited in silence while Rosenburg finished his perusal of the text.

'Stylistically, the text bears great similarities with the other epistles accredited to Paul. The opening, for example, is a typical opening.'

'The epistle is addressed to Linus. Is anything known about him?' observed Julie.

Rosenburg smiled. 'According to the Roman Church, Linus became the first Pope after St Peter in about 67 AD. Linus is mentioned in Paul's epistle to Timothy, the second epistle, that is.'

'What about the reference to the Nazarenes though? Who were they?' demanded Kane.

Rosenburg sipped at his whisky. 'This is where we get into really contentious matters because the modern Christian movement will not accept the Nazarenes in the manner which they are accepted by independent Biblical scholars. The Nazarenes call into question the basis of Christianity as we know it today.'

'Can you give us a brief outline?' Kane asked him.

'Very well. The term Christian is a Greek one and thus could not be applied to the followers of Christ in the decades immediately after his death. *Christos* – anointed one – is simply the translation of the Hebrew word *mashiah* or, as we know it, Messiah.'

Rosenburg paused and took another sip at his glass , as if marshalling his thoughts.

'So ... the early term of a follower of Jesus of Nazareth was Nazarean or Nazarene. The term is accepted both in early Christian and Hebrew sources. References to Nazarenes can be read in the New Testament and in the writings of early Christians such as Justin Martyr, Epiphanius, Jerome, Irenaus, Hippolytus and Origen. The Nazarenes were led by the original disciples of Jesus, those who had lived and worked with him during his lifetime. The 'pillars' of the movement were, of course, James, Peter and John.

The original Nazarenes did not believe in Jesus as God. They believed that he was the Messiah, the anointed one, the rightful king of Israel who would return to liberate the Jewish people from foreign oppression and inaugurate an era of peace and prosperity. Central to their belief was the idea of resurrection; yet they did not believe that Jesus was divine but simply that he had joined a select band of other Jewish prophets and heroes, such as Enoch and Elijah, by becoming immortal in the same way as, in later legend, did King Arthur of Britain, or Charlmagne and Barbarossa.

'The Jewish religious authorities regarded the Nazarenes as heretics to mainstream Judaism. The Nazarenes themselves saw their movement as a sect within the Pharisee group. They were led, after Jesus's death, by Jesus's brother Jacob, mentioned as James in the Bible. They believed that Jesus had not abrogated the laws of Judaism and they continued to observe all the laws of purity, circumcision, and diet, and so forth, maintaining that they were following the instructions and examples of Jesus himself.'

Julie stared at Rosenburg in astonishment. 'Isn't this very radical?' she asked.

The professor smiled gently and shook his head. 'To Biblical scholars, no. The evidence is fairly clear. Many modern Christian scholars have had to accept it in view of the evidence, but they have developed a weird philosopy that somehow the Jesus of history is divorced from the Jesus of their faith.'

The professor continued.

'The Nazarenes preached only within the Judaic fold. There is evidence of another group of followers of Jesus who might have been established at the time of Jesus's death as well. Their ideas followed closely the Nazarenes and their leader was another brother of Jesus, Jude Thomas. We even have a surviving gospel of this movement. Jude is referred to clearly as the brother of Jesus and Jacob. The fascinating thing here is that Thomas is the Hebrew word for a twin and there is one intriguing reference to the fact that Jude may have been Jesus's twin brother.'

Julie shook her head in open disbelief.

Rosenburg chuckled. 'Well, if you are brought up with

modern Christianity it does come as a shock, I suppose. If only people read modern Biblical scholarship...'

'If the original followers of Christ saw themselves simply as a Jewish sect,' Kane interrupted, 'how did Christianity come about?'

'Enter a Jew from Tarsus named Saul, a good Hebrew name. Saul never knew Jesus, but it was Saul who invented Christianity.'

'I've had enough shocks for one day,' murmured Julie.

'Go on,' pressed Kane.

'As you know, our friend Saul became known by the Latinised version of his name – Paul. It was Paul who began to propound a view of Jesus's life which was entirely inconsistent with the teachings of the original Nazarenes and the beliefs of Jesus's own friends and followers. It was Paul who gave him divine status, claimed he had abrogated the laws of Judaism and who interpreted his death in terms of gnostic soteriology. Tarsus was a Greek city and we must remember that Paul was greatly influenced by Greek culture and its religious ideas and myths.'

Julie sighed. 'What the devil is gnostic soteriology?'

'The salvation doctrine, my dear. Furthermore, with Paul busy inventing his own doctrines and, in fact, his own religion, he came into conflict with the original followers of Jesus, the Nazarenes. So pagan were Paul's concepts that he attracted few Jewish followers and it was among Greeks that he made his strongest converts. Even the New Testament writers cannot entirely expunge the fact of the conflict between Paul and Jesus's own disciples. James and Peter were particularly appalled at Paul's activities. A great split began to develop between them around 60 AD. It was felt that Paul had completely surrendered to idolatory and pagan-ism. There was a riot in the Temple at Jerusalem when Paul went there about that time. The Nazarenes felt Paul was desecrating the Jewish sanctuary. Paul was arrested and eventually sent to Rome for trial.'

Rosenburg paused to finish his drink.

'So you see, the Nazarenes could justifiably claim to be the authentic transmitters of Jesus's own teachings. After all, their leaders had known him and were eye-witnesses to his deeds and his speeches. Paul was not. Indeed, Jacob, or James, was Jesus's own brother... a fact that is even admitted in the New Testament, as well as in independent sources, such as the historian Josepheus who was a contemporary of both Jesus and James. Paul, on the other hand, maintained that all his ideas were derived from visions. But we must be practical: Paul was undoubtedly the originator and founder of his own movement which we now know as Christianity.

'For the next ten years the Nazarenes and Paul's Christian movement were in violent conflict. Just read Paul's epistle to Galatians. Paul had won the Galatians to his movement, but James and Peter sent Nazarene missionaries to reconvert them to their sect. The Nazarene message was simple. You could not believe in Jesus as the Messiah unless you accepted the Judaic faith and that involved circumcision, God's famous covenant with Abraham.'

'Well, why don't we hear of the Nazarenes now?' demanded Julie.

'The event which weakened the Nazarene movement was the Roman siege and capture of Jerusalem in 70 AD. The Nazarenes, as loyal Jews, took part in the defence of the city and were severely crippled. Jacob, or James, the leader of the community, had already been executed on the orders of Ananus, the high priest who was a fanatical Sadducee, the sect which was in conflict with the Pharisees. In 90 AD the Nazarenes were finally expelled from the Jewish synagogue, but they continued to exist until 400 AD. They maintained until the end that Jesus was the Messiah and would soon return to fulfil the Messianic prophecies. They further maintained that Paul was a deceiver who had perverted the message of Jesus. All the Nazarean literature which fell into the hands of the Christians was either destroyed or suppressed, but we do have fragments of the Nazarene Gospels including the Gospel of Peter which was discovered in 1884 AD.'

Kane whistled softly.

'What in fact you are saying is that, historically, everything that this papyrus states is already accepted?'

The professor shook his head.

'The conflict between Paul and the original disciples of Jesus has been accepted by most Biblical scholars for many years now. Indeed, the major part of the papyrus text is merely repetitive of Paul's letter to Galatians... even in some of its phraseology. For example, the reference to Paul staying in Jerusalem with Peter for fifteen days occurs in Galatians, so does the reference to his second meeting fourteen years later and the story of Paul's open quarrel with Peter in Antioch. The argument with James and Peter on Paul's final visit to Jerusalem occurs in The Acts, in chapters fifteen and twenty, which are, of course, rather idealised from Paul's viewpoint.

'But where the text starts to shatter the Christian world is that it confirms that Peter was in Rome. So far, there is absolutely no evidence for Peter having been in Rome. The entire matter is hearsay and legend. Peter's appearance in Rome seems to have been first rumoured in the second century AD when a legend reports that he went there to undo the harm done by the teachings of Simon Magus. Then there evolved the legend of Peter going to Rome to "found the Church", which even Christian historians discount. The famous story of Peter's death there, being crucified upside down, is of much later origin. Yet, if the papyrus is genuine, here we have Paul admitting that he employed two ex-Roman soldiers to murder Peter in order to stop his criticism. That is going to upset a lot of people.'

Kane shrugged. 'Personally, I am an agnostic so I don't much care. If it is the truth, then it is the truth. What people make of it is their own affair.'

'Well,' smiled Rosenburg, 'this would be a bombshell which would make Darwin's theory seemed insignificant.'

Julie made a nervous gesture. 'According to the Church, Jesus told Peter he was the rock on which it would be founded. Peter is said to have come to Rome and was martyred. Every Pope takes his authority from Peter. This papyrus now says that this is all the fabrication of Paul.'

'The greatest fabriction in history,' agreed Rosenburg. 'A fabrication which has had a greater influence on civilisation than any other single event.'

'Is there any chance that Paul was speaking about someone other than Peter the Apostle?' pressed Julie.

Kane shook his head. 'I don't think my translation is wrong. Twice the name Simon Bar-Jona is referred to in the text, which is the Hebrew name of Peter, while in the rest of the text the Greek – Cephas – meaning "rock", is used. I have merely put Cephas into its more popular Latin form – Peter.'

Rosenburg nodded vigorously. 'It is accepted by Christians that Jesus's disciple Peter was called Simon Bar-Jona. Look at Matthew in the New Testament – chapter sixteen, I believe. "And Jesus answered and said unto him, blessed art thou, Simon Bar-Jona . . ." Where I disagree with what you have just said, Kane, is in this: there is a tendency for Christian interpreters to think this is just a pure Hebrew name – Simon Bar-Jona or Simon, son of Jonah. But we must remember that Aramaic was the language spoken by the Jews at this time and in Aramaic the word *Baryona* means an outlaw. *Baryona* was a typical nickname for a Zealot, one of the group who opposed the Roman occupation by force, a sort of ancient Irgun or Haganah. The Zealots were freedom-fighters.

'In fact, the name comes from the Greek word *zelotes*, whereas the Aramaic and Hebrew word was *kanai*. That's why there are some peculiar references in the New Testament to followers of Jesus being Canaanites when the Canaanites no longer existed. The New Testament copyists simply misread the word *kanaiani* as Canaanite.'

'Are you saying that the disciples of Jesus were a group of nationalist guerillas?' gasped Julie.

Rosenburg smiled.

'That's one contention. The gospel of Luke refers very clearly to Peter as "Simon called Zealotes", while Matthew and Mark called him "the Canaanite" which, as I say, is just a misreading of the same word. The word *Baryona* was often applied to the Zealots. Take the nicknames for James and John, which Mark says was "sons of thunder". That again was a euphemism for Zealots. Then there is Judas Iscariot, another Zealot name – Judas the dagger-man.

'If you look in the New Testament you will find copyists have been very inconsistent in translating names. Thus Simon Bar-Jona's nickname, "the Rock", usually occurs in its Latin form as Petrus since Latin became the adopted language of Paul's Christian movement. But all the early manuscripts refer to the Greek word Kephas, sometimes spelt with a letter C. In the James's version of the Bible, for example, Cephas occurs in Galatians two, verse nine, and a few verses later we are talking of Peter. To the uninitiated Cephas and Peter might be two separate people. The translators of the *New English Bible* were obviously worried abut the theosophical problems of Paul having an argument with Peter and so made his argument into one with Cephas throughout that epistle.'

'So Simon Bar-Jona, Cephas and Peter were all the same person?' asked Julie.

'That's right.'

Kane had been taking some hurried notes.

'So what it boils down to is that the contents of this papyrus are not out of keeping with the known facts of the period and could well be genuine?'

Rosenburg nodded. 'That's about the size of it.' He glanced at the papers. 'Of course, one would have to check if there were consuls named Bassus and Crassus as mentioned in the text.'

'No need,' smiled Kane. 'I've already done that by the simple expedient of checking Tacitus's *Annals*. They were joint consuls during the year of Rome 817 which makes it 64 AD.'

Rosenburg's eyes sparkled. 'And that places it in the year of the fire of Rome.'

Julie smiled. 'Isn't that when Nero played his fiddle or something?'

'More or less,' grinned Rosenburg. 'Tacitus says that the prevailing opinion was that the Emperor Nero ordered Rome to be set on fire, but to remove the accusations of guilt from himself he blamed it on the Christians and started the great persecution in which it is thought that Paul died.'

Kane shook his head with a sigh.

'So we have a picture of Paul, having had Peter put out of the way for denouncing his version of Christianity, making not so much a confession but a justification of his deed to Linus, who turns out to be his successor in the leadership of the movement. He writes the note to Linus in the immediate aftermath of the destruction of Rome by fire at a time when Nero is making accusations against his movement. He is afraid for his life and decides to flee to Antium...'

'Which is modern Anzio,' interrupted Rosenburg.

'Paul gives the papyrus to Pudens...'

'Who is also mentioned in the New Testament writings in the same line as Linus in the epistle to Timothy,' interposed Rosenburg.

'Then Paul disappears from the historical stage, presumably a victim of Nero's persecution. However, we are led to believe that Linus survives because, in the fourth century, Eusebius, the bishop of Caesarea who wrote a great history of the movement, mentions him as the first bishop of Rome in succession to Peter not Paul. He was said to have been Pope between 67 and 78 AD.'

Julie gazed at the photographs of the papyrus. 'You mean that this papyrus was actually written by Paul of Tarsus himself?'

Kane smiled thinly. 'Unless it is a very early copy.'

'It's a bit eerie,' Julie shuddered.

'Why?' demanded Rosenburg. 'Paul was only a man who lived on this earth and, for a time, here in this very city. I have seen plenty of fragments of manuscripts written by people who lived during the same period as Paul, and even before him.'

'What are we going to do?' asked the journalist.

'The first thing to do is to authenticate the papyrus under

121

proper conditions.'

'In view of the circumstances,' replied Kane grimly, 'that would seem impossible.'

'Unless we break into the Villa Tiburtina,' suggested Julie, 'and open the safe.'

'The most important question is whether Tellaro is acting on his own or on behalf of the Vatican itself,' said Kane.

Rosenburg started. 'I think we are steering into troubled waters, my friends. We must proceed carefully. Governments have been known to commit crimes and seek to cover them up. One must remember that the Vatican is the oldest continuous government in the world. With your permission, Dr Kane, I would like to take the papers, your photographs and reports on the various tests, back to my rooms for a more leisurely study and then do as much background research as I can. Once I am as assured as I can be from the evidence we have, then we may go onto the next step.'

Kane frowned. 'Which is?'

'To go to see the Cardinal Archivist of the Secret Archives and present him with the facts, having made sure duplicates of all these documents are lodged in a safe place. Then we can call upon the Vatican to invite Cardinal Tellaro to produce the original papyrus for scholastic study.'

The little professor stood up and collected the papers into his briefcase. His whole being exuded eagerness and excitement and he grinned broadly at Julie and Kane.

'I'll be in touch tomorrow. In the meantime, judging from your story, I would say that Tellaro and his cousin are dangerous men. I would be very careful, if I were you.'

Kane nodded. 'You don't have to tell me, professor. We shall be careful.'

'Be in peace, my friends,' smiled Rosenburg as he left.

122

Chapter Seventeen

Kane spent the night on the couch in Julie Gambretti's living-room. The next morning, at breakfast, he said: 'I'd really like to get some facts about Cardinal Tellaro. Isn't there a library which might have some press cuttings about his career, of biographical references? It would be a good thing if we could find out as much about him as possible.'

Julie frowned as she sipped at her coffee. 'There's the *Governatorato*'s Personnel Office or the Vatican newspaper *L'Osservatore Romano...*'

Kane chuckled. 'If Tellaro is head of Vatican security that would be the last place to start searching.'

'I guess you're right. How about the American Library in the Via Veneto?'

'That's an idea,' agreed Kane.

'But is it wise to leave the apartment?'

'While I wouldn't go strolling down to the Villa Tiburtina, I doubt that there'll be a problem. Rome is rather a big place and the odds of bumping into the Tellaros are in my favour.'

'I suppose so. Do you know where the Via Veneto is?'

Kane grinned wryly. 'I guess anyone who has ever spent a day in Rome knows that.'

The broad tree-lined avenue, with its fashionable hotels and cafés, was the centre of *la dolce vita* in the city whose pavements were crowded with touts, pimps, prostitutes, transvestites and the general flotsam and jetsam of human degradation in search of new stimulus.

'Shall I run you down in my car?'

He shook his head. 'I'll bus down. It'll give me a chance to stretch my legs a bit as well.'

'Do you have enough money?'

'Enough for a trip to the library. I'll be on my way now and be back this afternoon. I don't suppose Rosenburg will call before then.' He paused. 'Maybe you'd better give me his telephone number in case I pick up anything worthwhile in the library.'

Julie scrawled it on a piece of paper which Kane placed in his wallet.

Julie went with him to the door of the apartment.

'I'll be here all day. I have to finish writing a story.'

He nodded.

'Take care, David.'

It was the first time she had used his first name and he turned, catching the concern in her face.

'You bet,' he smiled with reassurance.

The little that the American Library had on Cardinal Giona Tellaro was frankly disappointing. There was an entry in the Catholic Church's *Who's Who*, but it gave dates mainly, of ordination, of appointments, and little else. It presented a skeleton without substance. Kane spent a couple of hours ploughing through numerous editions of *L'Osservatore Romano* for the dates given for Tellaro's Vatican appointments, but the Vatican daily newspaper carried little information about him. He also checked through files of the official Vatican journal *Acta Apostolicae Sedis* without adding greatly to his knowledge. The saturnine Sicilian cardinal somehow contrived to remain in the shadows.

The pleasant-faced young librarian suggested Kane try the Biblioteca Nazionale Centrale on the Viale Castro Pretorio, but she seriously doubted whether it would be able to supply him with any further details. She felt he would be better off going directly to the library of *L'Osservatore Romano* itself.

Kane smiled, thanked her and left the library just after midday, realising that he was hungry.

From the Via Veneto, at the Piazza Barberini, where the cost of eating was exorbitant, he strolled down the Via del

Tritone and into the old crowded streets of the city, through the numerous tiny squares and into the great oblong of the Piazza Navona, which had always been his favourite spot in Rome. It occupied the site of the ancient stadium of Domitian where festivals, jousts and sporting events were held. Even in the seventeenth and nineteenth centuries, the piazza was flooded every weekend in August for the entertainment of the citizens. No wheeled vehicles were allowed into the piazza whose three sixteenth-century fountains were surrounded by the ancient church of Sant' Agnese in Agone and the Palazzo Pamphilji and the church of the Madonna del Sacro Cuore. In Rome it was easy to become besotted with history.

He strode across the piazza into the Corsia Agonale and halted with a happy smile. The small trattoria which he had frequented during his stay in Rome was still there, its tables sprawling across the pavement. He chose one of the few pavement tables which remained unoccupied and ordered a pizza and a Peroni beer from the waiter who contrived to appear at his side the moment he sat down.

The service was good and he was soon tucking into a giant-sized pizza with a happy smile. He realised that, in spite of the events of the last few days, he was experiencing a strange sense of well-being, something which he had not felt in years. New York and Janine began to seem a million miles away, a thousand years ago. He felt a momentary pang of guilt. Yet it was almost as if it had all happened to someone else. Rome seemed to throw light into the dark corners of his world, leaving him nodding drowsily at the remains of his meal in the warm embrace of the sun.

He called for a coffee and the bill and paid immediately while sipping his coffee.

He was vaguely aware of someone taking a seat at the table immediately behind him. A hand touched him on the shoulder and a harsh voice said sibilantly: 'Well, *doctore*, it is a lucky thing that Salvatore spotted you as we were driving by. You have caused my cousin and me a great deal of trouble.'

125

Kane found himself go icy cold. He turned his head to gaze into the dark expressionless eyes of Adriano Tellaro.

Julie Gambretti was drying her hair when the telephone started to shrill.

'Hello, my dear. This is Jacob Rosenburg. Is Kane there?'

Julie thought that Rosenburg's voice was edged with suppressed excitement.

'He won't be back for a while, professor. He's gone to the American Library to do some research. We didn't think you would telephone until much later today.'

'I have made my preliminary investigation now. I think I should talk to you before proceeding further. Is it possible for you to come over to my apartment?'

Julie frowned. 'David should be back in a few hours...' she began.

'No,' his voice rose in intensity. 'I must proceed as soon as possible. I would like to see you now. Immediately.'

She capitulated. 'I can be over there very shortly. Say fifteen or twenty minutes depending on the traffic. Is anything wrong?'

'I cannot speak over the telephone. Please come as soon as you can.'

There was a metallic click as Rosenburg hung up leaving Julie gazing down at the receiver in puzzlement. She sighed, replaced the receiver and began to write a note for Kane if he returned before she did.

Monsignor Ryan seated himself across the desk from the fragile figure of the Cardinal Archivist of the Secret Archives and smiled apologetically.

'It is good of you to see me, Eminence.'

'I am always at the disposal of officials of the Central Security Office, Monsignor,' replied the Cardinal blandly.

Ryan smiled good-naturedly. Was the grave-faced Cardinal Archivist possessed of a sense of humour?

'Naturally, I must ask for this interview to be strictly confidential.'

'Naturally.'

'Cardinal Tellaro has been displaying signs of stress due to the workload which he has taken on his own shoulders. His Eminence is a man who is extremely conscientious where his duty is concerned. To be blunt, I am seeking diplomatic means of relieving him of the burden of office by taking over some of the more arduous problems which he is handling.'

The Cardinal Archivist smiled thinly. 'I wish my own staff were so conscientious. Unfortunately with office comes responsibility, much of which cannot be delegated. Have you told His Eminence of your concern?'

Monsignor Ryan shrugged. 'I understand that His Eminence has been involved with enquiries connected with the Secret Archives?' he went on without directly replying to the question.

'That is so. He saw me some time ago concerning the death of Brother Girolamon...'

'Ah, the monk who committed suicide in the papal apartments?'

'Yes. But the case is now closed. Cardinal Tellaro concluded that the young man was overworking and had become unbalanced especially after the illness of his immediate superior, Father Manzoni. Tragically, Father Manzoni died soon after.'

'I am told that Cardinal Tellaro went to see Father Manzoni. Was that in connection with the affair?'

'You would have to discuss that with His Eminence.'

'I am also told that Cardinal Tellaro made a search of the offices which Father Manzoni and Brother Girolamon shared.'

'I am unaware of any such search.'

'I see.' Monsignor Ryan smiled gently. 'Well, in that case I do not think I need trouble you further. It would seem that the affair is closed and that it is not one of the cases which His Eminence is now currently pursuing. Therefore it cannot be the cause of any stress or anxiety.'

The Cardinal Archivist grunted.

Monsignor Ryan hesitated at the door. 'One more thing

though, Eminence... When your archivists take documents out of your vaults to work on, is it not the practice to sign a central register to ensure that each document's whereabouts is known?'

The Cardinal Archivist glanced up with a frown. 'You are well informed, Monsignor.'

'Would it be possible for me to examine that register?'

'I cannot see...'

Monsignor Ryan went on apologetically: 'It is just something in Cardinal Tellaro's report which I fail to understand. I am cursed with a mind which likes exactitudes.'

The Cardinal Archivist made an impatient gesture. 'I will give the order to my secretary.'

'You have been most helpful, Eminence,' smiled Monsignor Ryan. 'I am sorry to have disturbed you.'

Adriano Tellaro smiled thinly. He had his right hand in his coat pocket and he gestured through the material.

'This is a Beretta .25, *doctore*. A small gun which makes little noise. Please do not try to be a hero.'

Kane looked at him with narrowed eyes. He glanced at the people strolling by and those seated at the tables behind him. 'You wouldn't dare.'

'No?' Adriano chuckled unpleasantly. 'Perhaps you would like to find out?'

'You wouldn't get away with it.'

'One thing you could be sure of... you would never know, *doctore*. You would be dead. And I? I would most likely escape in the confusion, but you would be dead. Shall we put it to the test?'

Kane knew that Adriano had the upper hand. He shrugged his defeat.

'Excellent,' smiled the dark Sicilian. 'In a moment Salvatore will drive up in the car. When he does so, you will cross to the car in front of me and climb in. Understood?'

Kane had barely time to nod when a black Mercedes saloon squealed to a halt in front of them.

128

'Move!' snapped Adriano.

Kane rose with a hopeless gesture and walked to the car. There was nothing he could do. He had lost his initiative. He climbed in with Adriano close behind him. The small gun was out of his pocket now and jabbed against his side.

The car sped away into the Roman traffic, dodging nimbly in and out of the side-streets, keeping away from the more crowded thoroughfares until it swung over the Ponte Umberto I. Kane could identify the bridge over the river because it led straight onto the façade of the Palazza di Giustizia, the Palace of Justice, which was perhaps an ironic piece of driving from the bull-necked Salvatore. Kane glanced wistfully at the milling uniformed police as the car swung around the high walls. Then the car was moving across the Piazza Cavour and into the Via Crescenzio, along the high walls of the Vatican City until they arrived in the Via Angelo Emo and entered the grounds of the Villa Tiburtina.

Salvatore leaped from the car and opened the door of the villa as Adriano gestured for Kane to get out.

'Upstairs, *doctore*. I think you know your way.'

Kane felt bitter as he climbed the stairs before Adriano, returning to his bedroom.

'Sit down!' snapped Adriano, turning and handing his Beretta to the grim-faced chauffeur. 'Keep him covered until I return, Salvatore.'

'Going to get orders from your eminent cousin?' sneered Kane.

Adriano's eyes widened at Kane's inflection on the word 'eminent'.

'So?' He was about to speak, then he shrugged, suddenly leaned forward and punched Kane straight in the mouth, causing him to jack-knife across the bed. 'You must have respect, *doctore*,' he said softly.

He turned and hurried from the room while Salvatore squatted on a chair, gun held steady in one huge hand, and a smile on his pugnacious features which displayed his yellowing teeth.

Kane ruefully rubbed the blood from his mouth.

129

It was not long before Adriano was back. To Kane's bemusement he carried a couple of bottles of whisky; squat-shaped bottles of Old Grand Dad Special Selection, he thought irrelevantly.

'Right, *doctore*,' began Adriano briskly. 'Where are the photographs and the notes which you took? Where did you stay last night? Who did you speak to?'

Kane did not bother to reply.

Salvatore rose menacingly, but Adriano gestured for him to remain seated. Adriano then leisurely opened one of the whisky bottles and poured a tumbler, setting it on a bedside table.

'Empty your pockets.'

Under the threat of the Beretta, Kane did so, watching as Adriano examined each item. He went cold as the torn scrap of paper with Rosenburg's telephone number, which Julie had given him that morning, was fished out of his wallet. Adriano glanced briefly at it and then collected the other items, his wallet, money and the notes he had made about Cardinal Tellaro from the American Library and left the room saying: 'You can have a drink while I'm gone.'

Kane did not move.

It was twenty minutes before Adriano returned. This time he spoke swiftly to Salvatore in Sicilian dialect which Kane failed to understand. The chauffeur pocketed the Beretta and followed Adriano from the room. The door slammed and Kane heard the key turn in the lock.

Kane leaped to his feet immediately and tried the door. It was an automatic but obviously futile reaction. Then he turned and surveyed the room, his eyes coming to rest on the two bottles of Old Grand Dad whisky. What were they trying to do? Get him drunk in order that he would tell them what he had done with the papers? Some hopes!

He went to the wash basin and bathed the sore area where Adriano's fist had smashed into his face. His gums were still bleeding and his cheek was slightly bruised. He took a tooth mug and rinsed his mouth out.

One thing was clear now, Giona Tellaro was in deadly

earnest about stopping word of the papyrus leaking out.

He moved to the window which was fastened and shuttered. Damn it!

His eyes returned to the whisky bottles. He must stay sober! They were probably thinking that he would succumb to the temptation and that they would return to find him talkative. They had misjudged him. He sat down on the bed and glanced at his watch. Then he lay back on the pillow and closed his eyes. It was useless expending energy for no reason at all.

He wondered how long it would be before they came back.

Chapter Eighteen

Julie Gambretti eased her Fiat into the stream of traffic circling the Piazza della Republica, which sprawled in front of the ornate façade of Rome's Stazione Termini. She allowed the stream to take her to a side-street then she weaved through the narrow roads until she emerged onto the Viale dell' Università, whose broad avenue led straight into the academic complex known as Città Universitaria which, from 1935, housed Rome's ancient university. There were only a few cars moving on the avenue that majestically separated the grandiose-looking buildings which had been erected at the height of Mussolini's power, when the Fascist dictator sought to re-create a grandeur to equal that of ancient Rome. She was soon into the university complex, moving into the Via Borelli from the Viale Ippocrate.

She was in luck. There was a vacant parking meter within a few yards of the block where Jacob Rosenburg had his apartment. She edged the Fiat in, climbed out and fumbled with her purse to find a coin for the meter. A lounging traffic warden nodded approvingly as she hurried by.

She had been to interview Rosenburg twice before and she knew the way up to his apartment without needing to consult the *portinaio*. She took the lift to the fourth floor and pressed the door buzzer.

There was no answer.

Frowning, she pressed again, letting her finger rest a little longer on the button.

It was very quiet. Surely Rosenburg had not gone out after demanding her immediate presence? Maybe he had gone out

132

for cigarettes or something? She leaned over the stair railings and peered down to see if there was any sign of him. The building seemed deserted.

She turned back to the door and raised her hand to knock, hoping that his might raise some response. As her fist fell on its wooden panels, it swung open, propelled by the impetus of her blow. She bit her lip as she saw that the lock had been broken off its mounting from the inside, the screws ripping the wood away from the door.

'Professor Rosenburg?' she called nervously.

There was no answer.

She took a step forward.

It appeared as if a whirlwind had struck the room. Drawers were emptied, their contents scattered over the floor, books lay everywhere and a chair had been overturned.

Her heart started to pound rapidly.

'Professor?'

She had to cough to clear the sudden restriction in her throat.

Julie moved slowly to the middle of the room and stared about her. It was obvious that the room had been searched; thoroughly searched but with some considerable haste. She wondered what she ought to do.

Where was Rosenburg?

Who could have done this? Should she call the police? Yes, that was probably the best thing. She looked for the telephone.

The instrument was on the floor, its receiver off. She bent down on one knee and seized it. Though she tapped the receiver cradle up and down there was no dialling tone – just a silence. There was not even a tell-tale click to show her the telephone was connected.

She pulled at the cord and gasped. It had been cut through.

She shivered and abruptly stood up. She had to get in touch with Kane; tell him; ask him what she should do. Maybe the university would know where Rosenburg was?

The thoughts entered her mind without order.

It was as she was turning towards the door that she saw the foot.

It was sticking out from behind the sofa. Just a single foot clad in a black sock and a highly polished black shoe.

She stared in fascination at it. Then she swallowed hard, drew back her shoulders as if mentally preparing herself for what she now knew she would find.

Professor Jacob Rosenburg lay on his back behind the sofa. His eyes were wide open, staring sightlessly at the ceiling. His other leg was crumpled under him. One arm was flung out carelessly behind him, the other lay alongside him, a bunch of torn papers were still clenched in his hand. Half on, half off his face, his spectacles lay askew, both lenses smashed. The expression on his face was one of surprise, perhaps a little indignation.

Across the white of his shirt was a crimson stain.

Julie felt a twinge of nausea and fought to control her feelings. She breathed deeply to regulate her wild respiration and forced herself to gaze down at Rosenburg's body. Then, willing herself to perform each motion, she bent down and reached for the pulse on Rosenburg's wrist. The hand was limp, and although not exactly cold it had the chill feeling of damp clay, the texture of death. She knew before she knelt that there would be no pulse.

She stood up and began to move away. She was half-way across the room when the thought struck her and forced her to halt. Slowly she returned to kneel down by the corpse again. Biting her lips, she picked up the dead hand and began to prise the torn papers from its vice-like grip. There was not much left of the papers, just a few shredded scraps, but Julie felt a welling sense of panic as she realised they had been part of the notes which Kane had given Rosenburg the previous day.

Cosima watched sullenly as Adriano Tellaro entered their bedroom and began to throw off his clothes. He did not speak to her but strode swiftly into the bathroom. She heard the shower turn on. With a sigh, the girl moved across the room and began to gather up the discarded clothes.

The sleeve of the jacket was damp. She gazed down in curiosity. There was a faint red stain on her hand.

She gave a small cry and let the clothes drop to the floor. 'What is it?'

Adriano's harsh tones caused her to swing round, shivering violently and staring at him with large frightened eyes.

Adriano, still dripping from his shower, was wrapping a towel around him. He gazed from the girl to the clothes and then strode across and seized the girl's wrist, glancing at the red stain on her hand.

'Go and wash that off,' he scowled.

The girl gazed at him in bewilderment. 'What is it, Adriano?' she whispered.

The dark expressionless eyes returned her gaze unflinchingly. 'Why should it be anything? I just had a small accident. Go and wash it off.'

Cosima turned and went slowly to the bathroom. Adriano ignored her and bent to pick up the clothes, taking items from his pockets and stacking them on the bedside table. Then he took a plastic bag from a dressing-table drawer, stuffed all the discarded items of clothing into it and placed the bag by the door. Then he sat on the bed, reached for the telephone and dialled a number.

'It's done,' he said shortly when a voice answered.

On the other end of the wire Giona Tellaro drew a long sigh. 'Very well. What of the other business?'

Adriano's eyes involuntary moved towards the ceiling as if he could peer through to the upper floors of the villa. 'We will proceed with our original plan.'

'Do you think he made contact with anyone else?'

Adriano pursed his lips. 'There is no way of being absolutely sure. I doubt it. I think he found that the old professor was in Rome and went straight to him with the documents. The old man was working on them when we arrived. We recovered them all.'

135

There was a pause.

'Very well. Proceed.'

Adriano replaced the receiver, his face still expressionless.

Cosima stood hesitantly on the threshold of the bathroom. She was looking uneasily at him. 'What is going on, Adriano?' she whispered almost plaintively.

Adriano turned with a scowl and then changed it abruptly into a broad smile. 'Going on? Nothing for you to worry about. Tomorrow we shall be returning to Palermo for me to clear up some business and then we shall take a holiday. Didn't I promise you a holiday in Sorrento?'

He strode across to her and embraced her roughly.

She did not respond for a while, her mind full of suspicion. Then she sighed reluctantly. She did not understand what was going on. Not anything. Not the odd activities of the American upstairs, not the strangeness of Adriano's cousin... not any of it. But then it was not her business. Better not to dwell on things which did not concern her. After another moment she gave herself to Adriano's fumbling hands and allowed herself to be drawn towards the bed.

Julie Gambretti had never felt panic before; never complete and utter panic.

Still carrying the torn fragments of notes in her hand, she had been seized by an overwhelming desire to run. She had hurried from Rosenburg's apartment, down the stairs, luckily meeting no one, until she was once more in the calm of the Roman sunshine. Not pausing, she hastened to her car, and was soon speeding away into the traffic, back across the city towards Aventino.

She had to talk with David Kane before she called the police. Her mind whirled with questions and gradually a cold realisation struck her: the reservations about David Kane's story that had been lurking at the back of her mind were now gone. There could be no doubt that his life was in danger, and it seemed obvious to her that Rosenburg's death was directly connected with the ancient papyrus. And that meant that she was in just as much danger as Kane!

Damn! She wandered through her apartment. Where was he? She wished that she had not been so acquiescent in allowing him to go out.

Someone had murdered Rosenburg. Someone wanted to murder David Kane.

Cardinal Giona Tellaro?

She could not believe it. The idea that the head of Vatican security would resort to such methods to keep an old document from public knowledge was just too crazy for words. Yet Rosenburg was dead. Murdered!

She glanced at her watch. It was getting late. Where was Kane? She began to feel an overwhelming sense of despair.

There was a rattle of keys at the door and it opened with abruptness.

Kane must have been dozing for it startled him and he sat up blinking as the electric light flooded the room. His first thought was that it was very late and he wondered what Julie Gambretti was thinking about his disappearance. It was an inconsequential thought.

Adriano Tellaro was gazing down at him with Salvatore behind him. The dark-faced man glanced at the still-full bottles of whisky and shook his head as if in sadness.

'You disappoint me, *doctore*,' he said softly.

Kane stared back defiantly. 'You won't get me to talk that way.'

'Talk?' Adriano chuckled drily as if the idea amused him. 'But we don't want you to talk, *doctore*.'

He picked up the untouched tumbler full of whisky.

'No,' he said, regarding it solemnly for a moment. 'We don't want you to talk. We just want you to have a pleasant little drink with us, eh?'

Kane shook his head.

'Come, *doctore*,' the smile did not leave Adriano's features but his voice turned cold and compelling. 'You will drink . . . one way or another.'

'Make me,' challenged Kane.

Adriano thrust the glass against Kane's lips, grabbing him by the hair to force his head backwards. Kane struggled, feeling the whisky spilling against his clenched teeth and pouring down his shirt-front.

Adriano swore in disgust.

Before Kane could compose himself, Salvatore had pocketed the gun and come round him to grab him from behind, leaving Adriano with a free hand to force open Kane's mouth while he poured the drink down. Most of the contents went down his throat; he could feel the raw alcohol burning through him.

'That's better, isn't it?' smiled Adriano. 'But I think you would like another glass.'

After the third full tumbler of whisky had been forced down his throat, Kane began to lose track of what was happening. He knew, vaguely, that he must not say anything. He knew that they were forcing glass after glass of whisky down his throat. He felt weak, unable to co-ordinate his limbs, unable to speak. He heard them laughing. Then he passed out.

When he came round he was being carried over someone's shoulder. He felt sick and dizzy and passed out again.

He came round again and was dimly aware that he was in a stuffy confined space. He was aware of motion and reasoned that he was on the floor of a car. He tried to fathom out what was happening to him but before he could do so he had blacked out again.

Something crashed into his ribs. He groaned. His eyes flickered open and he tried to focus. Adriano's smiling gaze was laughing down at him. Then he was being manhandled along the rough ground. It was cold and hard. He was picked up and pushed against a balustrade. He felt a sharp shove and he thought he was flying through space, floating gently through the air. He chuckled, or thought he chuckled, and tried to flap his arms. He was so peaceful, floating, floating gently...

Something ice-cold and wet leaped up and slapped him in

the face.

Water!

He was suddenly immersed in water. He blinked and desperately tried to bring his surroundings into focus. It was black, so terribly black. He could not see anything. Blackness and water were everywhere. The water was suffocating him. He struck out and more by luck than good co-ordination was able to turn himself onto his back and paddle. He floated easily in spite of the weight of his clothes. He pushed with his hands and feet. The water no longer seemed so cold. It didn't bother him. Nothing bothered him. He just wanted to close his eyes and relax. Relax and go to sleep. Yes, that was it. He was tired. He would sleep. He would deal with the problems when he woke up.

He would sleep now. Sleep...

Chapter Nineteen

Julie Gambretti had finally dropped asleep with exhaustion early in the morning. All evening she had paced to and fro in agitation at Kane's disappearance. At six o'clock, just before the American Library in the Via Veneto closed, she had telephoned to see if Kane had been there. The librarian assured her that a man answering Kane's description had left about midday. Julie put down the telephone and realised she was frightened.

Kane had somehow become an important factor in her life and for that she was slightly puzzled. It was strange the interest he had generated in her, right from her first glimpse of him. Yet he was seemingly everything she disliked – an alcoholic, a sign, she thought, of a weak personality. But he had certainly shown no sign of weakness the previous day. She hoped that he would be able to keep it up . . .

She shivered, wondering for the thousandth time where he was; wondering what had happened to him. Several times she had started to telephone the police but some fear, something which kept sending her thoughts in a panic, made her pause. She could not even bring herself to telephone Charlie Burgano, her bureau chief, but also her oldest friend in Rome.

She paced the apartment until she was exhausted, but even then, sitting on the couch near the telephone, hoping Kane would call, she found that sleep would not come. It was not until after three o'clock that she finally dozed off.

It was the door buzzer which started her from her shallow sleep. She stumbled to the door and reached for the intercom. *'Pronto?'*

'Signorina Gambretti?' Julie Gambretti?'

She could not identify the male voice which asked the question with detached politeness.

'Yes.'

'I am Capitano Tornioli of the Polizia. May I see you a moment?'

She fought for a moment to control a sudden shaky feeling. David Kane! Rosenburg!

'Are you there, *signorina?'*

'Yes, yes, I am. Come up.'

She pressed the automatic switch. It was only after she had done so that she felt a vague shiver of fear. What if the man was not a policeman? What if . . . ? She hurried to the window which overlooked the roadway and peered down. The blue-and-white police car outside reassured her a little.

Before she had time to dwell on what the police could want with her, at six o'clock in the morning – she glanced at her watch to confirm the time – there was a tap on the door.

Captain Tornioli was young, dark-haired, with a thin moustache. He saluted her politely and removed his cap as she stepped aside to let him enter.

'Mi scusi, signorina,' he smiled, fumbling for the right words. 'It is a matter of some delicacy. Do you know a man called Kane – a Dr David Kane?'

She stared at him a moment and then nodded.

'Is the *doctore* a man given to excesses in alcohol?'

She groaned inwardly. 'Yes.'

'Ah, just so. We have him in the car at the moment. He is still much the worse for an indulgence with drink.'

Julie sat down abruptly on the couch. All her anxiety went out of her like a deflated balloon and she began to feel angry. So Kane was not the reformed character he had said he was. While Rosenburg had been murdered and she had been worried out of her mind, Kane had been out getting drunk.

Tornioli watched her sympathetically.

'He will be all right, of course, *signorina*, although last night could so easily have ended in tragedy.'

She glanced up sharply at the young police officer. 'Tragedy?'

The man shrugged eloquently. 'The *doctore* must have devoured the contents of a distillery and somehow contrived to fall in the river. He was fished out of the Tevere near the Ponte Duca d'Aosta just after midnight.'

Her jaw dropped. 'What was he doing there?'

'Who can say?' the captain replied. 'Only the fact that he was so full of alcohol kept him alive in the water. We fished him out of the river and let him sleep for a while. There was a wallet on him which identified him, but not where he was staying. We were going to refer the matter to the American Embassy, but when he came round he kept mumbling your name and address, so we brought him here.'

Julie bit her lip. Damn the man's alcoholism!

The young policeman gazed round with some embarrassment. 'The *doctore* is staying here, no?'

'Yes, Dr Kane is staying here,' she replied with perhaps a little bitterness in her voice.

'In that case, you will have his passport, *signorina*. I will have to check it for my report.'

She moved to Kane's canvas grip and rummaged through it. His passport and a few odd items were tucked among the dirty clothes.

The police captain thumbed through it, nodding to himself.

'Dr Kane is a ...' he frowned at the unfamiliar word. 'This is to do with medicine?'

'No,' Julie replied. 'Old documents. He is an expert in old documents.'

The policeman sighed and handed her back the passport.

'I suggest that when Dr Kane is in full possession of his faculties, you should tell him to stick to his old documents and not alcohol. With your permission?'

He went to the window and gave a piercing whistle.

'If you would open the street door, *signorina*?'

Julie pressed the intercom.

A few minutes later a policeman helped David Kane into

the apartment. Julie's eyes widened as she saw what a state he was in. His eyes were red and bulging, his hair was a tangled mat. His cheeks were pale, and beard stubble caused a bluish tinge to accentuate their sunken appearance. Even now he looked barely sober. His clothes clung to him in a damp, muddied mess. He was hardly in control of his faculties and had to be helped to a chair in which he sprawled helplessly.

'Are you sure it is all right to leave him, *signorina*?' demanded Tornioli.

Julie nodded. 'It will be all right,' she said.

Captain Tornioli replaced his cap and saluted. 'Good day, *signorina*.'

He and his companion left and Julie shut the door after them, standing with her back to it for a moment as she gazed with distaste at Kane.

'Did you have to choose this particular moment to get yourself drunk?' she suddenly snapped.

Kane blinked and tried to sit up. 'Julie?' The words were a slur.

'Damn you! Damn you, David Kane!' she cried in frustration.

Kane rolled his head from side to side. 'Julie... not drunk... no... wait...'

He tried to grab her arm as she began to turn away. There was no power in his grip and his hand fell away.

'Listen...' he tried to articulate, with desperation in his voice. 'Tellaro, got me. Adriano... got me...'

She turned back and stared down at him. 'What are you saying?'

'Tellaro got me. Gun-point. Villa Tiburtina. Made me... drink whisky. Threw me... in river. Tried killing... kill me.'

He tried to chuckle, but it sounded like a coughing fit.

'They forgot... forgot I'm a lush... more resistance to alcohol... threw me in river. I just... just floated... away!'

She stared at him in horror.

Suddenly Kane slid from the chair onto the floor and began to snore.

Julie bit her lip wondering what on earth she should do. There was nothing she could do until Kane came round. She walked into the bedroom, took a blanket and placed it over Kane's crumpled body where he lay. He would just have to sleep it off.

Cosima groaned as the persistent shrill of the telephone roused her from her sleep. Beside her, Adriano grunted and reached out of the bed.

'*Pronto?*' he mumbled thickly.

On the other end of the wire Giona Tellaro was saying coldly: 'You fumbled the job, Adriano, and that I do not like. You are supposed to be a professional.'

Adriano came wide-awake. 'What are you saying?' he gasped.

'Do not leave Rome,' his cousin's icy tone went on. 'I will come to see you this morning.'

Adriano put down the receiver with a gesture of annoyance.

'What is it?' yawned Cosima, struggling to sit up in the bed.

'A little unexpected business,' Adriano exhaled sharply. 'We might have to stay in Rome for a few more days.'

Cosima swore.

Adriano turned to her with a thin smile. 'We'll be on our way to Palermo soon, I promise. Tell you what,' he glanced at his wristwatch, 'why don't we have breakfast now and then I'll give you some money and you can take yourself off to the shops for the day while I sort out this business?'

She pouted sulkily. 'I don't like Rome. Can't you put off this damned business of yours?'

Adriano reached for a cigarette and lit it, letting the smoke curl upwards from his thin lips. 'In my business,' he said quietly, 'you don't refuse business.'

Two hours later Giona Tellaro sat across the desk from his cousin, his face creased with anger.

'It is remarkably fortunate that a man in my position has

good contacts with the police,' he said tersely. 'I made a point of checking reports of any incidents connected with the river last night. It was as well I did so.'

Adriano shrugged helplessly. 'The man has nine lives! I don't understand it. We poured two bottles of whisky into him and pushed him over the Ponte Milbio. He should have drowned within minutes.'

Tellaro pressed his fingertips together and sneered. 'Instead he went floating away down the river to the next bridge, which is where the police fished him out. It is lucky for us that they thought he was simply a drunk who had fallen in the river. But if he starts to talk . . .' Tellaro made an ugly gesture with his mouth.

'He should have drowned,' muttered Adriano again.

'He must be found and eliminated. Every moment he is at liberty, he is a danger to us.'

'What can I do if the police have him?' demanded his cousin.

'My contact said that the police captain in charge took him somewhere . . .'

'To the American Embassy?' Adriano asked anxiously.

'No. To a private apartment.'

'Not to Rosenburg's place?'

'I don't think so. If the police knew about Rosenburg then they would be holding Kane as a suspect. No, they took him somewhere else. My contact is going to make a few discreet enquiries. When he gets back to me, you must go and ensure that you are more thorough with your work.'

'If he knows someone well enough to go to their apartment then it means that he has shared his knowledge with them,' Adriano said thoughtfully.

'That will be for you to discover and to rectify. You will ensure that no one is able to speak about the papyrus.'

Adriano rose and then hesitated. 'I find it strange that a priest should sanction killing.'

Tellaro's eyes narrowed as he answered his cousin's challenge. 'Is it so odd? For countless centuries priests have blessed armies in the cause of just wars and given them succour and comfort in their trials. Now we are fighting another war, a war to preserve Holy Mother Church, a war against irreligion, against atheism, which is corrupting Christianity across the face of the world. I see no moral question to be argued.'

'What is in this papyrus which could harm the Church?'

'It is a forgery,' snapped Tellaro. 'It must be! Yet Kane will use it to destroy us, and therefore he must be destroyed, as well as anyone who stands with him.'

'I agree,' nodded Adriano absently. 'Never wait for your enemy to grow strong. Nevertheless . . .'

'Holy Mother Church must prevail,' said Tellaro. 'What is the damnation of one soul compared to the salvation of many, those generations yet to come who may grow up in the Faith?'

Adriano grunted assent. He didn't particularly care one way or another. He was not religious. Oh, he would describe himself as a Catholic, true. He supposed that there was a God, although he never really thought about such matters. He supposed that the Pope was infallible, as were the priests who exercised authority in his name. But Adriano felt that the time to consider the question of religion and God was when he was nearer death and, God willing, that would be some time yet!

Nevertheless, it was the first time he had seen the glow of fanaticism in his cousin's dark, brooding eyes.

It frightened him a little.

Chapter Twenty

Kane awoke and groaned in pain at the sudden spasm in his stomach.

'David?'

He squinted upwards, through the terrifying pins and needles which tingled around his eyes. He could see the concerned face of Julie peering down at him. He shut his eyes, counted to ten and opened them again. He felt terrible. His stomach seemed to be in the process of being sliced by a sharp knife. His heart pounded and his head throbbed with nausea.

'David, are you all right?' Her voice was persistent.

The events of the last twenty-four hours came slowly back to his agonised mind. He tried to push himself upwards.

'Julie, what time is it?'

'Five o'clock in the afternoon. The police brought you here early this morning.'

He blinked. 'I wasn't drunk. I...'

She smiled softly and squeezed his arm.

'I know. What happened? You mentioned something about the Tellaros.'

Kane made some chewing motions with his mouth. It felt dry and painful. 'Do you have some coffee?'

'Yes. Can you get up onto the couch? You slumped on the floor and I couldn't move you.'

While she went into the kitchen, Kane slowly climbed to his knees and hauled himself onto the nearby couch. His body seemed to be burning with a prickling fire. She seemed to return immediately. When he held out his hand to take the cup from her he found it shook so uncontrollably that he could not hold it. She had to place the cup against his lips while he took a few experimental sips.

'God, I'd give anything for a shot of Paraldehyde.'

'What's that?'

'No idea except that it's the quickest goddam cure for a hangover that I know of.'

'What happened, David?'

He told her briefly.

'I feel like death. I would have been dead only I've had some practice with alcohol,' he ended with bitter irony. Then his eyes widened. 'Did Rosenburg get back to you?'

He didn't notice how her face paled.

'Yes,' she said. 'Yes, he did.'

'What did he have to say?'

She bit her lip, paused a moment, and then told him. 'He sounded excited. When he heard that you weren't here, he asked me to go over to his apartment. I was not long in getting there . . . but he was dead. There was blood over his shirt. I couldn't tell whether he had been stabbed or shot. The place was ransacked. Then I noticed that he held some torn fragments of papers in his hands . . . the papers which you gave him, David. It was as if he had been trying to hang on to them and the killers had taken them.'

'Rosenburg was murdered?' Kane was shocked. His mind was racing. 'What time did you get to his apartment?'

Julie frowned, trying to recollect.

'Just after four o'clock, I think.'

Kane gave a terrible moan which frightened the girl.

'Do I have my wallet on me?'

She hunted through his pockets and came out with the wallet.

'Is the scrap of paper on which you wrote Rosenburg's telephone number there?'

She peered through the contents and shook her head.

'They must have traced Rosenburg through the number. Damn it! Damn them!' His voice was full of violence.

'How did they get it?' Julie asked quietly.

148

'I thought they had missed it when they searched me. Now I remember. Adriano took it with the wallet and he and Salvatore left. They must have gone straight to Rosenburg's apartment and killed him to retrieve the papers.'

They sat in silence for a long while.

'What shall we do, David?'

Kane swung off the couch and attempted to stand up. He doubled up almost at once as the stomach pains hit him. Julie helped him back on the couch.

'What can I do?' she said helplessly.

Kane had broken into a cold sweat.

'I think I must have alcoholic poisoning or something,' he grunted. 'I'll just have to hope that it works through my system.' He paused. 'Do you still have my bag?'

She nodded.

'Is there a plain brown envelope in it?'

She went to check and returned with the envelope.

Kane grinned painfully. 'There are two photographic prints of the papyrus. It means we still have some proof, some hold over Tellaro and his cousin.'

Julie shivered.

'Is there any way they can trace you here?' Kane shook his head.

'No, I didn't mention you. There was nothing to link me to you . . . unless they saw you at Rosenburg's apartment and followed you. But then they would have come here before now.'

'Perhaps they think you are dead?'

'Knowing Tellaro, I would guess that he'll soon find out that I am not. We must think of a plan to . . .' He groaned loudly as the pain struck him again.

'There must be something I can do?' she asked in desperation.

'Not unless you know some friendly doctor,' he replied between clenched teeth.

'Well . . .' she stood up abruptly. 'Will you be all right for about half an hour?'

'Yeah . . .' he winced.

The girl already had her coat on. 'Don't let anyone in until I get back.'

Kane forced a wry grin. 'You can count on it.'

The pain must have hit him with a terrific force and caused him to black out because the next thing he knew was that Julie was bending over him.

'David?'

He tried to open his eyes and smile, but only succeeded in giving an inane grimace which frightened her a little.

'I have something for you. You must swallow it.'

Dimly he realised he would take cyanide if it would cure the terrible pain.

She held a small glass in her hand full of a milky-looking liquid. She pressed it to his lips.

The liquid went down his throat and for a moment nothing happened. Then he suddenly felt his face turn hot and a blinding pain struck his temples. He opened his mouth and began to gasp for breath. Pains, excruciating pains, pierced his chest and his vision blurred as the room spun out of focus. Then he was swimming slowly through velvet blackness.

Cosima was having breakfast when Adriano entered the room. There were shadows under his eyes and she wondered where he had spent the night. He moved to the table and poured a cup of coffee, sprawling in a chair.

'I want you to go back to Palermo,' he said suddenly. 'I'll follow you later.'

She stared at him nervously. 'I don't want to leave you, Adriano.'

He grimaced. 'It will not be for long. Just for a few days at the most.'

'Where were you all day yesterday and last night?' asked Cosima petulantly.

Adriano shrugged. 'I had some important business to attend to,' he said shiftily.

Cosima looked unhappy, so Adriano stood up and came to her side, placing a hand on her shoulder.

150

'Listen, I'm not trying to ditch you. You know that. Here are the keys to my apartment in Palermo. You go there and I'll come before the week's out.'

She took the keys gravely. 'You'll join me in a few days?'

Adriano nodded reassuringly.

'I do not like your cousin,' she said vehemently.

'He is a prince of the Church,' Adriano said without disguising the sarcasm in his voice.

'He frightens me.'

'Never mind. You probably won't have to see him again.'

'You won't be more than a few days?' she repeated, anxious for his reassurances.

He took out some notes from his pocket. 'Here's some money. I'm sorry I won't have time to run you to the airport, but you can get a taxi.'

The girl looked suddenly thoughtful. 'If you are going to be a few days then I could take the train to Naples and go and see my mother. Then I could catch the ferry from Naples directly to Palermo. I haven't seen my mother for six months.'

Adriano nodded absently. 'As you wish,' he said.

Cosima noticed his preoccupied expression. 'Your business has something to do with the strange *doctore*, the one working upstairs, hasn't it?'

Adriano scowled. 'What do you know about that?' he demanded harshly.

The girl looked frightened. 'Nothing. Nothing. Except that he was working for your cousin and now he makes trouble for you. And he ran away with something belonging to your cousin.'

Adriano said grimly, 'It is wise, Cosima, to know nothing. To say nothing. You understand?'

The girl nodded unhappily.

'You must not worry about these things,' Adriano went on. 'Anyway, the *doctore* will not be making trouble for much longer.'

When Kane came to, he was amazed at how bright the room

was. The sun seemed to be shining through the windows with a blinding ferocity.

His mouth felt dry; he was dehydrated and uncomfortable. Then he was aware that his headache and the terrible cramping pains in his stomach were gone. He felt weak and sore but there was no pain. He raised his hand and stared at it. It shook slightly but not with the previous uncontrolled trembling. There were none of the tell-tale shaking symptoms racking his body. His mind was clear. He felt refreshed. Slowly, wonderingly, he eased himself up on the couch.

A clock across the room was striking the hours.

Ten o'clock? It must be ten o'clock in the morning. Somehow he had lost an entire day and night.

He opened his mouth and tried to summon enough saliva to lubricate his throat.

'Julie?'

There was no movement in the apartment.

'Julie?' he called more loudly, feeling a sudden panic.

He swung off the couch. There was no feeling of dizziness, no nausea. Just a feeling of general weakness. He pushed back the blanket covering him. God! He smelt as if he had just emerged from a sewer. His clothes were stained and filthy. They stank with a foulness that caused him to retch. His face was unshaved and pricked with dirt caked by dried sweat. He made an effort to stand, and succeeded.

'Julie?'

He heard a movement across the apartment and the bedroom door swung open.

Julie Gambretti stood on the threshold in her nightdress, rubbing the sleep from her eyes.

'David? How do you feel now? Get back on the couch. Are you all right?'

She moved across to him, concern on her features. Kane smiled briefly as he allowed himself to be pushed gently back into a sitting position.

'I'm OK. Really,' he protested unconvincingly. 'I feel fine. A bit weak but OK. What happened?'

'I know a doctor in Celio. She's a friend of mine. I went to see her and explained your condition. She gave me something. Dis... something or other,' she frowned. 'Disulfiram?'

Kane shook his head. 'I don't know what it was, but it certainly saved my life. I wouldn't like to go through that again.'

The girl smiled nervously. 'She told me that it would probably make you pass out and that you would sleep for a while.'

'I certainly did.' He sniffed. 'I'd better get into a shower and get these clothes off.' He paused. 'Damn it. I've nothing else to wear.'

'Don't worry. While you're having a shower and scrub, I'll go down to Upims, the department store. Just tell me your sizes and I'll pick up a few things for you. Do you want some coffee first?'

Kane grimaced. 'A weak tea would be better. Coffee might rip my insides out at this moment.'

She hurried to the partitioned kitchen and began to prepare tea while Kane listed his clothes' sizes.

'While you are at it,' he added, 'you better get some newspapers to see if there is anything about Rosenburg's death.'

A wave of anxiety crossed her face. 'What are we going to do, David?'

He shrugged. 'I'm not sure. Maybe telephone Tellaro and let him know I still have photographs of the papyrus. Try a sort of Mexican stand-off. It might work. But first things first! a cup of tea and a shower and new clothes. Then I'll feel human again.'

'You had better not even sniff alcohol for a while,' advised Julie.

After they had tea, Julie went to get dressed while Kane stripped off his dirty clothing and went into the bathroom to run the shower.

After a while Kane heard Julie call out that she was leaving and heard the door slam behind her.

He finished shaving, splashed again in the hot jet of water, towelled vigorously and spent a long time cleaning his teeth and gargling with a mouth-wash he discovered in the cabinet.

Then he stood gazing at himself critically in the full-length mirror in the bathroom. His body looked pale and emaciated with nasty red blotches. It was entirely out of condition. The last few years had taken their toll. He frowned. The last few years belonged to someone else, not to him. Janine, the New York drunk, they were no longer a part of him. Rome was suddenly the reality. Rome and Julie Gambretti! He shivered slightly and found no good reason why he should do so.

A few moments later, he had found a plastic garbage-bag in the kitchen and was picking up the relics of his clothing, first removing his wallet and papers, then depositing them in the bag. He made himself another cup of weak tea, and sipping at it slowly, went back into the living-room.

There was a desk in one corner on which stood an electric typewriter and several sheets of paper. He wandered over and looked down. It was some article Julie was writing about the Italian film industry at Cinecittà. Setting down his cup he wandered into the bedroom, smiling at the disorder of strewn clothes and the forest of bottles of perfume and make-up, the countless lotions and lipsticks which littered the dressing-table.

On one side of the bedroom, French windows gave access onto a small roof-garden, obviously looked after with loving care. A riot of pot plants stood on terracotta tiles and there were a couple of sun-loungers under an umbrella shade.

The sun was blazing down from a midday azure sky. Kane moved out onto the roof garden and stretched in its rays, feeling its fierce glow kiss his pale skin for the first time in years. He wished he had a pair of sun-glasses. Perhaps he could find some lotion and take advantage of the sun while he tried to work out what the next step was.

He moved to the edge of the terrace and gazed down into the street below.

He was about to turn away when he caught sight of a familiar car at the far end of the street. It was parked at an intersection which gave it a commanding view of the door of the apartment block below. It was a large black Mercedes and the dread of recognition caused Kane a sudden stab of physical pain around his heart. A tall, swarthy man stood leaning against one of its wings, smoking a cigarette.

Kane stood stock-still, fear setting his body trembling.

There was no mistaking the dark, sinister figure of Adriano Tellaro.

Chapter Twenty-one

The sound of a key being turned in the lock of the apartment door brought Kane hurrying back into the bedroom, desperately searching for some weapon. The door of the apartment swung open and Julie's voice called out gaily: 'I'm back!'

Kane leaned against the frame of the bedroom door and let out a deep sigh of relief. Julie heeled the door shut behind her and gazed at him in surprise.

'You look all in,' she commented as she threw her packages down. 'You're not feeling ill again?'

Without replying Kane hurried to the apartment door and put the chain on while she watched in bewilderment.

'What is it, David?'

'Adriano Tellaro is parked outside,' he said shortly. 'Didn't you see the large black Mercedes?'

Her face went white.

'I didn't see anyone. Are you sure?'

He took her by the arm and led her through the bedroom to the roof garden.

'Just glance down the street towards the intersection.'

She followed his directions. 'There's a black Mercedes with a tall man leaning against it.'

'That's Adriano Tellaro. He must have traced me here.'

Julie bit her lip, anxiety tightening her features. 'What shall we do? Call the police?'

Kane hesitated and then shook his head. 'No; you know that they wouldn't believe my story. There would be all sorts of complications. Can you imagine what their reaction

156

would be if I claimed that a cardinal of the Catholic Church was trying to kill me to prevent me revealing a Vatican document which might destroy Christianity as we know it?'

She grimaced wryly and followed Kane back to the living-room.

'We'll have to slip out and evade Tellaro somehow,' he said. His eyes fell on the parcels. 'Did you manage to get me some clothes?'

'Yes.'

She began to undo the parcels with a preoccupied air. She had bought him a couple of shirts, a pair of casual trousers, socks, shoes, underwear and a lightweight casual jacket. He took them into the bathroom and soon re-emerged. It felt good to be clean and in control once more.

Julie was preparing a light lunch. It was obvious that her mind was not on it. He watched as she automatically beat two eggs in a basin, mixed with Parmesan cheese and fine semolina. To this she added chicken broth and stirred it into a fine cream. Then she heated the rest of the broth and when it was nearly boiling she poured in the mixture and beat it vigorously with a fork, leaving it until it had nearly come to the boil.

'Stracciatella,' she smiled in reply to his unasked question. 'It's the best thing to eat with an upset stomach.'

They were silent over the soup.

'Where did you park your car?' Kane suddenly asked.

'Where I always park it, in the side-street.'

Kane's eyes widened hopefully. 'You mean that Adriano might not have seen you arrive in the car?'

Julie nodded.

'That means he doesn't know your car.'

'Is that good?'

'It might give us an edge. Is there any way we can get to your car without going out of the front door which Adriano is watching?'

'No, not...' Julie suddenly smiled and gestured with her head towards the bedroom. 'Yes, of course! There is a fire escape which leads down from the roof garden.'

'Then after lunch we better be on our way.'

'On our way where?' demanded the girl.

'Somewhere where the Tellaros won't find us until we sort out a plan.'

'Look, David, why not let me tell Charlie Burgano...he's the chief of the Italo-American News Agency here. If we can't go to the police, let's tell the story to the papers. We have to tell someone because the more people we tell the safer we would become. The Tellaros can't start killing everyone, can they?'

Kane hesitated. 'The point is not simply telling people but getting them to believe us.'

'You have those photographs of the papyrus?'

'True, but it would be better if I had those reports which Rosenburg had.'

He suddenly clicked his fingers. 'Rosenburg! Did you get the newspapers?'

Julie went to one of the bags and pulled out several daily newspapers. They each took a couple and scanned them carefully. There was a short paragraph in *Il Tempo* and *Corriere della Sera* announcing the discovery of Rosenburg's body. It was as Kane was looking through the pages of *La Republica* that after a sharp intake of breath he let out a whistle.

'Is there something in there?'

'I'll say,' Kane smiled. 'And it might be the answer to the problem. Remember that I said I only knew one Biblical scholar, named Myles, of the University College of Los Angeles?'

'Vaguely.'

'He arrived in Italy today.'

'In Rome?'

'No, Naples,' Kane grinned fiercely. 'We must get to see him; take him the photographs and tell him the story.' He turned back to the newspaper and began to read aloud in English. 'Professor Stanton Myles, well known American authority and writer on Biblical studies, will be giving a series of lectures at the University of Naples. He arrived today at the Naples International Airport at Capodichino. He will be speaking on... etcetera, etcetera.'

Kane put down the paper with an eager expression. 'If I can get Myles on our side then we'll be OK.'

Julie looked worried. 'Look what happened to Rosenburg.'

'Yes, but this time we must ensure that the Tellaros don't know that we are contacting Myles.' Kane stood up. 'We better start moving. Adriano is probably only waiting for the right moment, or until it gets dark, before he attempts to come up here.'

'I'd better let Charlie Burgano know that I won't be in Rome for a few days.'

Kane was about to protest but he shrugged. It could not do any harm. 'Tell him that you're going to Milan or Florence... somewhere north... just in case it filters back to Tellaro.'

'Charlie wouldn't...' Julie began to protest.

'Better not trust anyone for the moment,' Kane interrupted.

While Julie was making the telephone call, Kane cleared away the luncheon things and put the newspapers and what few belongings he had in his bag. He found himself humming softly to himself. It was as if danger had suddenly resurrected him from his netherworld of alcohol and turned him into a human being again.

Julie finished her phone call and began packing a small suitcase. As a journalist, she was used to travelling light. Kane noted that she also packed her camera-case.

He suddenly swore. 'I hate to ask you, Julie, after what you've done already but do you have any money? I've probably got enough on me for one good meal and that's about all.'

'Don't worry about that. I've enough.'

'It might be wise to make a detour and not go straight to Naples. If Tellaro reads about Myles in the newspapers, he might put two and two together.'

'We could go to a friend of mine for tonight. He's an Englishman who has a villa not far from Montecassino. It's on the way to Naples.'

Kane glanced quizzically at her. 'An Englishman?'

'Yes. He's a thriller writer who decided to live over here. I met him a few years ago and we became friends.'

She did not volunteer any further information and Kane realised, with some surprise, that he felt pangs of jealousy. Still, it was a good idea. After all, it would be late by the time they reached Naples if they left now. Better to stay outside the city and make the journey there more leisurely. It would be safer, too, if Tellaro was tracking them.

He went back through the bedroom to see whether Adriano was still at the car. In fact the tall figure of Adriano had been replaced by the stocky figure of Salvatore. Kane wondered what they were planning. Were they simply waiting until dark?

In the kitchen Julie was putting some sandwiches into a bag. 'We might as well use up the perishable food,' she said defensively.

Kane grinned. 'Anything you say. Are you all packed?'

'All packed,' she said.

Kane took her bag as well as his own and started for the bedroom.

The door bell buzzed.

They froze for a moment.

'Adriano,' whispered Kane as the second series of buzzes came from the apartment bell. He stood undecided. If they didn't answer it, perhaps Adriano would attempt to break in. They needed to buy as much time as possible.

'Answer the intercom,' he told the girl gruffly. 'If it is Adriano, stall him. Pretend that you don't know what he's talking about, especially if he mentions me. Threaten him with the police. Anything.'

Julie crossed to the intercom. She looked unhappy but she braced her shoulders. *'Pronto?'*

'Signorina Gambretti?'

Even from across the room Kane recognised the harsh tones of Adriano Tellaro.

'Yes?'

Kane hoped that Adriano would not notice the tension in Julie's voice.

'I am a reporter from *Il Tempo*,' the lies flowed easily. 'I understand that you have a Dr Kane staying with you. The man who was rescued from the river the other day. We would like to speak with him about the incident. May I come up?'

Julie glanced across at Kane. He shook his head violently. She turned back to the intercom.

'You are misinformed,' she said, trying to keep her voice cold. 'There is no one here of that name.'

'But the police said . . .'

'Furthermore, I don't believe you are a reporter. I have heard how people break into apartments to rob or rape. I am going to call the police!'

She clicked off the switch.

Kane hurried to the roof terrace and peered into the road. He could see Adriano standing below in indecision and guessed at the man's bewilderment. Then the Sicilian turned and began to walk slowly back to the Mercedes. Kane wondered whether he was going to telephone his cousin for more orders. He clicked his fingers as the idea struck him.

In the living room he asked Julie: 'Can you get the telephone number of the Villa Tiburtina?'

It was a simple task of looking up the name T. Jonah in the telephone directory.

Kane was not surprised when the impersonal tones of Cardinal Giona Tellaro answered.

'Tellaro, this is Kane,' he said clearly and without preamble.

There was a silence at the other end of the line.

'I still have some photographs of the papyrus and they are deposited with a certain newspaper in case anything happens to me. So call your cousin off, Tellaro.'

'*Doctore . . .*' the voice was hesitant. 'We could come to an arrangement . . . ?'

'No deals, Tellaro,' snapped Kane. 'Just call off your jackals or I tell the newspaper to go ahead.'

'You are bluffing, Dr Kane.'

'Try me!' snapped Kane, putting down the receiver.

Julie looked puzzled. 'Do you think that will work?'

Kane smiled and shook his head. 'No, but I am hoping that Tellaro will attempt to get in touch with Adriano to get an assessment of the situation, which might keep them preoccupied for a while. In the meantime...'

He picked up the bags again and hurried to the roof garden. He could see the figure of Adriano bent into the front of the car. He had suspected that the Mercedes was fitted with a car-telephone.

'Let's go!'

Julie went down the fire-escape first, clutching her shopping bag with the food. Kane followed her, clasping the two cases in one hand. He still felt weak, but he was able to negotiate the iron ladder without much difficulty. They clambered down into a small yard full of the smells of fresh washing and the odour of a tomato sauce simmering with herbs in a cooking pot nearby. A dog started to bark somewhere. Julie moved to the gate. It was open and she peered out.

'All clear,' she whispered.

Her car, a Fiat Supermirafiori stood parked a short distance away. She unlocked the boot while Kane stowed the bags away. By the time he sat in the passenger seat, she was all ready to move off. They turned down the road in the opposite direction to where the threatening Mercedes was parked, and threaded their way across Aventino, heading at first as though they were going towards the city centre but swinging at a right angle at the Porta Capena Obelish, which brought them into the great green expanse of the park beyond. Kane kept a careful watch behind as they sped through the park to the gate known as the Porta Latina, which gave access onto the Via Latina, and swung through the southern suburbs of the city until they picked up the ring road leading to the Autostrada del Sole, the highway of the sun, which sped southward towards Naples.

Only when they were lost among the fast stream of traffic heading south out of Rome did Kane relax in his seat.

Chapter Twenty-two

They drove south on the autostrada for an hour and a half without saying much, each locked in their own thoughts. It was Kane who finally roused himself as he saw the road signs pointing to the town of Cassino.

'Where exactly are we heading?'

'We'll be turning off pretty soon now,' replied Julie. 'I'm heading for a little village up in the mountains of Terme di Súio.'

'Is that where this friend of yours lives?'

Julie nodded.

'His name is Ian Wallace. You might have read some of his books?'

'No,' Kane was emphatic. 'I never had time for fiction, least of all thrillers.'

Across to the east of the autostrada they could see the dark outline of Montecassino rising against the sky, perhaps the most famous image of Italy from the old newsreels of the Second World War. The famous Benedictine Monastery had been used as one of the vital defence points in the German Gustav Line during 1944, and had held up the Allied advance for months. Finally the Allies had to make the decision to bomb the monastery in order to break the fanatical German defence.

It was now late and the sun was hanging low over the western mountains between the autostrada and the stretch of sea known as the Golfo di Gaeta.

At the signs announcing the exits to Minturno and Scauri, Julie turned and swung round to the west, climbing over the mountain passes and chasing the setting sun. Across the slopes of the mountains, the olive groves were shimmering silver-green in the gleaming light.

They eventually came to a hilltop where, hanging breathtakingly to its summit, an old town was perched. It was small; not much more than a village. It shone brilliantly, white and pink and gold.

'That's Castelforte,' Julie said as she wrestled with the wheel, easing the car up the curving roadway. 'That's where Ian lives.'

'Is he a boyfriend?'

Kane asked the question with an abruptness that caused the girl to frown.

'Not exactly,' she replied. 'We've been out a few times but I wasn't really his type.'

The streets of the village were almost deserted as they drove through it. She slowed and drew to a stop at a small villa perched on the hillside beyond. The place commanded a stunning view of the valley through which a wide river ambled peacefully. Julie hit the car horn a couple of times before climbing out, followed by Kane.

A well-built man of forty with greying hair emerged from the villa, saw the girl and waved, coming down from the terrace of the building. Kane couldn't see his eyes, for he wore dark glasses, white slacks and sandals. He was muscular and good-looking.

'Julie, darling!' the man enthused in English. 'How fantastic to see you.'

Julie and the man kissed on both cheeks, Italian-style.

'Are you passing through?' he demanded.

'Not exactly, Ian,' Julie replied, turning towards Kane. 'Ian, I want you to meet my friend David. David, this is Ian.'

Wallace smiled. It was the superficial baring of white teeth which Kane associated with Hollywood film stars. They exchanged meaningless pleasantries.

'Well,' Wallace said turning back to Julie, 'what are you doing in this part of the country?'

'Well...' Julie hesitated. 'As a matter of fact we were

wondering if you could put us up for the night?'

Wallace's reply was immediate. 'No problem at all.'

'That's very good of you, Mr... er Ian,' muttered Kane.

'Not at all. In fact, you're just in time to join me for dinner. And you can tell me what you are doing in these parts. I'm not exactly on the tourist route, am I, Julie?'

'Lost them?' There was a dangerous note in Giona Tellaro's voice.

Adriano shifted his weight uneasily. 'They must have escaped down the fire-escape.'

Tellaro's eyes flashed in anger. He drummed a threatening tattoo on the desk before him.

'It wasn't my fault,' protested Adriano. 'They were in the apartment just before you called me on the car-telephone. I went back immediately afterwards and managed to get in by bribing the *portinaio*. They'd gone.'

Tellaro's eyes widened a fraction. So that was why Kane had made that stupid blustering telephone call! He knew that it would distract attention.

'They must be found.'

Adriano shrugged hopelessly. 'They could be anywhere. I don't see how...' his voice trailed off as the dark scowl of his cousin turned upon him.

'Didn't you check the girl's apartment for addresses of friends, car registration documents and so on? Most people leave duplicates of car documents at home.'

Adriano bit his lip. 'I was only looking for Kane's papers,' he confessed.

Tellaro sighed in exasperation. 'Get back there and search properly,' he snapped. 'Look for anything that will help us identify the girl's car and give a clue to where they might have gone. We are in this too deeply now. We must stop them.'

Ian Wallace leaned back in his wicker chair on the terrace of his villa and surveyed the lights twinkling across the valley below. The chorus of chirping cicada which had risen all around them, had stopped abruptly with the final setting of the sun. Now the scent of rosemary lay almost oppressively heavy on the night air. A few mosquitos darted here and there, attracted by the lights.

'Don't you find it remote here?' Kane asked.

Wallace smiled and removed the small cheroot from the corner of his mouth.

'Remote? No. I've lived here a few years now. It's a nice place. The town is called "the town of teachers" because so many of them live here. That means there is plenty of intelligent conversation to be had. Besides, I prefer to be up here in the mountains. Now down below is real mosquito country. It's all low-lying swampland. In fact, Latina is the fabled area where Mussolini drained the bogs. Remember the apologists' catchphrase for Mussolini? At least he made the trains run on time and drained the bogs! Well, it was around Cisterna di Latina that he did that... the name speaks for itself. They still think well of Il Duce in these parts.'

'What made you settle here?' Kane was curious.

Wallace shrugged. 'I was exploring the area one day. I came to visit the place where my father was killed. I just fell in love with it.'

Kane raised his eyebrows and Wallace gestured with his cheroot towards the winding river below, now just a silvery glint in the darkness.

'That's the Garigliano where some of the bitterest fighting in Italy took place in 1944. The Germans were fighting against the Allied advance on Rome and the mountains here were natural fortifications. It took months to break through. My father was in Alexander's Fifth Army and was one of thousands killed crossing the river.' He paused.

'I'm sorry,' Kane said awkwardly.

'No need to be,' replied Wallace. 'I was a babe-in-arms at the time. I can't remember him. Yet it was his death, a sort of curiosity about the place, that brought me here. It's a fascinating area full of spa hotels, sulphur baths and hot springs. The hills are extinct volcanos, you see. And people still come down here for "the cure" as they did in the early days of this century. I was wandering around for a few weeks until I came on Castelforte and saw its old walls and mediaeval tower, and that marvellous archway to the castle entrance, which you really must see. Then there is the old square stone tower of St John the Baptist's Church, which dominates the town. It's almost unique.'

Again there was a pause.

'I suppose I sound like a tour guide?'

Julie, who had been sitting silently, sipping her coffee, shook her head. 'It's a beautiful spot, Ian.'

'But you haven't told me what brings you here.'

Kane's mind had been working rapidly. He could not say that he liked Wallace much. Oh, he had overcome the vague feelings of jealousy which he had felt for the man. No, that wasn't it. He found Wallace too sauve, too smooth. Too self-opiniated. Maybe he had reason to be. He was a well-known writer. While Kane had never read any of his thrillers, he knew that the man was popular especially in the United States. In his position Wallace could actually be a help. He made up his mind to tell Wallace the basic story.

Wallace sat in silence as Kane launched into the tale, giving a brief outline, including details of the papyrus, his escape from the villa, the death of Rosenburg, the attempt to kill him and the escape from Julie's apartment. There was a long silence before Wallace turned to Julie for some kind of confirmation of Kane's story.

'It's true, Ian, every word,' she said.

Wallace sighed deeply. 'I couldn't have written a story like that,' he reflected. 'It's just too incredible.'

Kane snorted sardonically. 'It's believable enough. Check out Rosenburg's death.'

'As a matter of fact, I've already read about Rosenburg in *La Stampa*. The newspapers are trying to connect his death with a Palestinian political assassination.' He gazed thoughtfully at Kane. 'You claim that you have no doubts about the genuineness of this papyrus?'

'In so far as my knowledge took me. Rosenburg was the Biblical scholar and he was the only one who knew whether

167

the contents could be genuine.'

'Did he give any indication of what he thought?'

Julie intervened. 'In our initial talk he did say something that the contents *could* be genuine. But he was going to make a more thorough examination. Then he was . . .' She made a gesture of helplessness.

'Incredible,' said Wallace again. 'Do you realise the effect that such a revelation would have on the Christian world?'

'I'm not a theologian. In fact, I'm an agnostic,' Kane replied. 'I'm a palaeographer and I can only pronounce on what falls within my competency. What I find frightening, though, is that this cardinal is apparently so fanatical that he is prepared to stop this document being revealed to the public. That means, surely, that he is scared of what this document could do?'

Wallace grimaced cynically. 'You shouldn't find religious fanaticism a frightening thing. The history of European civilisation is simply a history of religious fanaticism and bigotry. Religious belief is an intangible and emotional thing, and people who have faith are likely to go to any lengths to defend it. People are prepared to die for it . . . and prepared to kill for it. It has been so for centuries. It still is. Man has not changed.'

Julie bent her head in agreement. 'I suppose you are right, Ian. After all, governments commit murder to further their political aims, to prevent secrets being leaked, and we accept that. Why not other organisations who have as much, if not more, to lose?'

'What are you going to do next?' pressed Wallace.

'I was hoping you might help,' replied Kane.

Wallace pursed his lips. 'Well, I'll certainly give the matter some thought. I do have some useful contacts, of course. What do you intend doing tomorrow?'

Julie was about to speak when Kane said 'Well, we were thinking of going up north, somewhere where Tellaro can't trace us, while we think about developments.'

'You could stay here.'

'We wouldn't want to put you in any danger,' Kane said.

'No, we'll go north.'

Wallace rose. 'Well, make yourselves at home. I have a woman who comes in at eight o'clock – I don't eat breakfast, but you can have coffee and rolls. Well, I feel it's time for bed . . .'

They all said goodnight and Wallace left them on the terrace.

Puzzled, Julie leaned forward. 'Why didn't you tell him about going to Naples to see this Professor Myles?' she whispered.

'I'm just keeping our options open. The less anyone knows about our contacts the better. We will see what Wallace has to suggest first. Then we can see Myles. Until we get something sorted out it is better to assure our own safety as much as possible by not telling anyone about our movements.'

Julie reluctantly assented. 'All right, David, but I am sure we can trust Ian.'

'I'm not saying that I don't trust him. But the only way to survive is to completely cover our tracks.'

Julie rose. 'I'll turn in now,' she said, hesitating above his chair. Then, on impulse she bent down and kissed Kane softly on the forehead. 'Goodnight, David.'

He watched her walk into the villa with a warm feeling tingling within him.

Kane was dreaming. He was back in the apartment with Janine. She was dressing, smiling and talking about food. Yet this time he knew that she would not return; he knew that she was going out to be raped and killed, and he was trying to warn her, trying to stop her going. And all the while she was laughing and talking about food.

He reached out. Then Janine's face dissolved and it was Julie's face which laughed down at him.

Julie!

He had to warn her, stop her. He tried to cry out and hold her. But she was gone through the door. She was never coming back!

He awoke sitting up in bed, bathed in sweat. His hand was stretching out into the darkness before him. For a long while he remained in this position, his heart beating rapidly in his chest. Finally he shuddered and swung out of bed, glancing at the luminous dial of his wristwatch. It was nearly five o'clock. Nearly dawn. He felt thirsty.

He left the bedroom and went in search of the kitchen, padding bare-footed across the cold tiles to the refrigerator. There was a carton of orange juice inside and he found a glass.

The villa was deathly silent. Here, up in the mountains, the air carried the faintest sound. The thought was probably prompted by the noise which began to grow in volume. It was the soft hum of a distant car engine, revving as it twisted and turned along the mountain roads. Kane sipped at his drink wondering who could be abroad so early in this remote place, and driving so quickly through the mountain passes. The sound of the engine drew nearer and nearer, and then, to Kane's amazement, it stopped.

Wallace's villa was on the outskirts of the town, some way from any other building. Yet it seemed as if the car had stopped right outside. As he made for the window, Kane heard a movement in the house – someone opening a door and footsteps on the path outside. His curiosity aroused, he opened the door which led from the kitchen on to the terrace outside. He had on only his pyjama trousers but it was fairly warm outside. He padded to the corner of the villa, noticing the faint light in the sky which gave a strange cold clarity to everything.

He saw Wallace's thick-set figure striding down the path. Somewhere on the roadway a car door slammed and then a tall shadow emerged at the gateway.

'Wallace?'

'Yes, yes,' the man's voice was eager.

'Are they still with you?'

Kane did not wait to hear the answer. He had recognised the harsh tones of Adriano Tellaro. He felt as if his body had suddenly become weighed down by a coating of lead. He

170

turned and hurried back... yet every motion seemed so slow, so terribly slow, as if he were running through soft fine sand.

There was no time now to ask how Adriano had traced them.

He rushed into Julie's room and shook her awake violently.

'Adriano Tellaro!' he hissed. 'He's here . . . coming into the house!'

She blinked in confusion at him.

'No time to dress. Just grab your clothes and bag. Quickly!'

He ran into his room, scooped up his clothes, shoes and thrust them into the canvas grip. By the time he came back he found Julie doing the same. Without pausing to ensure she was ready, he grabbed her arm, threw open the French windows and hauled her onto the terrace.

Clad in nightclothes, bare-footed, they stood poised and stared about them.

'Head for the cover of the olive trees!' Kane ordered.

They scrambled across the low terrace wall, gasping as the stony ground cut into their bare feet. Across the garden which surrounded the villa, through the bordering shrubs and bushes, they ran. Then they were into the stubble grass of the mountainside and among the dark shadows of the olive trees.

Kane thought he heard a shout behind them but he did not stop to glance back. Still holding Julie's arm, he pushed forward, penetrating deeply into the orchard. Only after they had gone a considerable distance did he fling himself to the ground behind a clump of shrubs. The girl dropped beside him. They lay for a moment panting in unison, trying to recover their breath. Their clothes were torn and their feet bruised and cut.

The girl managed to recover first.

'What is it?' she gasped.

She had not really taken in what Kane had said when he had woken her. She had merely taken a lead from his

171

panicked flight.

'Adriano Tellaro. Wallace was just letting him into the villa.'

She opened her mouth to reply.

Not far away came a crashing through the undergrowth.

Chapter Twenty-three

Ian Wallace's voice came clearly through the olive grove.

'They've got away! You should have parked your car further away from the villa and come up on foot.'

Adriano was swearing volubly.

'They haven't escaped yet. They could not have gone far. Perhaps they are trying to circle round us and get back to their car. Come on, Wallace, let's disable it.'

The crashing noise retreated.

Kane could see, even in the half-shadows of the pale dawn light, that Julie's face was a mask of taut whiteness.

'How could Ian know that man? How could he betray us?'

'He's your friend,' snapped Kane and immediately regretted it. 'Sorry.'

The girl shrugged. 'It's me who should be sorry, David. I didn't know he knew Tellaro.'

'Maybe he didn't before we came. After all, I told him about the Tellaros and the Villa Tiburtina.'

'But why would he . . . ?'

'It's no use asking questions which neither of us can answer.' Kane said shortly. He stood up and grunted in pain. 'We'd better get some clothes on before we cut ourselves to pieces in this undergrowth or step on something nasty.'

There was just light enough to fumble into their clothes.

'Did you manage to grab everything?' asked Kane.

'Everything except my make-up bag and camera,' was Julie's mournful reply.

'Then we better put as much distance between Wallace's villa and us.'

'You heard what they said: we can't get back to the car.'

Kane nodded unperturbed. 'Do you know your way around these parts?'

'Fairly well.'

'Maybe we can hire another car from somewhere. It's no use trying to get the Fiat back.'

The birds were setting up their chorus now and the girl squinted across the dark hills. 'That's Mount Fuga,' she said, gesturing upwards. 'If we walk across these slopes, through the olive groves, we'll come to another small town called Súio Terme. There's a garage there where I have stopped for petrol when I've been here before. We might be able to hire a car there.'

'Let's hope we can keep out of Adriano's way.'

They picked up their bags and set off through the olive groves, now becoming alive with noise as the sun rose slowly over the distant hills. Below them they heard a car start up.

'That's probably Adriano,' Kane said.

'I just can't understand it,' replied Julie. 'Why would Ian want to betray us?'

Kane did not reply. Instead they walked on in silence through the trees which stretched for miles over the shoulders of the mountains, contouring the Garigliano valley. It was several hours later when Julie began to lead the descent on the cluster of buildings which constituted Súio Terme. The village seemed deserted. They found the garage but the place was shut with a sign *'chiuso'* hanging drunkenly from a petrol pump. Not far away another sign proclaimed 'Bar'. The door was open, with a beaded curtain protecting the interior. Kane led the way across the dusty square and pushed through it.

Julie followed him and slumped onto a wooden chair while Kane shouted: 'Hello!'

A stocky man, with a cigarette drooping from the corner of his mouth, appeared in the doorway behind the bar. He was clad in denims and a string vest and had what Kane always described as a *'pastasciutto* gut', a hard round protruding stomach.

174

'*Buon giorno,*' he said indifferently.

Kane felt as if his mouth was full of granite. He wanted a cold beer but asked for two coffees instead.

'Any chance of hiring a car here?'

The man gazed up from his ancient coffee machine with a frown.

Julie smiled at him. 'Our car has broken down not far from here and we want to be in Ceprano later today.'

Kane smiled approvingly as the girl mentioned a town to the north.

The fat man shrugged. 'My son, Luigi, runs the garage. He has a car, I think.'

He finished pouring the coffees and then turned with a shout which startled them both.

'Hey, Luigi! Get in here. Some customers.'

A younger version of the bar owner entered. It took them twenty minutes to agree terms on the hire of an old Alfa-Romeo saloon car. Kane remembered to use Julie's name so that she could pay with her bank book without too many awkward questions being asked. As Julie was also an Italian citizen there was no need for copious form-filling. They bought a few edibles, had the car filled with petrol and, with Julie at the wheel, drove out of the town, turning up the Garigliano valley on the road which was marked for San Vittore Lazio.

As they turned eastward, Kane, who had been peering behind them, suddenly let out an exclamation. 'Drive as fast as you can, Julie,' he snapped.

The girl increased their speed. 'What is it?' she said, trying to keep her eyes on the winding road while wanting to look behind her.

'Just as we turned out of the town, I saw a black Mercedes turning in from the west.'

'Adriano?'

'I can't think that anyone else would have a similar vehicle in these parts.'

'The people at the bar will tell him about us.'

'Yes. But we will have time to lose him in these mountains.

175

If we can get to the autostrada and head south, with any luck Adriano will chase off in the other direction to Ceprano.'

Julie grinned. 'Let's hope the bar owner remembers me dropping that hint.'

The girl concentrated on her driving, following the twisting road that overlooked the broad snaking blue ribbon of the Garigliano for a while, then parted company from it. At San Vittore they were able to join the Autostrada del Sole and turn south for Naples. It was seventy-five kilometres to the city where the autostrada they were on converged with the Bari-Naples autostrada from the east and the Reggio Calabria-Naples autostrada from the south.

Once upon a time Naples had been a bright jewel among the Mediterranean seaports. 'See Naples and die' went the saying. Like a giant amphitheatre, the city was set along the north-east coast of the exquisite Bay of Naples, between Vesuvius, the still-active volcano, the Phlegrean Fields and the hillsides that formed a crown around them. The city's scenic grandeur, its wealth of monuments and artistic treasures, had lured conquerors from all the corners of the earth. Not only had the city been an artistic centre but it had been a leader of literacy and learning with an ancient university dating back to 1224 AD.

But now there was a new meaning to the phrase 'See Naples and die'. It had become the toughest city on the Mediterranean. It was a city of slums, of violent crime, social deprivation and extremes of lifestyles. Young toughs on motorcycles would career along crowded pavements to snatch handbags, and even necklaces, from anyone who took their fancy. Death was ever present in the city, as rival gangs sought to gain control over their *distretti*. And the slums which bred such violence and crime, the great monuments to poverty, remained little improved since the end of the war years. Corruption in government at local and national level, the machinations of conservative churchmen and the tired Christian Democrats who had contrived to rule Italy since 1945, meant that the great social problems of the south, the poverty and violence of Naples, continued to grow like a cancer. Even so, Naples rose impressively between the mountains and the sea.

Julie drove down the broad thoroughfare of the Via Don Bosco, skirting the colourful Piazza Carlo II and into the Vi Foria, heading towards the waterfront area.

'We'd better find a small *pensione* or hotel, and I want to get to a *pharmacia* to buy some toilet items,' she said.

Kane agreed. 'It would also be best to ditch this car, as Adriano probably has its details. I don't know how far Tellaro will go to use his police contacts.'

Julie bit her lip. 'Yes, I hadn't thought of that.'

She turned into another broad thoroughfare and drove through some smaller side-streets, passing a small hotel in the Piazza Mondragone.

'I suggest we try and book in there,' she said.

'What about the car?'

'I'll leave it a few streets away, park it with the door unlocked and the keys inside, and it will disappear within the hour. That should confuse our friends for a while.'

Kane frowned. 'What about the garage in Súio Terme?'

'I'll settle with them later.'

They parked the car as Julie suggested, leaving it open, with the keys inside, took their bags and walked slowly back to the piazza. Next door to the hotel was a *pharmacia*. Julie went in to a buy a replacement for her missing make-up bag and some toilet articles, while Kane went into the hotel and booked a room. He waited in the lobby until she rejoined him.

'I've got the key,' he said, holding it up. 'I'm afraid that they only had one room left... I thought it best to book us in as Mr and Mrs Gambretti.'

Julie flushed slightly but smiled: 'Just so long as the bed is comfortable. I'd love a meal and a shower, too.'

The room, number six, was at the top of the first flight of stairs and had its own bathroom. Kane dumped the bags at the foot of the bed and locked the door.

'What's first?' he asked. 'Shower, sleep or food?'

'It's nearly lunchtime. Let's eat first,' she replied.

There was a small *ristorante* across the piazza, where they settled for pizzas and salads. Julie had wine, Kane drank mineral water. By the time they had drunk their coffees, they both felt exhausted and Julie's eyelids were drooping. Kane paid the bill with the little money he had left and they wandered back to the hotel. As if by mutual agreement they locked the door, stripped off their clothes, without self-consciousness, and fell onto the bed. They cuddled against one another in sensual companionship, but they were tired and barely had they fallen on the bed when they were both fast asleep. It was the first time in years that Kane had experienced a deep, refreshing and dreamless sleep.

When he awoke, he was alone in bed.

Cardinal Giona Tellaro gazed at his cousin in suppressed rage, his face flushed in spite of the years of self-discipline he had learned in the priesthood.

'I cannot believe this. How many more times is this *beone*, this drunk, going to make a fool of you?'

'I've had bad luck, that's all,' growled Adriano defensively.

'Bad luck! Superstitious fool! How they have escaped you is beyond belief.'

Adriano spread his hands helplessly. 'The garage owner said the girl mentioned they were going to Ceprano...'

'And you dashed after them,' sneered Tellaro, 'just as they wanted you to. *Pazzerello!*'

Adriano glowered under the insult but said nothing.

The scowling cardinal stood up and began to pace the floor.

'They could be anywhere by now. Rome. Naples. Milano.' He clasped his hands in agitation.

'If it hadn't been for that idiot Wallace,' began Adriano.

'That idiot Wallace practically handed them to you,' snapped Tellaro. 'You were the one who fumbled things.'

Fate had certainly played an odd trick in sending Kane and the girl to Ian Wallace, for what they had not realised was Wallace was a convert to Holy Mother Church and, like most converts, was more fanatical in his faith than people born and brought up in it. Wallace had recently been appointed one of the Papal Secret Chamberlains of the Cloak and Sword, and according to the protocol of the Papal Court, a personal bodyguard of His Holiness, although the appointment was an honorary one rather than functional. Nevertheless, Wallace had believed his duty lay in informing the Central Security Office of the whereabouts of Kane.

Tellaro smiled cynically. 'Mr Wallace has been a valuable ally in this matter. I trust you were efficient enough to reward him adequately?'

Adriano's lips thinned. 'Unfortunately there was some faulty electrical wiring in his villa. There was a particularly bad installation in his bathroom. It seems that he was trying to fix it, but he slipped and fell into the bath ... It was very unfortunate.'

'Very,' remarked Cardinal Tellaro drily.

Kane sat up and looked swiftly round. The shower was running in the bathroom. He sighed in relief and eased back on the pillow, looking at his watch. It was nearly six o'clock. The noise of the shower stopped and after a moment Julie came into the bedroom with a towel wrapped around her. She paused when she saw he was awake and smiled.

'We both needed that sleep.'

'How are you feeling?' he asked.

'Hungry,' she said, coming to sit on the side of the bed. 'I could eat a horse.'

'We'll go out and see if we can find a place that serves horses,' he grinned.

There was an awkward pause and then he reached upwards and pulled her towards him. There was no resistance. She came willingly, meeting his hungry mouth with one equally demanding. Her desire matched his own, her demands were as insatiable, and when their frenzied love-making was over, they broke apart for a moment and stared at one another's flushed faces. They they kissed chastly, softly on the lips, a kiss more sensuous, more loving

179

than the burning demands of a moment before.

She lay nestled in the crook of his arm for a while. They did not speak. There was no need. They lay in a companionable, comfortable silence. They Kane said reluctantly: 'I guess we'd better go and find that horse. We need to hire another car and I need to telephone Professor Myles.'

As he moved to the bathroom, Julie felt a momentary pang of loneliness and fear – fear for the future.

Chapter Twenty-four

Hiring a car was easier than they expected, as car-hire was part of the hotel's service. Then Kane put through his call to the University of Naples and, after being passed through several departments, was actually connected with Professor Stanton Myles himself.

'Professor Myles? This is David Kane.'

There was a pause at the other end of the line.

'Kane?'

'Yes. It's a long time since we met, but . . .'

'Dr David Kane? New York?' interposed Myles' heavy west-coast voice.

'Yes. It has been a long time, Professor Myles.'

'A very long time,' came the dry response. 'I heard that you have quit academic life.'

'That's a diplomatic way of putting it, professor. But if I can be blunt, I want to see you immediately. There is something extremely urgent that I must speak with you about.'

'See me? Are you in Naples?'

'Yes. Can I see you as soon as possible?'

There was a pause.

'I have a meeting just now. I will be tied up until ten-thirty tonight.'

'I could see you then,' Kane said, trying not to sound too aggressive.

'Very well. Do you know Monte di Posillipo? It's a suburb to the north.'

'I can find it.'

'Very good. I have been allocated an apartment there by the university. It's in the Viale Maria Cristina.' He gave the number.

'I'll see you there at about ten-thirty, professor,' Kane said.

Cosima Colombo flung the money down on the table in anger.

'I didn't come home to be insulted. I'm taking the ferry first thing in the morning.'

Cosima's mother, a large woman with a thin, shrill voice, sniffed plaintively. 'Praise God that your poor father, the Lord have mercy on him, didn't live to see his daughter become a prostitute, a slut in the gutters of this city. He was a respectable man.'

Cosima threw back her head and laughed bitterly. 'Is a drunken thief respectable? Is a man who couldn't keep a job to feed his family respectable?'

The elder woman wailed and held up her hands to heaven as if in supplication. 'Ah, that I have lived to see this!'

'Has no one told you the truth before?' sneered her daughter.

The stout woman's hand flashed out, but Cosima caught it and forced it back. It was the first time she had reacted against her mother and it surprised them both. The old woman stood staring at the younger one for a moment and then burst into tears and collapsed onto a chair.

'God forgive you!' she wailed. 'If your poor father was here...'

'He would be incapably drunk,' replied Cosima.

'I will not have you speak of him that way.'

'This is the last time that I will visit you, mother, and the last time I will bring you money. I do not come here to be insulted. I do not have to give you money for which I get no thanks, but abuse heaped onto my head instead. God, how I loathe this place! How I have come to hate everything it has made me!' And she rushed from the room.

The old woman continued crying until she heard the street

182

door slam and then her hand reached out to grab at the discarded pile of *lire* notes on the table.

In the street Cosima wished that she had stayed in Rome with Adriano and had not promised to go to Palermo to wait for him. If only she had not had that stupid idea of coming by train to Naples to see her mother!

It was after ten o'clock when Julie glanced at her wristwatch and announced: 'It's time to go, David.'

The hired Fiat was waiting for them outside and Julie volunteered to drive. In fact it was a short distance to the northern suburb, an almost direct route following a long road called the Via T. Tasso, which led straight into Monte di Posillipo. They found the address without any problem and went straight to Professor Myles's apartment.

Stanton Myles was a thin-faced, wiry man in his late fifties. He had the sort of craggy, humorous features and twinkling grey eyes which seemed more suited to a college football coach than a man who spent hours poring over dusty manuscripts from bygone ages. 'Hello, Kane,' he said, as he opened the door of his apartment. 'It's been about four years, hasn't it?'

Kane shook his hand. It was a warm, firm clasp. Then he moved aside and introduced Julie.

'Hello, Miss Gambretti.' Myles gestured for them to enter and offered them a drink. They settled for coffee while Myles poured himself a whisky and soda. They sat on some comfortable couches in hesitant uneasiness. Then Myles said: 'Well now, what's this mystery? I'm always pleased to see an old colleague, but you did say you had to see me urgently.'

Kane exchanged a glance with Julie. 'I had to see you urgently, professor, because I think that you are the only person who can save Miss Gambretti and myself from being murdered.'

Myles choked over his glass of whisky and started at Kane with a startled expression. 'Is this some kind of joke?' he began.

Julie leaned forward. 'It's no joke, professor. Believe me, it's no joke. I wish it were.'

Myles gazed thoughtfully at Julie for a moment and then stretched back in his seat.

'Okay, Kane. You're calling the shots. Let's have it.'

Kane, who had been carrying the buff-coloured envelope with the photographs of the papyrus, handed it to Myles.

'The first step is for you to examine these photographs. They are of a papyrus written in ancient Greek, the text of which is fairly legible from these prints.'

Frowning, Myles set down his drink and drew out the photographs. He peered at them awhile, then he stood up and went to a desk, returning with a large magnifying glass. It was about half-an-hour later when he raised his gaze to Kane. His face had visibly whitened and his mouth was pinched.

'Has this papyrus been dated? Where was it discovered? Has it been authenticated?' The questions came in a rapid staccato fire.

Kane held up a hand as if to stem the tide of questions. 'It's a long story, professor.'

Myles glanced at the photographs again, then carefully put them back into the envelope and laid them aside.

'My time is your time, Kane,' he invited.

As simply and briefly as he could, Kane recounted all the events from the time of his recruitment in New York. Myles sat impassive, his head inclined slightly forward, his eyes on the floor. When Kane had finished he raised his head and looked straight at Julie. He asked the question with his eyes.

'I can confirm the parts of David's story which involve me,' she said nodding.

Myles was thoughtful. 'I was told of the death of Rosenburg last night when I arrived. It is believed that it was something to do with the Palestinians. I knew him quite well before he went to Israel and became an Israeli citizen.' He paused. 'Poor Rosenburg. He thought the papyrus was genuine?'

'He wanted clinical tests before making a final pronouncement.'

Myles nodded. 'Of course. He was a good scholar.'

He looked from Kane to Julie and back to Kane. Then he rose and poured himself another drink. He was returning to his seat when he suddenly realised his duties as a host. 'Sorry, more coffee? No?' He sat down again and sighed deeply. 'I find it hard to believe. Hard to believe that this document is genuine. Hard to believe that it could have lain hidden for so long from Biblical scholarship without one word, not even a whisper, about its existence. Hard to believe that a cardinal of the Catholic Church is so hell-bent on its suppression that he will attempt the means you have suggested. He could not get away with it.'

'He has so far,' muttered Kane, drily.

Myles shook his head slowly. 'Well, your photographs prove that a document exists which is written in excellent Greek of the New Testament period. Alas, that is the only thing the photographs tell me. Not having seen the original papyrus I can say nothing of its state, whether it is genuine or not.'

'I have seen it. I carried out the tests.'

Myles smiled.

'Of course. But you realise that I cannot bear witness to your conclusions without seeing the papyrus myself? You have the name of the manuscript and a reference number which, you say, relates to the Vatican Secret Archives?'

Kane nodded.

'Then there is only one course open to me. I will make a number of copies of these photographs and distribute them to the dozen most reputable palaeographers and Biblical scholars in Europe. I will convene a meeting of them in Rome as soon as possible and then call on the head of the Vatican Secret Archives to release the papyrus to scholastic examination.'

'But Cardinal Tellaro has the original at the Villa Tiburtina,' pointed out Kane.

'At least, then, the Vatican authorities will know of the existence of this papyrus and will be forced to come up with an answer.'

'But if Tellaro is actually acting on behalf of the Vatican in suppressing the document?'

Myles grimaced wryly. 'There we must part company in our attitudes. I refuse to believe that the entire Vatican is party to such a conspiracy. I'm shooting in the dark, Kane. I know you had a reputation once, a promising career. Then I heard that you blew it. Everyone thought you were dead in a Bowery gutter. I'm being quite frank now,' he said as he saw Kane's face redden. 'Yet, suddenly, you appear out of nowhere with photographs of what appears to be an ancient papyrus. It is written in ancient Greek and it tells an unbelievable story. To back it, you also have an unbelievable story, which I would discount immediately except for Miss Gambretti here and one fact – the fact that it is so unbelievable that it has to have some substance. Any fiction would be more plausible that the tale you've just told me.'

The professor paused and shook his head. 'I can hardly believe I'm going to put myself on the line for two glossy prints and a verbal Secret Archives reference, *Confessio Paulus Apostolus,* CRA 2. I just hope that I am not going old and senile.'

Julie left the couch and went to grip the professor's hand.

'We appreciate this, professor. But you must be careful. Rosenburg has already lost his life through this papyrus.'

Myles patted her hand. 'I'll be careful, my dear. That is why I suggested that I make copies of these prints first and distribute them to some colleagues of mine before calling on the head of the Secret Archives.'

'How long would it be before you could organise your meeting?' Kane asked.

'I shall confine my experts to the major European countries, so I could have them in Rome within two or three days. I would telephone them individually to ensure their interest.'

'So it will be three days before Cardinal Tellaro learns that his game is up?'

'Three days at the earliest, I'd say,' agreed Myles. 'Of

course, it is one thing to get the Secret Archives to admit the existence of the document or the fact that it is missing; it is quite another thing to start accusing a cardinal, and the head of the Vatican State's security, of stealing it, and deliberately murdering a leading Biblical scholar, and attempting to murder you.'

'That is if the Vatican itself is not involved,' Kane said, and then held up his hand as Myles went to speak. 'I know,' he smiled. 'You refuse to accept that idea. Perhaps I'm just cynical.'

Myles shrugged. 'I know, from what you tell me, that your lives are in danger and that they will continue to be in danger until I can convene this meeting and establish the existence of this papyrus. All I can suggest is that you hide yourselves away somewhere until I have the answers.'

'I'd already thought of that,' Kane smiled tightly. 'Don't worry. We'll keep out the way until we hear of your progress.'

Myles scratched the bridge of his nose. 'Where will you be? How will I let you know of my progress?'

Kane grinned crookedly. 'We'll be where Tellaro least expects us to be. Don't worry. I shall contact you.'

Myles reached into his pocket and drew out a card and a pen on which he wrote several numbers.

'These are direct lines, it will save time rather than you coming through the university switchboard. By the day after tomorrow, however, I shall be in Rome. I'll be staying at the Ambasciatori Palace Hotel. You'll have to find the telephone number yourself.'

Kane pocketed the card and stood up with Julie. As Myles escorted them to the door he said slowly: 'You know, Kane, if this papyrus does turn out to be genuine, it is going to upset a lot of people.'

'It would seem that Cardinal Tellaro is so convinced of its authenticity that he feels it is better to break at least three of the Ten Commandments to protect his religion than for people to judge for themselves.'

'One thing puzzles me, though,' Myles said thoughtfully.

'If Cardinal Tellaro wanted the entire subject of the papyrus suppressed, why did he bother to employ you to assess whether it was genuine in the first place? Why bring you from the States and get you to attempt to restore it? Why didn't he simply destroy the papyrus?'

Kane shrugged. 'Vanity? It's been known before. Murderers have kept evidence that eventually condemns them because they were too vain to part with it. And, indeed, if you had in your hands a document written by the hand of Paul of Tarsus, no matter what it said, would you destroy it?'

Professor Myles was evidently amused by the idea. 'I don't really know.'

They both turned and shook his hand.

'Good luck!'

'We'll be in touch in a few days.'

As they walked down to the car to drive back to their hotel, Kane found himself feeling hopeful about the future for the first time in a very long while.

Chapter Twenty-five

They slept in late the following morning and then ate a leisurely breakfast-cum-luncheon at a nearby café. As if by mutual agreement they did not talk about the Tellaros, the papyrus or Professor Myles. They made inconsequential, idle chatter. Then Julie went to a nearby bank to draw out some money. When she come back, she asked Kane without preamble: 'Where are we going to disappear to for the next few days? You hinted that you had some idea last night.'

Kane walked with her back to the hire car which they had left in front of the hotel.

'Where do you think that the Tellaros would look for us?'

Julie assumed a thoughtful expression. 'They would probably assume that you would try and get in touch with a university, that you would attempt to find some scholastic support and . . .'

Kane gave her an approving glance. 'So what would be the last place that they would think of looking?'

The girl shrugged.

Kane held out his hand for the car keys, climbed in behind the wheel while Julie slid into the passenger seat. Kane followed the signs for the sea-front, skirting the austere buildings of the Palazzo Reale and joining the traffic in the sprawling Piazza Municipio. Julie sat silently as Kane turned into the harbour complex and drove up to the Stazione Marittima. He parked the car and jumped out. Frowning, Julie followed.

'Where are we going?'

Kane grinned. 'Sicily. It's a nice place for a holiday. And

that's the last place the Tellaros would think of looking . . . in their own backyard!'

Julie saw the logic of his argument. And Kane was right – Sicily was a nice place for a holiday.

In the Stazione Marittima they found the office of the shipping line Navi Traghetto and Kane asked for a car-ferry booking for Messina, on the eastern tip of Sicily. The journey would take twelve hours and, they were told, the ferry left at 8.00 p.m.

'We have the best part of the day to kill,' remarked Julie as they paused outside the shipping office.

'I've always wanted to see the ruins of Pompeii. How about a trip there and then a meal before we come back here?'

'Sounds fine to me.'

In a phone booth in the main building of the Stazione Marittima Cosima Colombo was speaking rapidly to Adriano Tellaro.

'Are you sure it's them?' he kept repeating. 'Are you sure?'

The girl snorted indignantly. 'I know the American *doctore*, don't I?' she replied peevishly. 'It was a stroke of luck that he didn't see me. I came into the shipping office just behind him and it was only when I heard him booking the ticket that I recognised his voice and then managed to catch a glimpse of his face – but he didn't see me.'

'And you are absolutely sure he booked a ticket for Messina?'

'The two of them and their car,' confirmed Cosima.

There was a pause while Adriano considered matters.

'Listen, *tesora*,' he hadn't used that term of endearment for some time. 'I want you to book yourself on the Messina ferry too. But don't let Kane catch sight of you. I shall fly down and join you when the ship docks. I'll pick you up in Messina. OK?'

'All right, Adriano.'

There was a click as Adriano rang off.

*

Cardinal Giona Tellaro listened gravely while his cousin's excited voice echoed over the telephone.

'This time I shall go with you,' he said.

There was a puzzled pause at the other end of the wire.

'You have had three attempts to deal with this nuisance, Adriano. To have failed three times does not win my confidence.'

'I've had bad luck,' Adriano's voice was defensive.

Tellaro sighed impatiently. 'The luck must now be changed. Salvatore and I will fly down immediately. You will meet the ferry and ensure you don't lose Kane or the girl. I will ensure that a car is waiting available for you. We will keep in touch.'

Kane stood at the rail of the ferry watching the spectacularly dramatic outline of the small island of Stromboli slipping away into the semi-darkness on the starboard side of the ship. The great cone of the volcano rose straight out of the sea to a height of three thousand feet, its southern face an almost sheer precipice made smooth by the successive torrents of lava which had flowed down its side over the centuries. It was in a constant state of eruption, the crater throwing up stones and lava at intervals of about forty minutes, to the accompaniment of deep rumblings which were particularly noticeable in the silence of the night. Every few years the volcano suddenly became violently active, destroying houses and vineyards with torrents of molten lava which streamed down its slopes, never quite reaching the two villages which nestled on its shores. The spectacle of burning lava and flames against the night sky was astonishingly beautiful. Kane wondered why the tiny island community still clung so desperately to their inhospitable rock. As a student he had visited Stromboli once. It was a place where old men sacrificied their lives to wrest a living from the treacherous sea and the impoverished, ash-like soil. Where the women's dark clothes, black hair and brooding eyes were a reflection of the darkness of the volcanic background.

He sensed the arrival of the girl at his side as Julie Gambretti came to lean against the rail with him.

'It's very beautiful, isn't it?' she said softly.

'That's superficial,' Kane replied. 'Beneath the postcard scene is ugliness and hardship. That is the reality. That is what the people there have to live with.'

Julie glanced at his face, lit by the now-distant glow of the volcanic flames. It gave his features a curious satanic quality.

'Tell me about Janine,' she said abruptly.

He blinked and swallowed. 'There isn't much to tell. It was three years ago. Janine was twenty-three, a librarian. We met, fell in love and got married. On the day after we were married she went out to get a take-away meal. She was attacked, raped and killed. That's all.' His voice was cold and matter of fact.

'And you've blamed yourself ever since?'

He began to say something in reply, and then stopped and heaved a great sigh. 'Yes. I blamed myself. I went to pieces, turned to alcohol and was sacked from my job. That's why the Tellaros picked me out of a New York gutter and gave me their job. They thought I was expendable. I was. It never occurred to me before the other day just how expendable I am.'

Julie gripped his arm fiercely. 'No, you're not! Not now!'

Kane stared at her for a moment.

It was true. He realised that he wanted to live and the realisation was growing in him that he had finally got rid of that monkey on his back, got rid of the thing that had been propelling him to destruction through the mouth of a bottle. He had overcome his awful burden of guilt. He couldn't say that he no longer felt anything. It would always be a part of his life, a part of his experience. But experience was not an ending, it was a development. He had to move on. And now he had something to live for in this vital and attractive girl. He bent forward and kissed her gently on the cheek.

'What are you thinking,' she asked uncertainly.

'That you must be crazy,' he replied solemnly.

'Crazy?'

'To get mixed up with a no-hope guy like me. Just suppose we managed to get out of this mess...'

'*When* we get out of it,' she corrected. 'I have faith in Professor Myles.'

'OK. Then what? After these last few years who is going to employ me? No university in the US would give me a job.'

The girl frowned. 'Do you want to go back to the States? Italy is a beautiful place. I came for a year and have stayed ever since.'

Kane was intrigued by the idea but then he gestured hopelessly. 'And how would I make a living?'

'There are plenty of other things to do. You could even try writing.'

'Writing?' Kane chuckled and then his face grew serious. She knew immediately what was in his mind. 'You're wondering about Ian Wallace, aren't you? What made him betray us to Tellaro?'

He nodded.

She caught his hand. 'Let's not think about any of it for the next few days. Let's just have a holiday. Professor Myles will sort things out, you'll see.'

The Cardinal Archivist of the Secret Archives gestured to Profesor Stanton Myles to be seated. He smiled somewhat bemusedly before gesturing to his private secretary, a sallow-faced priest, to enter and shut the door. The priest took his stand, hands folded demurely in front of him, at the side of the Cardinal Archivist's chair.

'My secretary has explained the nature of your business, Professor Myles. Frankly, I am at a loss to undertand the implications which you seem to see in this mystery, if, indeed, it is a mystery.'

Stanton Myles shifted his weight in the chair and gazed across the desk to the Cardinal Archivist.

'Eminence, tomorrow morning a dozen of the leading European Biblical and palaeographic scholars will be meeting at the Ambasciatori Palace to discuss the signifi-cance of some photographs of a document which has come to their notice. The photographs purport to show a document called *Confessio Paulus Apostolus* which is registered as a Secret Archive document CRA 2. I have checked the references and discovered there is such a document registered.'

The Cardinal Archivist inclined his head. He had copies of the photographs on his desk before him.

'Yes, my secretary has reported this. Yet the document is also marked as being for the eyes of an incumbent Bishop of Rome and for no others. How did you come by these remarkable photographs?'

'At this stage I am not at liberty to say. The fact is that they have been made and have been distributed to members of the academic fraternity. The document, a papyrus, contains revelations of such importance that it demands an immediate investigation.'

'Yes: you are demanding that the Vatican Secret Archives allow your eminent scholars to examine the original papyrus to ascertain whether it is genuine or not?'

'Exactly.'

'You must realise, professor, that His Holiness is the owner of the Secret Archives and has absolute authority over their management and use. The admission of students and scholars to the inspection of any documents is a personal concession of His Holiness over which I have no jurisdiction.'

Professor Myles smiled wryly. 'That is hardly so, Eminence. It is your advice in such matters which His Holiness accepts.'

The Cardinal Archivist smiled graciously and nodded as if to say 'Touché!'.

'Your reputation as a scholar precedes you, Professor Myles. Yet there are many who would seek to discredit the Vatican.'

'Which is exactly why this papyrus must be examined by a panel of independent scholars,' insisted Myles, leaning forward a little in his eagerness to make the point. 'Pope Leo XIII, in his famous *Letter to Three Cardinals* of 1883, declared, and resoundingly so, that the Papacy has nothing to fear from history.'

The Cardinal Archivist stared straight into the professor's eyes for a moment, with a hard expression on his face. Then the priest let his features relax.

'My dear professor, the Vatican is still of this world, even when it seeks to deal with the next. You will recall the scandals which have erupted in the past over the release of documents on the Galileo Trial and the Burchard diary passages on the Borgias? People who want to create a scandal will always find tools by which to do so.'

'My colleagues and I seek no scandal. We seek the truth.'

'I must press you again, professor, as to where these photographs came from?'

Myles shrugged without answering.

'You make it hard for me to find a reason for co-operation,' sighed the Cardinal Archivist. 'Were these photographs taken in the Secret Archives or has the papyrus been removed from our vaults and photographed?'

'To be truthful, I cannot say. But since the photographs exist, and also show the existence of a remarkable document, we must find that document and ascertain its worth.' Professor Myles paused and then said slowly: 'If you seek a reason for co-operating, I would say that the reason must be truth. If this papyrus casts a new light on the foundation of Christendom then it is our duty to evaluate it.'

The Cardinal Archivist sniffed. 'Very well, professor. I share the view of Pope Leo XIII. The Papacy has nothing to fear from history. Yet while I might advise His Holiness in these matters, I must remind you that the decision to release any document in the Secret Archives is in the hands of His Holiness and no one else's. You have scheduled your meeting at the Ambasciatori Palace for tomorrow at five o'clock? Good. My secretary shall be in contact with you before that meeting starts and you will be informed of the Pope's decision.'

As Professor Myles was shown out, a small door behind the Cardinal Archivist's desk opened and Monsignor Ryan entered with a thin smile on his cherubic features.

The Cardinal Archivist glanced up with a frown. 'You heard?'

'Your intercom works very well, Eminence,' replied Monsignor Ryan, taking the seat which Myles had just vacated.

'And?'

'*Does* the Vatican have anything to fear from history?' mused Ryan.

'I do not find that very amusing. Has the papyrus been located yet?'

'Presumably it is still in hands of Cardinal Tellaro and he is no longer in Rome. I am making enquiries.'

The Cardinal Archivist's mouth worked and he came very near to profanity. 'Is Tellaro mad?'

Monsignor Ryan shook his head with a vague smile.

'No, Eminence, he is merely a believer.'

'A fanatic!'

'In the old days a grateful church would have bestowed the title *Fidei Defensor*, defender of the faith, upon him. We shall find the papyrus and when we have, let us be sure that His Holiness, Pope Leo, was right.'

'I know my duty, Monsignor,' replied the Cardinal Archivist with affronted dignity.

'*Dues det*,' Monsignore Ryan whispered piously as he rose and left the room.

The mountains of the eastern tip of Sicily rose spectacularly to greet the ferry as it eased around the lonely lighthouse at Cape Faro and into the straits which separated the island from mainland Italy. The ferry steamed across the shallow bay at Messina, edging into the harbour around the welcoming statue of the Madonnina de Porto and into the docks.

The call had gone out for all car passengers to report to their cars and Julie and Kane had made their way to the car deck to join the line of vehicles whose drivers were revving their engines as if under starter's orders in a grand prix.

There was no customs check for this ferry, being an internal Italian service, and so, as the great doors opened, the vehicles crawled out along the ramps through the marked route around the dockyards and onto the roadway that curved alongside the harbour. Kane followed the signs directing the traffic southward down the broad thoroughfare of the Via Garibaldi towards the autostrada 18, but before he reached the autostrada he turned off to take the more scenic and leisurely route along the coast.

Although it was not yet nine o'clock in the morning, the heat struck them immediately. On board the ferry the sea breezes had tended to cool them, but now the Sicilian sun was already fierce and ruthless. Kane drove into the first petrol station he came to and asked the attendant to fill up the tank and check the oil and water.

They climbed out and stretched themselves, and Kane wandered into the shop attached to the garage to buy two cold drinks, which they sipped in the shade while the attendant finished with their car.

'Well,' smiled Julie, 'here we are in Sicily. Where shall we go now?'

'We'll have to buy a map. Let's head up into the mountains... somewhere cooler.'

He finished his drink and went to settle with the attendant, picking up a touring map at the same time. When he returned to the car Julie was already in the front passenger seat. Her face was slightly troubled.

Kane climbed in, started the vehicle and sent it moving off down the coastal road. Kane noticed that the girl kept glancing into the rear-view mirrors.

'Anything wrong?'

'I don't know. Maybe I'm just getting jumpy.'

'What was it?'

'When were at the petrol station I saw a black car pull up across the street. It's following us now. I'm sure of it.'

Kane glanced into the driving mirror. About a hundred yards behind was the threatening black-and-silver form of a Mercedes matching their speed.

Chapter Twenty-six

They drove on for a while in total silence, the coast on one side of them and the tall black volcanic mountains, coloured by stretches of eucalyptus, pine and the occasional dark cypresses, on the other. They passed through white-washed villages like a row of pearls on the edge of the blue expanse of sea.

'The Mercedes is still behind us,' Julie said, breaking the silence.

Kane bit his lip, his eyes flickering to confirm her statement.

'How can they have found us?' demanded the girl.

'Maybe I've just been underestimating Tellaro the whole time,' Kane replied bitterly. 'Maybe ... damn it! We don't even know who it is back there.'

The signs announced their approach to the town of Taormina, which sprawled across the steep hillsides among the thickly growing silver-green olive groves and clusters of dark cypresses. Cypresses were rare in Sicily. They were a strange import of the English settlers who came to the area with the Duke of Bronte, the English heir to Lord Nelson's vast possessions, whose estates covered the southern outskirts of the town. The actual town of Bronte lay on the western side of the vast slopes of Mount Etna and it was from this town that Nelson took his title and which the Irishman, Patrick Prunty of County Down, later adopted in admiration of the admiral. Patrick's literary children made it world-famous.

They drove into the town by the colourful bathing places

198

of the Lido Spisone.

'Let's find somewhere for lunch.'

'What about them?' Julie jerked her head across her shoulder.

'We'll keep to the crowded places. Maybe we can work out a way to dodge them.'

He followed the signs pointing the way to the Hotel San Domenico. It turned out to be a luxurious hotel set in breathtaking gardens. It had apparently been a Dominican Convent and still preserved the cloisters. From its car park the huge mass of Mount Etna towered above them, its gradations of colour ending with the sparkle of white snow that was partially hidden behind drifting smoke that rose from the volcano's summit. It stood like a huge sentinel rising from its foothills of dense green, its blue rocky shoulders dotted by steep crags crowned with the ruins of churches and monasteries. Immediately below the hotel lay the red-tiled roofs of the town itself, a strange place with its English gardens dotted along the curved bay from the rocky foreland at one end to the sandy beaches at the other.

They left the car and entered the hotel restaurant. A waiter showed them to a table by the window from which Kane noticed with satisfaction they could see the car park. Almost immediately the dark form of the Mercedes edged in and halted. The tall dark figure of Adriano Tellaro climbed out followed by Cosima Colombo.

'Take it easy,' Kane smiled to Julie. 'They're coming in.'

The waiter was taking their order when Adriano Tellaro and the girl entered. They made no approach and went to sit at a table near the door. Kane saw Adriano Tellaro's dark eyes turn in his direction. Adriano had the audacity to smile thinly and raise a hand in greeting.

Julie's face was white.

'Don't let him see you're worried,' admonished Kane.

It happened unexpectedly, just as the waiter was returning with the plates of pasta that they had ordered.

The air was filled with a curious tinkling sound and then the entire room seemed to vibrate.

199

The sensation was gone before they had really understood what was happening. An excited babble of voices broke out. The waiter staggered a few paces, recovered himself and managed to reach their table looking a little shaken.

'What the devil was that?' Kane demanded.

The man hunched his shoulders eloquently. 'An earth tremor, *signore*.'

Kane's eyes widened in surprise. 'You mean Mount Etna?'

Mount Etna is still a very active volcano and often given to eruption.

'This area is very volcanic. Etna sometimes blows and then, every now and then, we have an earthquake. It is nothing to worry about.'

Julie was composing herself as the waiter left.

'It's true. I did a feature about this some time ago. There was a great disaster here in 1908 when both Messina and Reggio, just across on the mainland, were totally destroyed in an earthquake which lasted no more than thirty seconds. There were eighty thousand killed and a lot of them buried alive under ruined buildings.'

'How often does that happen?'

'Before the 1908 eruption there was one in 1783 in which there were 942 separate recorded earthquakes in the space of one year.'

Julie was clearly preoccupied with other things although she was trying to make light conversation. She kept glancing towards Adriano's table.

'Don't worry,' he said reassuringly.

'I thought you said that Sicily was the last place they would look for us?' the girl said with some bitterness.

Kane had no answer.

'I'm going to make a call to Professor Myles,' he said abruptly. 'At the same time I'll try to settle our bill without attracting Adriano's attention. When I come back, we move like hell for the car and see if we can give him the slip while he's tied up paying his bill. OK?'

She nodded uncertainly.

Kane stood up leisurely and strolled towards the exit

marking the men's room. Adriano tensed and then relaxed as he saw where Kane was going. In the men's room Kane found a telephone and put through a call to the Ambasciatori Palace in Rome. He was almost immediately connected with Professor Myles. The man sounded excited.

'The news is good, Kane. I have just heard that the Cardinal Archivist of the Secret Archives will invite my colleagues and myself to the Vatican Library to examine the papyrus later today. The Vatican laboratories will also be placed at our disposal for tests.'

Kane was bewildered. 'Where did they find the papyrus?'

'Presumably in the Secret Archives.'

'There was no mention of Cardinal Tellaro or his role in the matter.'

'None. But there are two pieces of news that will be of interest. That man you said that you stayed with... Wallace... Ian Wallace...' Professor Myless paused. 'He's dead. An accident, apparently.'

Kane felt cold.

'You said two piece of news?'

'Yes. I noticed an official Vatican announcement in the papers that Cardinal Giona Tellaro had gone on a personal visit to his family in Sicily. Doesn't that disprove your contention that he had the papyrus and was preventing its presentation to public scrutiny?'

Kane felt numb. So Cardinal Tellaro was here with his cousin!

'I'll get back to you when I can, professor,' he said shortly, as he saw the waiter that had been serving him enter the washroom.

The waiter was suprised by the money which Kane pressed into his hand in settlement of the bill. Kane moved rapidly back towards the table, signalling to Julie.

They moved towards the door with such abruptness that several eyes turned their way. Adriano was taken by surprise and was calling for his bill as they disappeared from the restaurant. In desperation he threw down some notes and, grabbing Cosima by the wrist, began to hurry after them.

A well-intentioned waiter blocked the exit, not realising Adriano had left money on the table. Adriano managed to push him aside but even as he got to the main entrance of the hotel he could see the Fiat easing away.

Adriano, still dragging an angry Cosima, began to sprint for the Mercedes.

The landscape seemed to shimmer out of focus for a split second with the whole earth trembling. Adriano lost his balance and spun into the ground dragging Cosima with him.

In the Fiat Kane swore as the wheel spun crazily in his hands and the car lurched uncontrollably across the driveway. He only just managed to save them from a head-on collision with a cypress tree before the vibration stopped. Julie groaned, her knuckles snow-white as she clenched at the dashboard. Kane managed to recover control and accelerate away.

Behind them Adriano picked himself up and took a pace towards the Mercedes. Then he hesitated and turned back to the hotel. Cosima was getting to her feet.

'Wait in the car!' he snapped as he ran back into the hotel foyer.

There was a vacant phone booth just inside. He dialled a number, waited a moment before a low voice answered.

He spoke rapidly before replacing the receiver and joining Cosima in the Mercedes. Cosima shivered as he swung the car recklessly out of the car park and into the main street.

'This *doctore* is not the drunken buffoon you thought he was,' she said maliciously.

Adriano simply swore as he found himself slowed by the dense tourist traffic which cluttered the centre of town.

Ahead of them, Kane manoeuvred down the winding road around the Giardini Naxos to the autostrada, and out onto the white sun-baked highway. He glanced in the mirror. There was no sign of the Mercedes or, indeed, any other vehicle.

He gritted his teeth and pressed firmly on the gas pedal.

'We'll turn off as soon as we can and double back to

Messina,' Kane said shortly. 'We'll head back to the mainland.'

'You've missed the turn-off to Gaggi,' Julie protested.

'We'll take the next one.'

'It's not for another fifteen kilometers,' she protested. 'A Mercedes will be able to overtake us on this stretch of road.'

She paused and sniffed. 'Is something wrong with the car?' Her voice was anxious.

Kane followed her example. 'Sulphur,' he said.

Above them Mount Etna's white clouds were turning black.

'Do you think it's an eruption?' Kane asked.

'We would have heard warnings,' Julie replied. 'Seismologists know when volcanos are about to blow.'

Kane glanced back into his driving mirror again and permitted himself a grin of satisfaction. There was no sign of the Mercedes. It had obviously been bogged down in the town traffic.

It was Julie who suddenly pointed ahead.

'David, that motorcyclist is behaving oddly.'

Ahead of them, on the other side of the central barrier, a motorcycle was tearing towards them. As it drew near, it braked and suddenly swung through a broken intersection then began to accelerate up behind them.

'A speedcop?' asked Julie.

Kane couldn't make anything out except black leather. But the bike had no markings, no siren or flashing lights.

Julie screamed as the offside wing mirror shattered.

Kane glanced back in his driving mirror in time to see the cyclist, still crouching low, aiming something at them. There was a metallic ring on the back of the car.

'Get down!' he yelled. 'He's firing at us!'

Julie unfastened her belt and slid down below the back of her seat while Kane swung the wheel slightly from side to side to spoil the marksman's aim. The back screen of the car suddenly exploded into fragments. Kane realised it would not be long before a bullet found its mark.

The idea came to him in a flash.

The cyclist was about twenty-five yards behind the vehicle now and moving up fairly fast. Uttering a silent prayer, Kane kept the vehicle straight, watching the mirror as the cyclist began to lift his hand. Kane could almost visualise the pistol in his gloved fist.

Then Kane slammed on his brakes yelling for Julie to hold on.

The cyclist had no time to take evasive action. One moment he was speeding along, guiding the bike with one hand while trying to draw aim with the other, and the next the vehicle in front had squealed to a halt. The motorcycle smashed into the back of the Fiat, causing Julie and Kane to be flung forward. The rider left his machine as if he had suddenly found the secret of flight. Like a stone from a catapult he somersaulted the stationery vehicle and smashed into the rocks of the mountainside just beyond the autostrada barrier.

There was an abrupt whoof of exploding petrol and Kane accelerated the Fiat away from the burning motorbike, halting a short distance away.

Shakily, he climbed out and examined the damage. Apart from the areas shattered by the bullets and the dent of the collision, there did not seem to be any serious damage to the car.

Kane took several deep breaths and glanced anxiously at Julie. The girl had opened her door and was sitting half out of the car.

'I'm... I'm all right,' she tried to smile, though her face was a white mask.

Kane turned and walked to the side of the road to where the figure of the rider lay just beyond the corrugated crash barrier. He was still clad from head to foot in riding leathers, but there seemed to be a lot of blood about. Kane wrinkled his nose in distaste and bent over the crumpled form. He tore off the cap and shattered goggles.

The staring dead face of Salvatore, Cardinal Tellaro's ugly chauffeur, stared unseeingly back at him.

Chapter Twenty-seven

'David!'

The hysterical note in Julie's voice made him look up, and at the same time he heard the growl of a car engine approaching at speed. Down the autostrada he could see the black speck of an approaching car. He did not wait to find out whether it was the Mercedes but sprinted across to the Fiat and flung himself in, yelling for Julie to close her door.

'Damn it!' he exclaimed as he thrust his foot down to the floor, trying to summon every ounce of energy from the vehicle. 'We'll never be able to get away from a Mercedes on this straight.'

Julie's face was taut. 'Who was that?' she jerked her head behind towards the still-smoking motorcycle.

'Salvatore, Tellaro's chauffeur.'

Kane suddenly swung at the wheel, swerving the car onto a twisting roadway which led up across the lower reaches of Etna through the dense foliage of its foothills. The road twisted and turned, but Kane did not decrease speed. At one corner his back wheels slid across the road so that the back of the car smashed into a stone wall causing Julie to cry out in fright.

They were out of sight of the Mercedes now and Kane peered forward, anxiously looking for a side-turning in which he might find cover. But the narrow mountain road continued to wind up between stone-walled boundaries towards the distant top of the volcano, still belching its unpleasant black smoke.

Then the Fiat's engine gave an abrupt cough, died, picked

up again and died altogether. Bewildered, Kane let the car coast to a stop, his eyes searching for a reason. They had not far to look. The petrol gauge was reading empty. He switched off and got out. The odour of petrol hung heavily on the air, mingling with the pungent fumes of sulphur. He saw the tell-tale mark on the roadway.

Julie was scrambling after him.

'What is it?'

'Salvatore must have holed our petrol tank.'

They could hear the churning of the Mercedes' engine coming up the hill below.

Kane glanced round. 'Into the forest. It's our only chance.'

Julie grabbed their bags and hauled herself over the low stone wall, heading for the tangle of eucalyptus and olive trees beyond. Kane paused a moment, bent into the car and took off the handbrake. The Fiat started to move backwards down the hill. He hoped that Adriano would not be able to stop or get out of its way. Then he was running after Julie.

The area seemed to be a mixture of olive groves and vineyards, stretching in a patchwork quilt across the shoulders of the mountain. He took the bags from Julie, who was panting from the sudden exertion. Behind them they could hear the engine of the Mercedes stop but there was no tell-tale bang suggesting a collision with their abandoned Fiat.

Peering forward Kane saw the red tiles of a villa or farm house not far ahead.

'Let's make for that building, Julie. They might have a telephone.'

The girl nodded and they moved on without speaking. They pushed through scratching shrubs and trees which tore at their clothing. Then they were precipitated onto a gravel drive which led up to the gates of a single storey farm building.

Kane hurried up to the door and hammered on it.

'Thank God they're on the telephone,' he muttered nodding to the telephone wire which looped across the mountainside on tall poles towards the house.

A surly young man, dark-haired with a dark moustache, sauntered out of a barn nearby. He carried a shot gun in the crook of his arm. He halted in surprise and stared at them without smiling.

'Can we use your telephone, please?' Kane demanded without preamble.

The sound of a car engine came to their ears, climbing the road towards the farm.

The young man frowned and replied in something which Kane could not follow because it was in the swift rolling accents of Sicily.

'We must use the telephone,' cried Julie desperately. 'We must telephone the police.'

The young man's head jerked up at the word *polizia* and his frown deepened. He began to say something which was clearly a negative as the Mercedes swung into the yard.

Adriano leapt out. He made no attempt to hide the automatic he held in his hand. There was a smile on his sallow features.

Kane pressed his hands to his sides in impotence as Julie gasped and shrank back.

The young man stood unmoving, his eyes hooded, gazing first at the couple and then at Adriano Tellaro.

Without any attempt to pocket his gun, Adriano strode up to the man and his smile widened.

'*Salutiano gli amici.*'

The young man's jaw dropped and he slowly straightened as if in the presence of one he recognised as his superior.

'*Salutiano, signore,*' he replied deferentially.

'You have seen and heard nothing in the last few minutes,' went on Adriano.

'*Si, signore. Niente.*'

Adriano turned to Julie and Kane, his smile hardening.

'You have caused me much trouble,' he said softly. 'However, your journey is almost over. Go to the car.'

Kane glanced at the young man who simply turned on his heel and went back to the barn. He reached out and took Julie's hand, gripping it tightly as they walked towards the

Mercedes.

'Cosima,' instructed Adriano, 'you will drive. Signorina Gambretti will sit up in front while you, Kane, will join me in the back. Please, no tricks. I can always kill you now.'

There was no option but to obey.

Cosima Colombo started the car, turning it in the yard and moving slowly down the farm track towards the narrow mountain road.

'Trust us to go to a farm owned by a friend of yours,' he said bitterly.

Adriano chuckled as if he found this statement amusing.

'You have it wrong, *doctore*,' he smirked. 'I never saw that young man before. You forget you are in my country now, in Sicily, and I am of the Honoured Society.'

Julie breathed in sharply. 'He means the Mafia,' she said shortly.

Cosima paused at the crossroads. 'Where now, Adriano?' she asked.

'Take the road for Zafferana. I'll direct you from there.'

The girl was about to slip the car into gear when it began to vibrate. Cosima gave a scream and clung fiercely to the wheel. The countryside seemed to shake as if seized by an invisible giant. The vehicle was actually moved some yards across the roadway. Then there was a total silence before the cicadas took up their interrupted chorus.

By the time Kane recovered his wits Adriano had shoved his pistol firmly against his side. There was no need for him to give Kane a verbal warning.

Above them Mount Etna was puffing like a steam train and great wreaths of belching black sulphur smoke were pouring from the crater.

'What is it, Adriano?' whispered Cosima.

'Nothing. Drive on.'

'Are we in danger?'

'Of course not. People have warnings before an eruption these days. Drive on.'

Kane found his voice. 'You'll never get away with this, Adriano. Neither you, nor your cousin, the cardinal.'

'Shut up!' snapped Adriano. 'It makes no matter to me whether you get it now or later.'

Kane was about to argue the point when he caught sight of Julie's imploring look.

He forced a smile of reassurance and fell silent.

Professor Stanton Myles, with a dozen distinguished colleagues from many of Europe's leading universities, was seated in one of the main archival laboratories of the Belvedere Palace of the Vatican. In front of them the Cardinal Archivist had just moved to a lectern.

'Gentlemen,' he smiled benignly at them, 'it gives me great pleasure to welcome you here. You are to be the first to see one of the ancient papyri which has reposed in our Secret Archives for over a thousand years. For centuries only an incumbent of the papal throne has been allowed to examine it.

'Photographs of this document somehow found their way into the hands of Professor Myles, our most esteemed and worthy colleague. He feels it will throw a new light on Christian history. He has requested, on behalf of you all, that the Secret Archives allow this papyrus to be examined by yourselves as independent scholars. By special permission, His Holiness has agreed to this unusual request, for the Vatican has nothing to fear from history and any document which helps to make the history of our great faith clearer and more understandable is to be welcomed, and is the property of all Christendom. not just of the property of the Catholic Church.'

He paused.

'This document, *Confessio Paulus Apostolus*, has excited curiosity because some claim it is a confession written in the hand of Paul of Tarsus and admits to an act which would destroy one of the cornerstones of our faith. You must judge for yourselves how valid the claim is; how genuine the document. Our contention, which will be judged by you, is that this is an unworthy forgery dating from the eighth century, when there was an attempt to challenge the authority of the Roman Church.'

There was a muttering among the scholars.

The Cardinal Archivist allowed it to die down before continuing.

'It is for this reason that the papyrus has never been presented to the world of scholarship outside of the Vatican before.'

He turned and made a theatrical gesture to a side-door where a stocky, round-faced priest in the cassock of a monsignor entered carrying a small lead casket.

'Allow me to introduce you to Monsignor Ryan of our Central Security Office. Monsignor Ryan is now in charge of all security arrangements relating to this papyrus and will have control of it at all times.'

Monsignor Ryan smiled pleasantly at the strained faces of the scholars as they stared at the lead casket in his hands. He placed it carefully on the table beside the lectern. The scholars, led by Professor Myles, rose as a body and crowded around.

'Now gentlemen,' the Cardinal Archivist said, displaying a sound sense of the theatrical. 'I can reveal the remarkable papyrus. It is for you to judge it.'

He bent forward and opened the lid of the casket.

Zafferana was a village which lay high up on the shoulders of Mount Etna, whose summit rose nearly eleven thousand feet above sea level. It was a small place around which were strewn a few isolated villas with palatial white walls, red tiled roofs and well-fashioned gardens, almost hidden among the dark vineyards and olive groves.

Under Adriano's guidance, Cosima drove the Mercedes up the winding roadway and eventually halted at the tall iron gates of a villa wall, which had a wrought-iron sign outside proclaiming it to be 'Villa Mandrazzi'. While Adriano kept Kane and Julie covered with his pistol, Cosima climbed out, leaving the engine running, and swung the gates open. Then she got back into the car and drove it through into a sheltered courtyard which had a bubbling fountain as its centrepiece. The villa was obviously richly equipped.

As the Mercedes halted before a low terrace which led to the main doors, the tall dark figure of Giano Tellaro, clad in his black and scarlet cardinal's cassock, came hurrying forward.

His dark eyes fell on Julie and then on Kane.

'So?'

His thin lips drew back across his gums in a mirthless smile before he turned to Adriano.

'Where is Salvatore?' he demanded.

Adriano pulled a face. 'Dead on the autostrada. I couldn't tell whether it was an accident or whether they killed him.'

Tellaro turned to Kane. 'Did you kill him?' he snapped.

Kane did not bother to reply.

Tellaro clenched his hands for a moment and then said: 'Lock them up in the cellar. We'll see to them shortly. There have been some developments in Rome which we must discuss first.'

Adriano moved forward and thrust his gun into Kane's back. 'Move!' he said curtly.

He propelled them through a richly furnished living-room, cool after the heat of the mountainside, towards a small door under the stairs. Adriano moved forward, still keeping his gun on Kane, and swung it open. 'Down there!'

Kane peered down. A small iron stairway led into a gloomy cellar from which rose the odour of stale wine. Kane went first and Julie followed closely.

'Take a drink while you are waiting, *doctore*,' chuckled Adriano as he slammed the door behind them.

'David!' gasped the girl. 'I can't see.'

Kane reached out a hand and clasped her arm in the darkness, guiding her down the rest of the steps to the cellar floor.

'Shut your eyes for a few moments and let them get used to the darkness.'

There was enough light seeping through an old grille to see by, as soon as their eyes became accustomed to the gloom.

'What's going to happen to us, David?' whispered Julie. It was no use beating about the bush.

'They're going to kill us unless we can find a way out of here,' he said simply.

Upstairs Cardinal Tellaro was pacing to and fro while Adriano gazed at him indifferently.

'The Cardinal Archivist has already begun enquiries about the papyrus and Ryan has been ferreting around,' Tellaro muttered.

'What can they discover?' Adriano asked. 'You still have the papyrus.'

Tellaro bit his lip. 'Only Kane has seen the papyrus. He must be eliminated now.'

'Don't worry,' smiled his cousin. 'It will be a pleasure after the trouble he has caused me.'

'But first I want to know if he has spoken to anyone else. He has turned into a stubborn and resourceful man. However, I am sure he will do anything to protect the girl. You understand?'

Adriano nodded. He started to rise. 'Do you think your position is in danger?' he asked.

'Time will tell. Let us deal with one threat at a time,' the cardinal said curtly.

Adriano began to move towards the door.

There came a roar like an old steam train, a cracking sound as if an entire barrage of guns were firing at once. The sky seemed to change colour; searing reds and oranges spread across it like a world gone mad. The villa shook and trembled. Adriano staggered and fell against a couch while his cousin only retained his balance by clutching on to a table. A chandelier, which hung centrally from the ceiling, shivered and crashed to the floor, splintering into a million pieces. Odds and ends of bric-a-brac danced off shelves and cupboards.

Cardinal Tellaro staggered to the window and gazed up at Mount Etna's rim, thousands of feet above. A column of flame was roaring upwards into the sky. Rocks seemed to be

212

crashing down all around the villa ... red-hot pieces of lava. The noise was unbelievable.

The shuddering stopped, leaving great strips of glowing red and orange lava streams gushing down the mountain-side.

Tellaro's face had assumed a ghastly hue.

'The volcano,' he whispered. 'It's erupting!'

Chapter Twenty-eight

Cosima Colombo came running into the room, a bathrobe hastily thrown around her. She was white-faced and trembling.

'Adriano!' she cried, clutching at him. 'What is it? What is happening?'

Adriano picked himself up, rubbing a bruised arm.

'The damned volcano is erupting,' he snapped. Then turning his gaze to his cousin he added: 'We'd best get out of here, just in case. I've never known the tremors to be as strong as this before.'

He had hardly spoken before another rumbling sent them sprawling across the floor. The patio windows shattered into pieces.

'Get Kane and the girl up here,' Tellaro said, moving to a small safe in a corner of the room. Then to Cosima, sprawled almost indecently on the couch, he said: 'Get some clothes on.'

Cosima opened her mouth to reply, thought better of it and retreated to the bathroom.

Tellaro swung open the door of the safe and took out a sheaf of papers and a wooden box. He checked inside for the familiar roll of papyrus. He had long since removed it from the heavy lead casket which was too awkward to carry.

A series of loud explosions thundered across the mountainside, like a battery of heavy artillery firing. Something large and heavy crashed into the side of the villa and a smell of burning wafted through the windows.

Adriano was motioning Julie and Kane into the room as

Cosima reappeared having hurriedly clad herself in a shirt and slacks.

Tellaro dumped the papers into a polythene bag and turned to Kane with narrowed eyes. 'I do not have much time, Kane,' he said. 'Tell me who you have spoken to about this papyrus.'

Kane laughed, perhaps a little too harshly. 'Screw you!'

Tellaro's face went white. 'Adriano, give me your gun then go and start the car,' he said softly.

Adriano stared for a moment and then shrugged. He tossed his cousin the pistol. It was obvious from the way Tellaro took it that the cardinal had handled a gun before. His hand was firm and unwavering.

'The car, Adriano!' he reminded him sharply.

Adriano turned and hurried out of the building and across the terrace towards the Mercedes, which stood miraculously unscathed by the hurtling stones and debris. Cosima, with a glance at Tellaro, made to follow him. As she reached the door to the terrace there came a strange hissing sound and the girl, standing just inside the door, gave an hysterical scream and fell in a faint on the floor.

Tellaro's eyes flickered, but did not stay long on the girl's slumped form. Still covering Kane and the girl he backed towards the door and glanced outside. For a moment he seemed to sag. A piece of burning rock, about the size of a football, had smashed into the form of his cousin Adriano, sending him crashing into fragments of the fountain, where his broken body lay with steam hissing all around it from the bits of cooling lava. Inconsequentially, Tellaro thought that it had been a merciful end. Adriano could not have known anything about it. '*Requiem aeternam dona ei . . .*' Tellaro found himself mumbling the words automatically.

Cosima stirred on the floor and began to moan loudly.

'Shut up!' Tellaro snapped at her as he moved back into the room.

Smoke was pouring in. It was obvious that the villa was ablaze.

Kane glared into the dark fathomless eyes of the cardinal.

'All right, Tellaro. You're on your own now,' he said quietly.

'I always have been,' laughed Tellaro bitterly.

Still without taking his eyes from Kane he reached forward and gathered the polythene bag from the table.

'You'll destroy that if you don't handle it carefully,' said Kane in a conversational tone.

'Stand still!' snapped Tellaro. 'No tricks.'

He jerked his head at Julie and indicated Cosima, still on the floor. 'You, pick her up.'

Julie moved to Cosima's side. The girl was moaning and almost oblivious to everything. She helped the girl to her feet.

There was a noise which sounded like a drummer's tattoo. Tellaro glanced anxiously outside and saw hundreds of chunks of rocks spewing from the sky. The earth shook fiercely and it was only with difficulty that they all kept their balance. Flames were eating through the room now, catching at wooden beams as well as the furnishings. Tellaro seemed to be undecided as to what to do. He kept glancing indecisively at the Mercedes, whose windscreen had now been smashed by falling rocks.

'Into the kitchen!' he called, motioning with his gun.

They moved towards the back of the villa. Tellaro had finally made up his mind to try and get to the Mercedes. In the garage alongside the villa he had another car, and a door led directly from the kitchen into the garage. It would afford him some protection from the shower of rocks and lava.

With a gesture of resignation, Kane moved after Julie, who was helping the stumbling Cosima.

To Tellaro's relief the door which opened into the garage was still untouched by the fire and smoke. He made the others line up against the far wall of the kitchen, then he opened the door and glanced into the garage. There was no sign of fire or other damage, and the car was intact. Backing through the door, he raised his pistol.

'This is where we part company,' he said. '*Deus vult!* God wills it!'

Kane prepared to throw himself flat and drag Julie with

him, while his eyes searched wildly for a weapon.

Then it was all over in one ghastly second, like a scene out of Dante's *Inferno*.

One minute there was the cold stone wall of the garage. The next there was a sea of remorseless, raging lava, smashing its way through the garage in a swiftly moving tide. Tellaro had time to glance up as the wall disintegrated with a crash, a split second to realise the inevitability of his death, a split second to let out a strangled cry before the stream hit him. Then there was no more... no more of him, the papyrus or his gun. Just a white blinding hot stream of molten lava flooding through the garage.

'Back to the front of the villa!' screamed Kane, feeling the searing heat on his flesh.

Tugging at Julie and Cosima he managed to get them away from the dangerous nightmarish vision, pushing them through the living-room which had become a blazing inferno.

'David!' sobbed Julie. 'What are we going to do?'

Kane was coughing and almost blinded by the smoke.

'Maybe we can get the Mercedes started. It's our only chance. The lava flow must be right behind the villa. Are the keys still in the ignition?'

Cosima nodded and caught at his hand. 'Please, *doctore*, you will not leave me? I had no wish to harm you. Please!'

He stared for a moment at the tear-stained face of the girl. Her eyes were wide with fear. He shook his hand free in annoyance.

'Calm down,' Julie assured her. 'No one's going to leave you.'

Kane moved to the terrace, trying to ignore the shattered remains of Adriano, still sprawled in the broken fountain.

'When I say "run!" run like hell? OK? Run!'

They scrambled out onto the terrace and ran blindly towards the Mercedes.

The edge of the lava stream was already beginning to push against the back of the villa, which was disintegrating with incredible noise. Rocking explosions, the surge and hiss of great jets of white-hot combustible materials, showers of sparks, the crack of breaking rocks and splitting earth as new fissures opened up across the mountain, all contributed to a wild cacophony of sound. The air was so hot and dense with acrid smoke that they thought they would suffocate.

Kane clambered into the Mercedes, not bothering to clear away the shattered windscreen glass. He paused only long enough to make sure that Julie had clambered in beside him and that Cosima had reached the back seat, then he sent the car rolling forward, not even bothering to open the gates but simply forcing them apart with the bonnet of the car. Outside, he turned down the mountain road, trying to avoid the rubble now strewn over it.

Before them they could see great walls of lava moving across the mountainside.

Kane was hunched over the wheel, his face set in grim lines as he grappled with the problem of keeping the vehicle on the road.

Julie sat silently beside him, her face taut and pale. Behind them Cosima sat sobbing to herself, staring in horror at the fiery landscape.

Navigating each bend of the road required the utmost concentration. It was just when Kane thought that their luck might see them through that Julie screamed a warning and he braked hard, almost sending the car sliding into a wall. A few yards ahead of them, stretched across the roadway, a great wall of yellow-white lava gushed forward with eager fingers reaching out all around.

'Get out!' Kane found his voice rose in a hoarse scream.

He flung himself out of the driver's door, turning and pulling Julie after him. The lava was up against the other side of the car.

'Get out!' he cried to Cosima.

The girl seemed too frightened to move.

Kane glanced round and then gave Julie a push. 'Down the hill, run! We can't get through the road. Head for the olive grove!'

He turned back to the car and leaned in, trying to ignore

218

the blistering heat of the approaching lava. He grabbed the shaking girl and heaved her bodily across the driver's seat, out of the car. There was a *whoof!* as the petrol tank caught alight. Half pulling, half dragging the girl, Kane began to run to the boundary wall of the road and, with the girl almost in his arms, he leaped forward, tumbling down the other side just as the car exploded behind them. A thousand pin-pricks of white heat caught at his back as he threw himself protectively over the girl. He screamed in shock and pain.

Some automatic force took command of him and the next thing he knew was that he was struggling to his feet, hauling the girl with him, and running down the mountainside after Julie, trying to keep ahead of the river of lava. Already, further down the slopes, the olive groves were burning and the crackle of flame was rising towards the fiery sky.

'Keep going!' sobbed Kane. 'Keep going!'

Behind them Mount Etna was shivering again. Hot blasts of pungent air enveloped them as large boulders exploded from the crater high above. Kane cast a swift look behind and nearly stopped, so spectacular was the scene.

Mount Etna loomed like a great black shadow towering upwards. From its squat maw a column of fire roared like a flame-thrower into wreaths of black smoke. Dribbling over the lip of the crater were several great rivers of fire, all flowing downwards, twisting and turning across the escarpment, joining with others in intricate patterns.

There came yet another violent trembling of the earth, and they were pitched headlong to the ground. A fissure suddenly appeared not more than ten yards away, from which bubbling fire spewed forth.

Cosima screamed wildly.

'This way!' gasped Kane, pointing towards higher ground from which he could see a way to clearer ground below.

They stumbled through a small vineyard. The fire had not reached the vines yet and it seemed treacherously cool and welcoming. As if by common consent they threw themselves down into the shade of a tree and lay trying to recover their breath. The crackle and roar of the oncoming fire was deafeningly loud.

'We can't stay here,' Kane said, hauling himself painfully to his feet. 'Let's go.'

The girls did not protest. They had not the energy. Impelled by his will, they stumbled upwards and through the deserted vines. Already the far side of the vineyard was crackling with flame behind them. They ran forward to the crown of a hill. Below them and on all sides the lava flows were running in criss-cross fashion.

Kane dropped to his knees and moaned aloud.

Cosima started to have hysterics, giggling uncontrollably. Julie turned, dried-eyed, but with her pinched face working, and struck the girl sharply across the cheek. Cosima collapsed to the ground and began to sob quietly. Julie turned and rested a hand on Kane's shoulder.

'There's no way out is there?' she asked trying to keep her voice even.

Kane made a desperate attempt to pull himself together. He took her hand and gazed up. 'I'm afraid not.' His voice was flat but it had a dangerous edge.

'You did your best, David,' smiled Julie, sitting down by him. She stared forward as if fascinated by the pulsing lava. 'Will it be painful?'

Kane frowned. 'Painful? Oh... no. The smoke will probably asphyxiate us long before the lava reaches us.'

Cosima was mumbling a prayer between her sobs.

Kane took Julie and kissed her gently on the lips. 'I'm sorry I got you into this.'

She tried to frown in mock annoyance. 'That's silly, David Kane. It's silly because I love you.'

'I love you, too,' he replied fervently.

Julie suddenly giggled. For a moment he wondered whether she was succumbing to hysteria, but he realised it was a warm chuckle of humour. 'I bet you say that to all the girls when you trap them on erupting volcanos.'

He grinned. 'Well, as a matter of...'

The noise, when it finally registered in his mind, was disturbingly familiar. It was Cosima who identified it,

leaping to her feet screaming and waving. 'A helicopter!
Look! Look!' She waved her arms frantically above her
head.

A black shadow, with the growling throb of a rotary aero-
engine, darted across the sky.

Kane and Julie were on their feet screaming insanely with
her.

The swirling smoke obscured the helicopter for a moment.
They could see it like a dark black bug, buzzing close to the
contours of the hillside. It roared over them. Kane felt his
heart stop, and succumbed to a terrible despair.

'It didn't see us,' he said brokenly.

But incredibly the helicopter was turning, swinging down
towards them and hovering a few feet above the ground. A
young man in uniform, wearing a sergeant's chevrons on his
sleeves, had leaped from the door and was running towards
them.

'Are you people all right?'

Kane smiled inanely. 'Now we are,' he said happily.

The sergeant shook his head wonderingly. 'Are there any
more of you?'

Kane hesitated, thinking of the villa, of Adriano and
Cardinal Tellaro. 'No, there is no one else.'

'Then we'd better get aboard. The lava will be here in a
minute.'

The sergeant hauled them all into the helicopter and called
an 'OK' into the intercom. The machine rose rapidly as the
young man slammed the door shut.

'Our base is at Milazzo,' he said, getting out the first-aid
box. 'Messina and Catania have been badly hit.'

'What happened?' gasped Kane, coughing to clear his
lungs of the sulphur fumes. 'I thought the seismologists were
supposed to be able to give warnings about erupting
volcanos.'

The young sergeant shrugged. 'I don't know exactly what
happened. All I know is that it was a combination of things.
First, severe earthquakes, which caused a volcanic eruption.
The scientists have been saying that they had no warning at

221

all. Several villages have been totally destroyed. The death toll is pretty high. It's the worst disaster since 1908.'

'Lucky thing for us you happened to come along,' sighed Julie.

The sergeant grinned wryly. 'Very lucky. We were just making our final sweep before heading back to our base.'

Chapter Twenty-nine

Julie Gambretti turned from the intercom of her apartment to where David Kane lay on the couch reading a copy of the *Corriere della Sera*.

'That was Professor Myles. He's on his way up.'

Kane nodded, swung himself off the couch and put down the newspaper.

'*Venienti occurite morbo*,' he smiled.

'What's that?'

'Latin.'

'I know, you idiot. What does it mean?'

'It means that I don't think Myles will have good news.'

There was a tap on the door and Julie opened it.

'Hello, professor.'

Professor Myles smiled and nodded as he entered. His face clouded as he caught sight of Kane.

'The final results are in on the papyrus,' he said. His voice was grim.

Julie frowned at Kane and was about to open her mouth when Kane said evenly: 'You are going to tell me that it is a forgery.'

Myles looked startled and then he nodded. 'No question about it. Materials date it to the late eighth century although the Greek is a reasonable facsimile of an earlier style. You were wrong in your assessment of the papyrus, Kane.'

Kane smiled thinly. 'So the official result is...?'

'Is in accordance with the statement of the Vatican Library. It is a forgery, probably a political move by one of the breakaway groups to discredit Rome as centre of the

223

Church. You know that even from the start of the Christian movement the claims of Rome have always been contested. As early as 189 AD, when Victor tried to assert Rome's authority, the Asian Church contested it, and the Greek Orthodox Church never ever accepted it.'

Kane sat down on the couch. 'So the matter is at an end?'

Professor Myles nodded. 'The discovery of the document was important but not that important. If you had been a bit more accurate in your assessment you might have been able to prevent some tragic deaths.'

This time Julie could not contain herself. 'Just exactly how do you figure that, professor?'

Myles shrugged apologetically. 'I have had a talk with Monsignor Ryan who is now head of the Vatican's Central Security Office. I told him your story. He is prepared to admit certain things provided they go no further than the three of us. I have given him my word.'

'Admit certain things?'

'Cardinal Tellaro was overworking recently and his mental stability became, shall we say, unsound. He developed certain ideas about this forgery, believing its authenticity. Which is where you came in. Instead of making a proper assessment of its value, you led Tellaro to believe it was authentic which pushed him over the precipice. The result was the death of poor Rosenburg and of Ian Wallace, who was something of a fanatic himself. He was a member of the Papal Secret Chamberlains of the Cloak and Sword and took his duties seriously.'

Kane and Julie exchanged a glance.

'The Vatican have no wish to expose Cardinal Tellaro's mental illness for understandable political motives. It has already been announced that Cardinal Tellaro, while holidaying at his cousin's villa near Zafferana, was caught in the terrible eruption and earthquake and is now listed, with his cousin, among the many thousands killed. Monsignor Ryan hopes that will end the matter.'

'But what of Rosenburg and Wallace?'

Professor Myles shrugged.

'Wallace's death is already considered an accident and Rosenburg's death will remain one of the many unsolved murders which the public will accept as being apparently perpetrated by a Palestinian group.'

Kane stared at Myles for some time. 'Are you prepared to go along with it?'

The Professor nodded. 'I have told Monsignor Ryan that I can accept your word on his behalf.'

Kane whistled. *'Tantaene animis caelestibus irae?'*

'What?' snapped Julie.

'I was quoting Virgil. "Are there such violent passions in celestial minds?"'

'So it would seem, Kane,' Myles said drily. 'The odds are stacked against you, should you start making accusations against Tellaro. You must bear in mind that had you properly identified the papyrus you might have stopped the final disintegration of Tellaro's mental state.'

'Tell him, David!' snapped Julie.

Professor Myles raised an eye. 'Tell me what?'

Kane shrugged. 'Nothing,' he said to the girl's astonishment. 'Absolutely nothing. You can tell Monsignor Ryan that we accept his version of the facts. He may rest assured that I shall not make any accusations about Tellaro. In fact, he will hear no more from me.'

Julie began to open her mouth, then shut it abruptly.

Professor Myles nodded. 'That is good to hear. I'm afraid that if you ever wanted to get back on a university campus I could not give you a reference. I still think you hold a great deal of responsibility in this matter for not spotting the papyrus as a forgery.'

When he had left Julie turned with a look of outrage towards Kane. 'Why didn't you tell him?'

'Tell him what?' smiled Kane.

'Tell him that Cardinal Tellaro still had the real papyrus in Sicily and that whatever Myles and his experts saw in the Vatican was not the one you worked on.'

Kane shrugged. 'And what good would that have done? The real papyrus has perished. The one Myles saw was an eighth-century copy. Since that is the only one in existence, how can I prove my story? Besides, as Myles said, I might have made the wrong deductions on the one I saw.'

Julie sniffed. 'I don't believe it. Anyway, Cosima is a witness...'

'We'll leave Cosima out of it. She's just a scared child pretending to be a woman. She's afraid as hell of the so-called Honoured Society. She won't say a word.'

Julie gave a sigh of exasperation. 'Do you think that the Vatican knew there were two papyri – the one you saw and which perished with Tellaro at Zafferana, and the one which they presented for Professor Myles's examination?'

'Who knows?' shrugged Kane. 'Who cares? It'll be many a year before I mess with old documents again. I'm starting a new life, a new job. I think I'll try a stab at writing as you suggested.'

The girl gazed at him anxiously. 'Will you go back to the States?' she asked.

'*Ubi bene, ibi patria!*' he replied unctuously.

She picked up a cushion and threw it at him.

'All right, all right!' he grinned. 'I said; "Where it goes well with me, there is my fatherland."'

The telephone shrilled. It was Charlie Burgano.

'Hi, sweetheart. That story you filed on the Etna eruption was really terrific. Terrific. I've been able to syndicate it in a dozen magazines so far. A pity you didn't get your own photographs though. We are using some from Reuters.'

Julie grinned into the mouthpiece.

'Even if I'd had a camera, I would have been too busy running to use it, Charlie.'

'Well, never mind, sweetheart. I have another great assignment coming up. It's just up your street.'

'Oh?' she frowned. 'I don't think I want another assignment yet, Charlie.'

Kane came up behind her and kissed her softly on the nape of her neck. 'Tell him that you'll be too busy getting married,' he whispered.

Julie let the phone drop and turned into his arms.

226

For a long time they ignored the sounds coming over the wire until Kane reached out with one hand and put the receiver back on its rest.

The Cardinal Archivist sat back with a sigh and gazed at the rubicund features of Monsignor Ryan, the acting head of the Central Security Office, who sat across the table with a glass of wine in his hand.

'"Better is the end of a thing than the beginning thereof,"' quoted the Cardinal Archivist.

The Monsignor nodded approval. 'Or as Shakespeare would have it: "All's well that ends well,"' he replied. 'And now?'

'Now life continues.'

'It is a heavy burden to lay on the soul,' observed the monsignor.

'Burden?' The Cardinal Archivist pondered for a moment. 'A burden implies a knowledge of the truth, and what is the truth? We know that Tellaro appropriated a papyrus and that papyrus was in a lead casket scratched with the letters CPA 2. *Confessio Paulus Apostulus 2*. We know that there was, in the vaults, another casket scratched with the letters CPA 1 in which we found the eighth-century papyrus. Why should the papyrus in CPA 2 be of an earlier date than CPA 1?'

Monsignor Ryan rubbed the bridge of his nose. 'Unless some librarian centuries ago wrongly indicated the caskets, one being an original and one being a much later copy.'

The Cardinal Archivist grimaced. 'What was it that the *Confessio* said? "Thus did he end his life for the good of the community, which is more important than the individual; for what is the suffering of one soul compared with the joy of those who shall come after?" Isn't that a good epitaph for poor deluded Tellaro and the destruction of the papyrus we know to be CPA 2?'

Monsignor Ryan inclined his head.

Outside came the solemn tolling of the evening Angelus. Both men reached for their rosaries and bent their heads in obeisance.

Angelus Domini nuntiavit Mariae . . .

The angels of the Lord announced unto Mary . . .

Et concepit de Spiritu Sancti.

And she conceived of the Holy Ghost.

Their voices rose and fell in unison, intense and sincere as they recited the ancient words of the 'Hail Mary'.

Ora pro nobis sancta Dei Genetrix . . .

Pray for us, O Holy Mother of God . . .

Ut dignu efficiamur promissionibus Christi.

That we may be worthy of the promises of Christ.

STAR BOOKS BESTSELLERS

FICTION

VOICE OF THE NIGHT	D.R.Koontz	£2.25*
DARKNESS COMES	D.R.Koontz	£2.50*
WHISPERS	D.R.Koontz	£2.25*
NIGHT CHILLS	D.R.Koontz	£2.60*
SHATTERED	D.R.Koontz	£1.80*
PHANTOMS	D.R.Koontz	£1.95*
CHASE	D.R.Koontz	£1.95*
POST OFFICE	Charles Bukowski	£1.80*
DANCEHALL	Bernard F.Conners	£2.25*
GOLD COAST	Elmore Leonard	£1.95*
SPLIT IMAGES	Elmore Leonard	£1.95*
ALL OR NOTHING	Stephen Longstreet	£2.50*
THE BODY	Richard Ben Sapir	£2.50*
HEADHUNTER	Michael Slade	£2.75*
THE LONG AFTERNOON	Ursula Zilinsky	£2.75*
BIRTHRIGHT	Colin Sharp	£1.95*

STAR Books are obtainable from many booksellers and newsagents. If you have any difficulty tick the titles you want and fill in the form below.

Name _____

Address _____

_____

Send to: Star Books Cash Sales, P.O. Box 11, Falmouth, Cornwall, TR10 9EN.

Please send a cheque or postal order to the value of the cover price plus:
UK: 55p for the first book, 22p for the second book and 14p for each additional book ordered to the maximum charge of £1.75.

BFPO and EIRE: 55p for the first book, 22p for the second book, 14p per copy for the next 7 books, thereafter 8p per book.

OVERSEAS: £1.00 for the first book and 25p per copy for each additional book.

While every effort is made to keep prices low, it is sometimes necessary to increase prices at short notice. Star Books reserve the right to show new retail prices on covers which may differ from those advertised in the text or elsewhere.

*NOT FOR SALE IN CANADA

STAR BOOKS BESTSELLERS

FICTION

SHATTER	John Farris	£1.50*
REVENGE OF MORIARTY	John Gardner	£2.25
GOLGOTHA	John Gardner	£1.95
BACK OF THE TIGER	Jack Gerson	£1.95
SPECTRE OF MARALINGA	Michael Hughes	£1.95
DEBT OF HONOUR	Adam Kennedy	£1.95
DEATH MAIL	Peter Leslie	£1.95
CONDOR	Thomas Luke	£2.50*
AIRSHIP	Peter MaCalan	£2.50
IKON	Graham Masterton	£2.50*
HAWL	James Peacock	£1.95
DOG SOLDIERS	Robert Stone	£1.95

STAR Books are obtainable from many booksellers and newsagents. If you have any difficulty tick the titles you want and fill in the form below.

Name _____

Address _____

_____

Send to: Star Books Cash Sales, P.O. Box 11, Falmouth, Cornwall, TR10 9EN.

Please send a cheque or postal order to the value of the cover price plus:
UK: 55p for the first book, 22p for the second book and 14p for each additional book ordered to the maximum charge of £1.75.

BFPO and EIRE: 55p for the first book, 22p for the second book, 14p per copy for the next 7 books, thereafter 8p per book.

OVERSEAS: £1.00 for the first book and 25p per copy for each additional book.

While every effort is made to keep prices low, it is sometimes necessary to increase prices at short notice. Star Books reserve the right to show new retail prices on covers which may differ from those advertised in the text or elsewhere.

*NOT FOR SALE IN CANADA